THE EDGE OF
THE ALPHABET

JANET FRAME

Janet Frame (1924–2004) was a celebrated New Zealand author of novels, short stories, poetry and the three-volume autobiography *An Angel at My Table* that was adapted for cinema by Jane Campion. Janet Frame won numerous local and international literary prizes including the Commonwealth Prize for Best Book. She was an Honorary Fellow of the American Academy of Arts and Letters and held two honorary doctorates. She was awarded a CBE in 1983 and in 1990 she was made a Member of the Order of New Zealand, the country's highest civil honour. Her work is in print around the world and has been translated into many languages.

CATHERINE LACEY

Catherine Lacey is the author of five books, most recently the novels *Biography of X* and *Pew*. Her honours include the Brooklyn Public Library Book Prize, a Guggenheim Fellowship, a Whiting Award, the Young Lions Fiction Award, and a fellowship from The Dorothy and Lewis B. Cullman Center for Scholars and Writers. Her first work of non-fiction, *The Möbius Book*, is forthcoming in 2025.

'She is a singular writer. No one is quite like her.'
— Eleanor Catton, author of *The Luminaries*

'Frame achieved that supremely difficult task of finding a voice so natural it feels almost as if it were not written.'
— Jane Campion, *Guardian*

'[Frame] is endowed with a poet's imagination, and her prose has beauty, precision, a surging momentum, and the quality of constant surprise.'
— *The Atlantic*

'[Frame] meditates upon the disrelation between inner and outer landscapes, mental and physical colours, cruelty and the withdrawal from cruelty, the experience of chaos, of inexplicable evils, of broken perceptions.'
— *New York Times*

'She has shown, so quietly, a mastery of the English language which dazzles one beyond ordinary praise.'
— Naomi Mitchison

'Everything she presents is illuminated and thrown into sharp focus by the limpid clarity of a highly individual vision; she can be detached and passionate at the same time.'
— Fleur Adcock

Praise for *An Angel at My Table*

'One of the great autobiographies of the twentieth century ... A journey from luminous childhood, through the dark experiences of supposed madness, to the renewal of her life through writing fiction. It is a heroic story, and told with such engaging tone, humorous perspective and imaginative power.'
— Michael Holroyd, *Sunday Times*

FITZCARRALDO EDITIONS
CLASSICS
No.6

ISBN 978-1-80427-118-6

DESIGN BY RAY O'MEARA
TYPESET IN FITZCARRALDO
PRINTED AND BOUND BY TJ BOOKS

FITZCARRALDO EDITIONS
8-12 CREEKSIDE, LONDON, SE8 3DX
UNITED KINGDOM

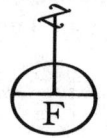

THE EDGE OF
THE ALPHABET

JANET FRAME

The first Janet Frame story I ever read was titled 'My Last Story', a brief and humorously irate few paragraphs railing against the self-inflicted indignity of writing fiction:

> I'm never going to write another story. I don't like writing stories. I don't like putting he said she said he did she did, and telling about people, the small dark woman who coughs into a silk handkerchief and says excuse me would you like another soda cracker Mary, and the men with grease all over their clothes and lunch tins in their hands, the Hillside men who get into the tram at four forty-five, and hang on to the straps so the ladies can sit down comfortably, and stare out of the window and you never know what they're thinking, perhaps about their sons in Standard two, who are going to work at Hillside when it's time for them to leave school, and that's called work and earning a living, well I'm not going to write any more stories like that.

I read those words when I was in my mid-twenties, the same age as Frame had been when she published them, yet I was already feeling similarly resentful about how much power writing and reading seemed to hold over me. I'd hardly begun and already wanted to quit, though I felt clinically unable to do so. Why did something so clearly fake feel so real? And why did novels and short stories obsess me so much? Neither of these questions, nor any of their many deviations, ever found suitable answers, and though there is still something deeply unclear to me about the purpose of creating or ingesting fiction, Janet Frame's work has come to convince me that this lack of clarity is a kind of answer in its own right.

'I'm never going to write another story after this one,' she wrote, with decades of stories and books ahead of her. 'This is my last story.'

I believe Frame was convinced of the truth of this dissent when she made it – not that she thought she would really stop writing, but that a general refusal to behave by pre-existing rules would become the core of her practice. The discomfiting magic and absurdity inherent in the fabrication of stories remained one of her central subjects. That battle between the fictive and the real is clearly ongoing in this, her third novel, *The Edge of the Alphabet*, a kind of companion to her first novel, *Owls Do Cry*.

A preliminary note at the start of *The Edge of the Alphabet* explains that this manuscript was 'found among the papers of Thora Pattern' and was published post-humously. As the first chapter begins, Thora announces herself by name and tells us she has 'made a journey of discovery through the lives of three people – Toby, Zoe, Pat.'

That Frame has enlisted a middle woman as an intermediary between the writer and the rest of the book is a very Janet Frame thing to do, especially since this Toby is the same Toby Withers from her debut. Does this make Thora, the writer and narrator, more or less real than Toby, Zoe and Pat? Does Thora even count as a character, little about her as we know? Is she a stand-in for Frame herself? Almost immediately, as if to rebuff the reader who even dares to ask such questions, Thora recedes into the third person, from which point she will tell the story of her three outcasts. Irregularly, as if she simply cannot help herself, Thora pops back in to re-announce or nearly renounce her task as a narrator:

> Do I, Thora Pattern, imagine that I can purchase people
> out of my fund of loneliness and place them like goldfish
> in the aquarium of my mind's room and there watch them
> day and night swimming round and round kept alive by the
> tidbits which I feed to them? They rise to the surface. Their
> mouths are open wide. Shall I overfeed them as people do
> with goldfish? Shall I starve them? Shall I remove their
> precious element and leave them gasping, stranded?

As a person who regularly sits alone at a desk, creating
and resolving little battles with imagined (yet actual!)
voices on the page, I've never come across a better met-
aphor for this activity than describing it as a purchase
from a fund of loneliness. It costs something. It creates
a possession. It is financed with solitude. By the time
Thora (or Frame) asks herself these questions, the story
is well under way, her characters bought and paid for.

Writers with such concerns – writers who constantly
question the purpose of their writing – writers who
intend their sentences to rattle like wind-up toys across
the page – writers who want to transfer their exhaustive,
existential curiosity to the reader – writers of this sort
are often accused of writing plotless books. This might
not be an unfair accusation, but it's also more complex
than that. Traditionally constructed plots do not serve
the goals of such writers, and in fact they frequently get
in the way. The energy and forward propulsion of *The
Edge of the Alphabet*, for instance, does not come from the
question of how any given plot-knot will loosen itself,
but rather from the rapid movement between layers of
consciousness and reality. Though, in fact, if plot is what

you're after, someone does die in the end, or, as Frame puts it, a character achieves 'that most dramatic and convenient change in habits which we call Death'.

Thora's goldfish – Toby, Zoe and Pat – are three lonely drifters who first intersect taking a boat from New Zealand on its way to London. Though most of the book remains in Thora's omniscient third person, she bends all the customs of such narration, refusing to move clearly from one point of view to another, refusing to strictly observe the boundaries of a mind; she is more like an invisible eel, slipping constantly between present, past and imaginary. The characters' dreams, memories and obsessions are just as often a subject as are their actions in the so-called 'present' of the novel. The focus shifts quickly and without warning; Frame either trusts you to keep up, or knows it simply doesn't matter if you fall behind.

As if to challenge the quasi-narration from Thora, and to echo the ongoing concerns of Frame, both Zoe and Toby consider writing books of their own. 'Shall I write a book?' Zoe asks herself. 'Everybody is going to write a book. Memoirs on writing-paper, toilet-paper, café wall, pavement, or stone column in a city cemetery where borders of trees provide a trip-wire into silence. Shall I write? Shall I engage in private research of identity?' Meanwhile, Toby is repeatedly convinced that he'll soon begin to write his novel about the Lost Tribe, a concept which seems to be privately held, though he's terrified someone (his father or Zoe) will steal his idea for their own book. Towards the end of the novel, Toby's work on the Lost Tribe remains un-started:

He had not yet begun it but he would, he would in time. Sometimes at night he heard his mother's voice say to him,

'Remember, Toby, Napoleon was an epileptic, many great men and leaders, Toby, had your trouble. Great and good men, Toby.'

Toby is thirty-five, has recently buried his mother, and insists on embarking on this journey away from his native New Zealand, despite limited funds, zero prospects in London, and the burden of his epileptic seizures. Pat is Toby's cabin mate on board the boat, an Irishman who could 'never keep the triumph from his voice when he talked of people who were 'friends of his'. He was like a big-game hunter, proud of the carcasses, but doomed to have no relationship with the living animal.' Similarly, Toby was 'lonely and incomplete, like a house with one wall torn away. He used people, strangers or friends, to keep out the draught.'

Zoe, another passenger, who is often seasick and experiences an unexpected first kiss from a stranger while fighting nausea, looks at the ocean and thinks, simply, 'There is too much of it.' After the kiss, almost all she thinks about is the kiss, and Frame's prose shines with peculiar precision when aimed at obsession.

Oh my Lord Omelette and Parsley but I was kissed scrambled egg I was kissed
kissed buttercup and cathedral for the first time in my life.
It will not happen again.

Frame has a careening, yet grounded way with language, as if the most sound-loving passages by James Joyce have been steadied by the plucky rhythms and quotidian concerns of Grace Paley. She writes from a both deeply inward and incredibly outward gaze, making scenes that are both abstract and figurative. She knows the way a

13

brain can tumble and tussle with itself, but she knows there's comfort in others, too, even if it's sometimes hard to come by.

'My Last Story' was included in Frame's first collection, *The Lagoon and Other Stories*. Upon its publication, Frame had been in and out of psychiatric hospitals for years, receiving frequent shock treatments. Perhaps the most often repeated detail about her biography was that her scheduled lobotomy was cancelled when *The Lagoon and Other Stories* won a prestigious prize in New Zealand. It would take her a few more years to come loose from the over-medicalization of her mental health, but few writers could say 'writing fiction saved me' with quite the same veracity as Frame.

But if that anecdote paints a rosy picture of the redemptive power of storytelling, don't let it. Redemption arcs are few and far between in Janet Frame's fiction. When doctors told her, years after the original diagnosis of schizophrenia, that there had been a miscarriage of medicine, and she was not schizophrenic at all, she recalled thinking, 'Oh why had they robbed me of my schizophrenia, which had been the answer to all my misgivings about myself?' However she soon felt a sense of wonder about this newfound freedom: 'I had only my ordinary or my extraordinary self with which to explain myself, and this was the first such opportunity for me since I had been an adult.'

The work she created – the novels and memoir and dozens and dozens of stories that came after 'My Last Story' – often contain a commentary, however oblique, on that issuing and retraction of a label on her brilliant and bizarre mind. Frame's voices on the page are a constant triumph over labels; she simply did not need them. Through all her marvellously layered and playful writing, Frame was able to chisel out an entire planet located in the liminal place between a writer and her fictions, something truer than apparent truth, something clearer than apparent reality.

THE EDGE OF
THE ALPHABET

CONTENTS

The following manuscript was found among the papers of Thora Pattern after her death, and submitted to the publishers by Peter Heron, Hire-Purchase Salesman.

I.

A Home There

MAN is the only species for whom the disposal of waste is a burden, a task often ill-judged, costly, criminal – especially when he learns to include himself, living and dead, in the list of waste products. The creator of the world did not employ a dustman to collect the peelings of his creation.

Now I, Thora Pattern (who live at the edge of the alphabet where words like plants either grow poisonous tall and hollow about the rusted knives and empty drums of meaning, or, like people exposed to a deathly weather, shed their fleshy confusion and show luminous, knitted with force and permanence), now I walk day and night among the leavings of people, places and moments. Here the dead (my goldsmiths) keep cropping up like daisies with their floral blackmail. It is nearly impossible to bribe them or buy their silence. They are never finished with trinkets pockets lockets gold watches that swing on giant chains against their dust-filled hearts. They leave their marks like fly-specks upon my life. Why do they spatter my vision with the excrement of the past, buzz in my head, seek the snow-crystals of desire?

I made a journey of discovery through the lives of three people – Toby, Zoe, Pat.

His feet had finished bleeding. They were withered now. He thought they were sea-anemones or dried oak-leaves or burst pinecones from outside, where the magpies garbled A-Wimbledon-a-Wombledon-a-fourteen-miles, and a bush-wren obsessed the leafy places with a sound light as poplar-cotton or purple thistle-head, a tiny piping jig that betrayed more than sight or statistic the vulnerability of the instrument that produced it.

Yes, outside where the hawks fly.

Toby walked carefully, a saint or politician, between the layers of knives. He walked on the sea too, giving the offal of the past to the searching grey and white birds that rose and fell in the sky, like supplementary breathings of the tide.

Toby was dreaming of the Lost Tribe.

He was a tree. He was sitting on the bin in the corner at home. His arm was shaking, not a human arm, but a branch with twigs for fingers and scabs and cuts where age had scarred the bark. He felt so strange, as if he were an entire forest, with the Lost Tribe inhabiting him as if his head were a secret gully somewhere up-country, just below the snowline, before the clumps of tussock and snow-grass begin to shine in the wind and sun.

So his withered feet dropped off, like dead twigs. He dived now and swam deep in the curving waves until he reached the bed of the ocean where all forms were of shadowy dreams and ribboned sleep, and the sun was only a green inkling, an intuition of light in the brain.

The funeral was over. Toby's father was listening, listening, and opening and shutting doors. Toby said to his dead mother, You old witch how I loved you with the Latter Days waving like maggots in your entrails and your targeted breasts hitched like moons in the sky, you old witch with your nose meeting your chin, your Blaikie nose, your Dunwoody chin.

'If you ever go overseas, Toby, visit the places where your ancestors lived. I have their chin and their nose, registered parcel of history delivered to the womb's door. And, Toby, Toby, sit in the old churchyard where the yew trees grow and where are buried John Blaikie, Master of

Model Training College, Evan Dunwoody, Minister to the King, Dr Charles Gibbs, F.R.C.S....'

You pegged your ancestors on the line between the work-socks and the blankets and they bubbled with cleanness and kicked in the breeze and were slapped in the face by the oak leaves that got up one morning to wash their face in death. Oh Dolly Dolly Varden in pleated china with the dust in the cracks and the chipped eyes. I did not have dolls. My sisters had dolls blushed pink with hollow bellies and patent bellybuttons and limbs held by a knot of elastic, and the house was littered with amputations lying in corners by spiders' webs and on ledges with empty bottles and beetles resting between engagements, and under the house near the blocks of Waimaru stone and the lank sleepless potato flowers looking for the light. And I, Toby, travelled a long way in my dream, and when I came to the pond and the patch of babies growing up like little green frogs from the bank, with leaves sheltering them as they shelter flower-buds, I, the tramp, the epileptic, drew my bundle of sharp stakes like the *manuka* my father used as religious instruction to discipline the beans in their search for heaven

my father the curate

so I pierced the little frog-heads and sat down and cried because my mother with her Blaikie nose and Dunwoody chin was dead.

His body worried him. There was no one now to care for him, to defend him, to give him special glances of love. His only close friend now was Fluffy the cat. He talked to her and sang little songs to her and brought her in at night to sleep beside him on the pillow or on his coat laid across the foot of the bed (though his mother warned him over and over, Don't let her share your breathing, Toby), and his father with the irritation of jealousy complained. (Cats inside at night destroy the oxygen.)

And his mother and father were right of course, for people need to stay alive, they need to turn green in the sun, and gold in their blossom. But still Toby liked to have Fluffy on the bed. She was a fierce hunter of rabbits and birds and mice, and a rowdy lovemaker in the early hours of the morning, under the holly tree and the hedge, but she was getting old and her teeth were nearly all decayed, and her cheeks now had a mark down each one where unsummoned tears ran. Her nose was beaded and cold. A scab had settled inside her right ear; it kept her scratching. When she saw Toby she throbbed with pleasure and twined luxuriously around his feet. She liked sleeping on his pillow. Sometimes in the early morning when she crept outside and brought through the window a newly killed wax-eye or goldfinch, Toby would hug her close and say, Thank you Fluffy, puss puss, with a wild feeling of gratitude, as if he had been offered someone's love.

Toby woke gradually. It was half-morning, with birds turning in their sleep in the trees outside. He could see faintly the shapes of the room, his clothes, his blueys stiff with dirt on the hook behind the door; the gum-boots, free issue from the Freezing Works; the books; and nearer, on the bedside table, in their glass, the distorted outline of his submerged false teeth with their dolly-pink gums. He felt with his tongue the inside of his dry furred mouth. He shrugged his right shoulder, grinding the bone. He was conscious of pain in it, as if he had been doing heavy work, lifting and straining. Then he knew the wet bed, the separated reality, demanding to be accounted for, of urine that had lost its first warmth and nearness. The habitual accusation, followed by dismay, sprang to his mind,

Who wet the bed?

Then he knew that he had been taking a fit. He wanted to cry, as he used to cry when he was a little boy and woke out of the strangeness. But he did not cry. He moved his shoulder again, testing it. At the foot of the bed Fluffy stirred in her sleep, and began to purr, knitting sound against his overcoat. Toby closed his eyes. He made a sound like a sigh. His hand crept down to the wetness of his bed and touched in between his legs where it felt limp, like a ship come drooping home. Resting his hand there he sighed again and fell asleep and at the door of his dreams his dead mother was waiting with her little tray of poisonous apples.

The bracelet of decay glitters with diamonds. Tiny worms carry lanterns in the storm. At the edge of the alphabet there is no safeguard against the dead.

HIS FATHER told him, 'You're mad to go overseas. What do you expect to find there? How will you keep yourself? What would your mother say?'

'I'm going overseas, Dad, because I've a mind to. I'll be an old man soon and I've never seen the world. I'll write a book, too.'

It was the old discussion which took place more often now that Amy Withers was dead. The background was familiar – the evening meal; oxtail stew. Tinned peaches and cream. 'I don't do so badly do I?' Bob said, dishing out the peaches. He poured the left-over syrup into an empty jug.

'More syrup than peaches. Diddled every time.'

'There's going to be a law against that sort of thing,' Toby said sympathetically looking at the few peaches left after the syrup had been poured off. 'It's the same with pears and pineapples.'

'They seem to be able to do anything nowadays and get away with it.'

'You're right Dad. They do. There's no honesty in the world today. Did you see about that man in the paper?'

'This morning's?'

'No, last night's.'

'Yes, I saw it. What they want –'

How could Bob Withers explain what 'they' wanted? It was so much, so various and so urgent; the thought of its urgency gave him a feeling of hopelessness. Would 'they' never mend their ways – listen to advice, run the country as it should be run, bring in the right laws, the right working-hours and conditions...?

Bob laughed suddenly and turned to Toby.

'So you'll be writing a book at last will you?'

'Yes, and getting it published.'

Toby knew that if his mother were alive she would at that moment glance proudly at her husband, and more proudly at her son,

'You see. Toby's going to write a book. He was always good at English at school, top marks for his composition that time. And his great great grandmother wrote a book of poems, signed by the Archbishop of Canterbury.'

'Here we are, out with ancestors,' Bob would say, moving his hands as if he were drawing handkerchiefs from a box. 'Here they are, all the doctors and ministers to the king and masters of model training colleges. Don't mention the murderers and convicts. And don't mind me, my mother began work in the mills when she was ten.'

And Amy would say,

'Don't be silly Bob. All your family were talented. What about the schoolteacher who emigrated to Canada? It's in the family I tell you. Toby's going to write a book. He'll get his own back. You remember the composition he wrote at school and the teacher read it out in front of the class? Didn't he Toby?'

And Bob would clear the phlegm from his throat, spit it noisily into his handkerchief, and laugh sarcastically,

'The Lost Tribe, the Lost Tribe. We'll never hear the end of the Lost Tribe.'

And now, slipping curled peaches into his mouth, he said wearily to Toby,

'I suppose your book will be about the Lost Tribe. Very original. In fact I might try writing about it myself some time. Let me tell you if I wrote a book I'd have a thing or two to say for myself. I've seen a lot in my time.'

Toby spoke his reply slowly. He opened wide his left eye which seemed always to act independently of the other and was usually half-closed – a doctor had said it was nearer to giving blindness than sight – and he leaned forward, staring at his father who perhaps at this time, who can say? – needed more the scrutiny of blindness, of being focused from the other face of light. Toby flushed as he spoke.

'If you ever write about the Lost Tribe,' he warned, 'I'll kill you. The Lost Tribe is *my* book.'

'Don't be silly. You can't even spell your own name.'

That was true. But Toby remembered his mother's fond words to him whenever he had worried over his spelling. Even the smallest words were difficult for him.

'Toby, many of the world's great writers were poor at spelling. Many of the greatest men were no good at school or games; many had little education, and left school early, like you. Look at Abraham Lincoln and President Garfield.'

Then Toby's mother, talking of her favourite presidents, and becoming absorbed in their story, would add:

'Like all great men they never forgot what their mother had done for them, and the sacrifices she made, and when they wore fine clothes they were never ashamed to acknowledge their mother, even though she wore rags. You'll never forget your mother will you Toby? And one of these days if you're driving along in your carriage and you swerve to avoid the tattered woman trudging along with her little bundle of washing, you'll lean out and speak to her, and smile at her, won't you, because it might be me, it might be your own mother!'

In Amy Withers' mind, even in the days of fast cars, Buicks, Chevs bigbodied gleaming, the symbol of prosperity had always remained a coach and fine horses. In her rather muddled dreamy but determined ventures in Time, Amy used to move back and forth from the past to the future, from the days recorded by fossils, temples, Victorian writings, to the Latter Days and Armageddon, avoiding the splash and spatter of the Present Day as if it were an inconvenient puddle in the road.

'So you see,' Toby repeated, 'although my spelling is bad it won't stop me from writing my book. I've saved enough money from the Freezing Works to go overseas. My passage is booked.'

'Where to?'

'England.'

'But what about when you return? You'll have to start from scratch. And why do you want to go to England? What's wrong with your own country?'

Toby did not answer.

Bob looked up from licking his plate which he did at every meal and was about to make a derisive remark when he saw with a shock that made his face go white and a pain creep up his arm and into his chest, that the man sharing his meal was not Toby, not Toby at all. Surely it was Bob's father, Henry Withers? There was the heavy frown, the pleat of flesh at the neck, the constant laborious focusing from distant objects to those close at hand as if the points of sight were rusty with age and had to be switched with effort.

Toby put his plate aside, got up, stretched himself on the sofa.

'I think I'll bring the cat in,' he said, darting a glance of challenge at his father who did not respond with his usual 'Yes, bring in the cat to tease the bird, to frighten it out of its wits.'

Toby decided not to bring the cat in. He reached to the wall where the rifle hung, kept for killing rabbits and ducks. He unhooked it and laid it across his lap. He glanced again at his father, waiting for the outburst of anger. His father was staring at him in a dazed way.

'What are you staring at, Dad?'

Bob's face was white. Surely it was Henry Withers! And what was Amy doing, going down in her bare feet to the gate to collect the milk and the letters and having to stop by the flowering cherry to get her breath? She was dead wasn't she? Even if he still felt at night for her body under the barren plain of patchwork beside him, that used to escape when she moved, from ravines and closets of flesh, she was dead, wasn't she?

'I've got a pain,' Bob said. 'Indigestion. I'll mix some powder.'

He went to the scullery, taking the dirty plates and the empty peach tin.

'You might help with the dishes,' he called. He tried to ignore the fact that Toby had the rifle and was pointing it towards him in the way that Toby all his life had teased animals and birds and people when the mood came upon him. Bob recognized the mood now. He felt anger and resentment. He tried to sound casual.

'Is that thing loaded?'

Toby smiled, pleased. He had gained his response.

'Yes,' he said. 'It's loaded all right. I put in some bullets the other day to get a few rabbits on the hill.'

'For heaven's sake take out the bullets then!'

'I'll take them out all right,' Toby answered, making no attempt to remove them, but still pointing the rifle and stroking it as he would stroke Fluffy.

Bob, an apron round his waist, came to the door of the scullery. He was wearing Amy's old men-size slippers.

'You're wearing Mum's slippers!' Toby accused.

'And why not? Your mother's not here now.'

Bob's use of the term 'your mother' acted as a temporary disownment, a shifting of the responsibility and reality of the grief that had overtaken a personal relation-ship which had always been so complicated that it needed division anyway into two or three or four in order to survive. Your mother, Mum, Amy, The Wife.

'Still you're wearing her slippers,' Toby said.

Bob burst out in the exasperation which Toby had longed for.

'Why can't you grow up? Playing with the cat, playing with the rifle, annoying people; and you've flicked little balls of paper all over the kitchen floor and I've had to pick them up. I swept that floor not an hour ago. Small things amuse small minds. Why can't you be your age?'

Toby did not reply. He swung the rifle suddenly, pointing it at the budgerigar in its cage. He knew that his father had a special fondness for the bird, that he liked to talk to it when he felt lonely, that he gained comfort from its limited conversation of Pretty Billy Up the Stairs to Bed Pretty Billy Up the Stairs to Bed.

Bob started forward, his arm raised. Toby swung the rifle towards him, then laid it down on the sofa beside him.

'Yes my passage is booked,' he said. 'For July.'

'And might I ask how you'll keep yourself when you come home?'

'My book,' Toby said, with a quick joyful smile. 'My book. And I'll have a wife to keep as well.'

He reached to the wall and hung the rifle on its nail, and stretching himself on the sofa he began, with tense concentration, to pick his nose, working his finger with a drilling motion and peering curiously at the little blots of salvage.

III

So I, Thora Pattern, walked one evening near the mud-flats where I live and I considered the creatures who are beyond the range of words. I saw the relics of the extinct monsters.

This monster in the mudflats
deceived and dying
while other creatures willed their change of way
(as weather-vanes believe they trap the wind, as
lilies on a snow-filled morning
imagine their whiteness is the sole reason)
this monster with so little purpose,
double-crossed by an Outlandish Good Thing
– sky-high armoury,
millipedal wish on one foot
star-scraping flightless wing –
who tried to kill
with no technicolour balloons rising from his mouth
*   to explain his actions,*
who was pushed off the bandwagon of Survival,
who never knew the secret caves of language, the
comparison and blind sight
that rumoured cities of man
that promised the cradle-comforts of intelligence
– a big heavy brain to play with,
a bomb to suck in the lonely dark –
this monster arouses our love and pity.
We take our feeling for him like a kind of food,
changing it to flow through ourselves;
for in the shadow of conjectured bone
in the threadbare seam

uncovered between mantle and mantle of history
we glimpse our own lives?
our minds in the mudflats dying
unwilling to change or camouflage
in detergent snows or gusts of opinion,
still wrapped defensively in the Outlandish
     Good Thing.

Will Time publish us too as grotesque, purposeless,
beyond the range of human language, between the
     pages of ice
turned and torn uncuriously by the illiterate years
till our story is sealed at last
till no human mind remains to trace
the compelling reason,
the marginal dream?

The dead return, they mingle, their smell is layered over the living and the present. Do people passing in the street recognize the smell that hangs like a cloud like a shroud, or do only the little dogs know it, jerking and running around corners to catch the tantalizing bitch-smell of death that stings them to life, to uncomplicated slot-machine love where the face is faceless –

Pardon me, as I passed by did I leave a germ of suffering trapped in your breath, a sealed envelope of love in the lattice-work of your face?

Poste Restante.

Why all the Poste Restante faces, waiting; the white snow in the bin; not for me; they never came. They never came. And now it is dark here, beyond the boundaries of words.

An enormous cloud has blotted the sun that we pin our faith to, personally well-dressed in our carnation of faith.

And all this will change, the grinding ice will move in its sleep, extend, and sheet your face and mine.

IV

NOW THAT Toby had made arrangements for his journey overseas, and Bob had decided that someone in the family ought to see him off at Wellington, and Bob had written to his sister Norma to tell her the date of sailing, family ties (as they say) prevailed, and Norma invited Bob and Toby to stay.

She did not want Toby. She did not want to associate with someone who was an epileptic; it was an embarrassing disease that had to be explained and excused and that caused people to wonder about the family history. Toby himself did not help either. She thought him uncouth and dull. His apparent slowness of thinking and his habit of taking such a long time to utter one sentence, and the way in which once he began talking he stayed doggedly on the same subject, ignoring the attempts of others to change it, all seemed to Norma like evidence of mental backwardness. She considered Toby to be a 'drag' on his family and on society. He was nothing but a 'great lazy lump', she thought, and although she usually felt sorry for the afflicted (after all, one must), there was something about Toby which changed her pity for him into annoyance and exasperation. There was just no place for him to fit in. People should fit in and harden and stay, like drops of cement in a brick wall.

Toby gave his Aunt Norma a feeling of untidiness in herself and the world about her, a sense of gaps and holes and torn threadbare linings that made her want to take her needle and thread (she had worked as a tailoress and still took in sewing) and sew day and night to make pockets safe once more, clothes warm and buttoned, and even to secure the sky tightly to the edge of the world, with no

39

draughts and flapping fringes.

Nevertheless Norma posted her notelet (Dear Bob, You and Toby are of course welcome) in its magnolia-scented envelope, and warned her husband Philip that for the last week in July his sisters (high in society, safe beyond the cocktail curtain) were not to visit Number Fifteen Short Street, Okare.

It rained, Scotch mist braiding and trembling upon people and hills. The rain moved through the sky in shapes determined by the wind, now a grey broom sweeping, a ribbed and feathered wing flying, a scarf enveloping the light, preserving dimness and secrecy. The sea heaved and the headlands loomed out of sleep like an extra dream or nightmare, confused in the minds of the ferry passengers with other private seas and voyagings and thus arousing even in daylight and waking, the deepest longings that have exiled in the sleep of night.

Crowded on the deck, pale from their inadmissible dreams, the passengers stared at this new 'other island', trying in a way to disentangle themselves from it, recalling the wild dreams that had gone ahead to investigate, inhabit, preside over, perhaps change the shape of it; then admitting in the final sour waking from the lulled sleep of the Straits, that here again, as usual, as always, as the Shipping Company would inform anyone if he cared to examine his ticket, here was the North Island, seat of government, population (in souls) one and a half million.

There was no new land made visible, no discovered world. Amazed suddenly at the familiarity of it all, at the rows of red-roofed houses and their miraculous hold on the steep hills, at the buildings themselves, and the chimneys – there! a train whistled, going north – the people began their ordinary striving to get to the rails and wave or blow kisses or shout greetings to those who waited below.

The ship berthed. Soon all the passengers were pro-pelled from the porcelain and steel environments of their night's cramped but deep deep dreaming (the harsh fawn blankets of the bunks were folded, the sheets and pillow-cases removed, the huckaback towels changed, all as if in denial of the past twelve hours, as if by changing the towels and sheets the Shipping Company could shed re-sponsibility for the dreams), down the hooded gangways to the close-up of wharf sheds, cluttered ropes, and the tired faces of those who had got up so early to greet them.

Aunt Norma was waiting. Bob was quick to notice her pallor in the grey light and to feel the anxiety which troubled him often since Amy's death and which caused him to search the faces of his elderly relatives and friends for signs of growing weakness, warnings of collapse. Bob Withers who used to read only the Sexton Blake detective stories and the morning and evening news-papers, was obsessed now with the language of death – he had learned the rudiments of its grammar so easily; after so little formal education he could translate libraries of faces and gestures and conversations; a profitable fearful pastime. His early enthusiastic reading of love explained, of course, his facility in the translation of death: the al-phabet, the grammar, are the same.

His face was strained and anxious as he studied his sister Norma.

'We could have found our own way. You needn't have got up to meet us.'

Norma spoke briskly.

'I've brought the car. I'm driving you out.'

The car was frog-green, a latest model. Bob climbed into the front with Norma while Toby was directed to the back seat.

'So you're going overseas? I suppose you know what you're doing?'

Toby clenched his hands with their thick fingers and their bitten nails. He was a grown man, and everybody treated him like a child. He felt useless and unwanted. But he had a secret, he had not yet banished his night-ferry dreams, and had kept some, like dust diamonds under the mat, to deal with this expected greeting from his aunt. Why worry?

The old hag. Now, Evelina –

Evelina Festing!

She had turned him down. He had not really expected her to say Yes I'll marry you Toby. They scarcely knew each other. At first he used to visit the Festings' on Saturday evenings to keep Evelina's father company, for Sammy's legs had been shot off in the war and he could not go out much to meet his cobbers. Toby would sit and gossip with Sammy who would catch up with his work of sewing leather, repairing handbags, saddles. Sometimes he played Patience. His habit was to explain every move aloud as if no one but himself could understand it.

'Black two on the red three, ace goes out. See?'

But when Toby offered advice over his shoulder – 'That red seven on the eight of clubs' – he was always startled and touched by the way Sammy accepted it without complaint without saying (as Toby's father would have done) 'I saw that all along, stop interfering won't you!'

On those evenings at the Festings' Toby was happy. There was Mrs Festing making the supper; he and Sammy were sitting talking and playing Patience; no quarrelling, no jeering, no wireless turned loud to hide the silence. And moving in and out of the room, and sometimes sitting in the chair by the fire with her work, there was always Evelina. Toby placed the responsibility for his happiness upon Evelina. It was she, it seemed, who made the harmony of the evening, who bewitched the queen cakes to rise and turn golden brown in the oven in the kitchen, who compelled all the cards to be revealed in the correct order and the game to be solved. The fire burned in the grate for her. The clock ticked on the mantelpiece so that she might hear it and privately, without fuss, remove the detonator to protect the world from the explosion of Time.

And all this she performed without boasting or obvious display of power – oh Evelina was brave, so brave!

Her cheeks were rosy, her hair dark, not as curly as she would have liked it, Toby knew, for she had a home perm kit in the bathroom. And her body was firm and round in the right places. Her mother had mentioned once that Evelina had 'trouble' with her feet, and when Toby, sitting opposite her by the fire, considered and warmed to her charm, he often knew a fleeting uneasiness at the thought of the 'trouble' lodged in her feet. He was careful, then, to keep his glance from them, so as not to spoil his pleasure. Sometimes he wondered why she was not out on Saturday nights, like the other girls, dancing at the Scottish or out the country, or at the pictures, or down Lovers' Lane with a boyfriend. One night he thought, She stays home because I am here. She is in love with me. She used to sit with a small green pillow resting on her knees, making lace, twisting and turning bobbins wound with fine white cotton.

'They don't often make lace nowadays,' her mother said. 'She's clever with her fingers.'

Toby thought, That means: when she's your wife Toby she'll be handy with a needle.

And soon he took it for granted that Evelina would be

marrying him. She never mentioned it herself.

She has a wonderful modesty, Toby thought. She knows her place. Although she said nothing about their coming marriage, she talked freely of her work in the haberdashery department at the draper's, of people who ran up bills and couldn't pay them, of the woman who worked with her and was taking lessons in drama, of the man in the office who was going to Night School.

Night School, thought Toby. I left school early because of my fits, but I'll get my own back.

He sometimes wished that Evelina would not talk about her life at work. It excluded him. She seemed, at times, to have forgotten that he and she were marrying in the near future.

The near future!

So he had gone to the jeweller's and had a pair of ear-drops specially made from greenstone, attached to tiny golden rings, and laid in a small green box upon cream padded satin. And one night with his heart aching with love for Evelina, and for the room where she sat, and for the teacups on the table and the clock on the mantelpiece, and the little green pillow that she held upon her knees, making lace, he gave her the ear-drops.

'My engagement present,' he said. 'For our engagement.'

Toby didn't want to remember any more about that. He remembered only that Evelina had looked horrified, and in her horror she had thrust her feet out, and while she was growing more and more alarmed, explaining that surely he knew about her boyfriend in Fiji, in the Air Force, he was staring in a dazed way at her feet, wondering how to recognize the 'trouble' in them. Perhaps it was bunions, well thank goodness he had escaped from a woman who had bunions and corns!

But no, no, Evelina! He was heartbroken. His mother was dead too. Evelina had led him on, deliberately lured him. But how beautiful she was, with the freckles on her cheeks, and her quick hands twisting the bobbins, and the little green lace pillow resting on her knees that she held so close that they might have been joined together, like the legs of the tiny celluloid dolls his sisters used to play with.

Well he was leaving the country now. But he would wear, for ever, the greenstone earrings which she had refused. The world laughed at him, everybody laughed at him, but still he would wear the earrings, as they hung now, fastened to his watch-chain...

And what was Aunt Norma saying?

'I know it is *something* to have someone who's going overseas. Not everyone can go *overseas*. To the Lakes, yes, and to Rotorua, and the Glaciers, but not *overseas*. Why must it be Toby?'

'He's writing a book, too. The Lost Tribe,' Bob said. 'He wrote a composition about it years ago. The teacher read it out in front of the class.'

Toby sensed the sudden pride in him, and flushed. Then he remembered again how his father always mocked him while his mother defended him. The Lost Tribe. No one but himself knew or understood the real meaning of it; no one possessed the subject as he did, and no one must ever share it.

'How strange,' Aunt Norma was saying. 'The Lost Tribe!'

'It's my idea,' Toby warned, leaning forward. 'The Lost Tribe is my idea. And I'm going to London all right.'

'But why? You, of all people!'

'Well why do other people go overseas? I'm the same as other people. I want to see the world.'

'But what about settling down, earning a living? And your father isn't getting any younger.'

'Come off it, Norma, I'm not in my grave yet,' Bob joked, while a flash of fear played like vivid lightning in his eyes.

'Olive Warren had a stroke and lost the use of her legs,' Norma said suddenly, turning to Bob and intoning her information like a child who stands on a street corner skipping and chanting, 'Lucy Locket lost her pocket, Kitty Fisher found it!'

And now here was Number Fifteen Short Street, without a fence but with such a neat lawn and garden.

'It's the trend,' Norma explained as she drove up to the garage, 'not to have a fence. It's rather a sign that you're anti-social if you have a fence and a gate.'

Currently, to be anti-social was a sin. One had to co-operate, to contribute, to direct one's living outward; fences were barriers.

Of course they were, and useful too, Bob thought.

'What about burglars?' he asked.

Norma exclaimed impatiently, 'Oh Bob, don't be old fashioned!'

'But burglars are modern enough! Didn't you see in the paper where –'

'Oh Bob, the fact remains that fences are not the thing.'

Bob was persistent. 'Where's the letterbox if you haven't a gate?'

'There's the letterbox, silly!'

'A gatepost and no gate!'

Norma repeated that being anti-social was a sin. Murder, suicide, adultery, they were too fierce to be teased, and if one found oneself in the same cage with them it was the end; one lay savaged, bleeding; whereas the little sins, the tiny white mice climbing their ladders and running round on their wheels in the convenient cages, they could be commanded, teased, or ignored, and little harm was done; there was no question of death, of the body or the soul.

Being anti-social was wrong. Not wearing the right clothes was wrong. And eating peas with a knife. And gargling with too much vigour in the morning. Dolly sins. It was safe to defy their attraction. It was safe to talk about them. Sins of gauze, worn like a veil over the murdering hearts.

'Now you'll have to entertain yourselves for a while,' Norma told them after breakfast. 'I've an early choir practice.'

'Singing in the choir, the heavenly choir. Where?'

'I belong to the League of Mothers,' Norma answered, adding quickly before Bob could examine and ridicule her information, 'Oh anyone my age can belong. You don't have to be a mother.'

'Funny,' Bob said.

Cold current without warning in a mild summer sea. In the early years of her marriage Norma had borne twin dead babies; forever nameless, shelled fast about the impenetrable kernel of their identity; treated as nobody, buried in a hurry, their faces never flamed with the stress of beginning.

'What do you sing in this choir? Trilly things I suppose.'

Norma opened her handbag and withdrew a leaflet of music which was tattered and held together by a strip of cellotape. 'Sheep may safely graze,' she read.

'Sheep may safely graze! Oh, may they? No hawks around, no killer dogs, no keas, no swamp, no river coming down dirty? Still, the farmers are wealthy enough

47

– they support the government all right, the capitalists, see them every Tuesday and Friday on Farmers' Day with their posh cars parked between the trees down the main street. They're having to uproot those trees, you know. Interfering with the sewers. Mustn't have anything interfering with the sewers; foundation of society, eh Norma?'

'Don't be crude, Bob. Well I must go. And Bob when you talk open your mouth and pronounce your words more carefully. Oh Bob, if you mumble like that and don't clean your teeth properly – look in the mirror for yourself – you'll be a dirty old man. Bob, I'll never forgive you if you turn into a dirty old man!'

And she was gone, clackety-clack down the path, and they heard her starting the car.

Bob leaned back in a chair by the electric fire. 'Well now we can relax. What's up with you?'

'Nothing. She's an old fusspot. The Lost Tribe is none of her business.'

'Beats me with all your talking about this Lost Tribe why haven't you written about it and got it over with?'

Toby frowned. Why didn't his father understand that it was not like that, it was not like that at all?

v.

LIVING where I am, how can I cleave to anything? Please tell me now. Am I plugged in to the sky? Is it a waste of light out here, in the natural dark, with the mauling sea so close?

Toby will know.

Toby is sitting by the fire at Aunt Norma's. He is thinking, My father doesn't understand the subject at all, there are precautions to be taken, menaces to be foreseen and overcome, slits in the roof to be mended unless the storm is to intrude day and night and the water run like mice down the walls. Toby is remembering that when he was a small boy he found some coins which were called *Money*, which he saved in a tobacco tin with *Bears* printed on the lid. Polar bears, grizzly bears who cried at the slightest upset, Bruin with his nose in a pot of honey, sleeping a long sleep in winter, koala bears feasting upon the gum leaves. And the gumnuts are hard on bare feet; they hurt.

So Toby saved the money in the tin until he knew he could keep it no longer, there was a demand from God that he spend it.

'Tomorrow,' he said to himself; while the rats and bogies inhabiting the wall under the wallpaper and the scrim scuffled about tearing up documents and carrying the Great Plague like a peppermint under their tongue. And when Toby woke in the morning the bed was wet and cold. 'Why didn't you use the chamber?' his mother asked him.

All the way down to Mrs Bollidge's he made footprints in the clay. He found three fingernail pieces of snailshell which he planted among the dead leaves under someone's hedge; people drew hedges round themselves, like magic chalk rings.

Mrs Bollidge moved her arms as if she were swimming through the morning and wanted to get a good start.

'Well little man,' she said. Toby had not yet started school.

He slid the coins on the counter. 'What can I buy with these?'

Mrs Bollidge stopped swimming, she was far enough ahead, no one would catch up with her now. She examined the coins carefully.

'You can't buy anything with these. They're foreign.'

'But they're money to spend!'

'Not in this country. Perhaps not anywhere.'

'Nowhere in the world?'

'I don't know. But not in my shop. Now run along home – here's a broken animal biscuit.'

Half a lion, a dead lion, a pink lion, in return for all those years of saving in the Bear tobacco tin and of turning and touching each night in bed; sleeping, or face from the wall when the bogies troubled! Oh it did not seem fair, nothing was fair. Could I, Toby wondered, could I perhaps travel to the other side of the world and spend my money, for it is *my* money, I found it in the pocket of my father's old soldier uniform; finders keepers.

But when he reached home he was crying, and he wouldn't tell anyone what was the matter, and at night he still played with the foreign money, gravely, carefully. The coins now contained a secret weight, as if they were heavy as lead or iron or Waimaru stone. Yet they were made from a substance that could not be mined or quarried or welded, that could build no ships or cities; yet imprisoned deep in itself was a pattern of former dream, a shell of hope, leaf of fantasy. In the end, Toby, the coins of fantasy mean nothing, have no rate of exchange or any value; they do not even deceive by being counterfeit.

Simply, few people will accept them, not even on the other side of the world. Only at the edge of the alphabet are
they legal tender.

'Well, don't keep on dreaming. Why haven't you written
your Lost Tribe?'

Toby smiled. I am an ambassador.

'You'll see,' he said. 'You'll see.'

Shading his eyes and face from the people who were
taking his photograph, going overseas.

I present the credentials of my loneliness. Will you attend my party at the Embassy?

VI

WHEN TOBY was a child and his sisters were playing house and didn't want him for a husband because he might take a fit and spoil everything, spill the dock-seed tea and the dahlia wine, knock over the furniture and wet on the carpet, Toby learned to play by himself, gathering appleboxes and making his own furniture and owning large areas of land (by right) where his sisters wanted to play.

By decree, Toby owned the summerhouse too, and the furniture in it, and although his sisters didn't want him for a husband they couldn't stop him from visiting when he chose or from trying to collect the rent. By nature and circumstance Toby was a landlord. Sometimes when his loneliness and fury became too much for him he gave notice to his sisters and the girl over the road who played with them; he evicted them, saying that the rent had been increased and he knew they couldn't pay it, ordering them to appear before a bankruptcy court, and not to try to drown or shoot themselves in the meantime. They were afraid of Toby. They were alarmed by his fits. Yet they accepted him as the landlord, and when he turned them out of their house, although they began to cry and threatened to 'tell Dad', they obeyed his orders and went bag and baggage to new territory which Toby instantly claimed, for he owned the whole world, as far as eye could see and beyond, over the hills where they sledged, past the caves with the seashells and the creek with its cocka-bullies. He owned the theatre too, the old velvet curtains hanging in the summerhouse; for special concerts and plays he increased the rent.

'You have to pay a levy,' he would say.

Who taught him this urgent system of personal economy?

Lying in his camp bed at Aunt Norma's ('I've put you in the camp bed Toby because you're younger and ought to be able to rough it a bit. You've done too much for him, Bob. And then they go away and leave you. Overseas! Just imagine! *Overseas!*') Toby was remembering one of the special concerts in the summerhouse when the girl over the road sang the Hawaiian song *Proudly Sweeps the Raincloud O'er the Cliff*. He was thinking of Minnie Holloway, the girl over the road who lived in a house with red cushions and carpets and the blinds down with the tassels touching the windowsill. Minnie Holloway used to say *Basilica, escritoire, chiffonier*. And *couch* instead of *sofa*. And *tallboy* instead of *wardrobe*. *Tall boy?*

Toby was thinking of Minnie now, but not really thinking of her, for people shift, like panels of lantern-slides or cards mysteriously removed and replaced, and one person is another, and people do not stay.

Minnie Holloway. But Evelina Festing! Evelina singing the farewell song at the concert in the summerhouse.

Proudly sweeps the raincloud o'er the cliff,
Borne swiftly by the western gale,
and the sound of lovers' parting grief
sadly echoes amid the flowering vale.
Farewell to thee, farewell to thee –

Evelina was singing to him. His sisters were not there, to spoil everything. He and Evelina were alone, and Evelina was saying, 'Are you really the landlord and can turn people out of their houses when you choose?'

'Everything belongs to me,' Toby said grandly. 'If it were not for me they would have no food or furniture, never be able to play house. I tell you they would starve.'

'And you're really going overseas?' Evelina asked, her eyes filling with tears. 'You'll never come back and see me again?' 'I'm coming back to marry you, Evelina, and we'll live out the North Road in a new house, roughcast with a flat roof painted your favourite colour.'

He thought it wise to mention Evelina's favourite colour. He had read an advertisement where a man and a woman were choosing paint in a shop. In one square they decided upon the paint. In the next square the woman had her arm around the man and was kissing him, standing on tiptoe while a bubble-shape blown from her mouth had captured the words 'He lets me choose my favourite colour in Hurndell's Paints. No woman can resist a man who lets her choose her favourite Hurndell Paint.'

In the next square they were arm in arm outside their new house and an arrow shot into the roof trailed the words *Hurndell's Paints.*

Toby enjoyed reading the advertisements on the screen and in the newspapers. He liked reading little stories about pimples and bad breath and Night Starvation and B.O. and Mr Universe, and although he did not believe what the advertisements claimed, there were times when out of a sense of desperation and a need to simplify the process of living, to break it down into little squares, he tried to follow the commands of the advertisers, to perform the ritual of using their product in the hope that good fortune, love, happiness, would be trapped into showering bounty upon him.

He stirred the dock-seed tea.

'Evelina,' he said. 'I love you.'

No, that was not the way to say it.

Then Evelina took the tiny teapot with roses on it, and poured another cup of tea for Toby and herself.

'I've something for you,' he said, drinking the tea in one gulp because he was a man, thirty-five and going overseas. He drew the greenstone earrings from his pocket and offered them to her.

'Our engagement present.'

It was cold in the canvas bed. The bitter July wind whistled under the door and along the floor, flapping the blankets. There was no fire in the room. ('You must rough it, Toby,' Aunt Norma had said.) Toby shivered. Then quickly he leaned from the bed and searching in his coat which hung over the chair, he found the watch-chain with the earrings attached. He looped them, smooth and green, like frozen teardrops, over the palm of his hand. Should he name them? He remembered that when he was little he had visited a local museum and breathing over the glass cases and rubbing his breath away, he peered at the ornaments pinned to the green baize. Ornaments, tools, weapons. All were named. The names gave them value.

His fat suffocating aunty was with him that day. Her husband was a rabbiter, stringing the rabbit skins along the fence that winked with sun and gold and wire; spilling the rabbits' giggles over the grass while the hawks teetered down the wind and stayed poised.

'Why has everything got names, Aunty? Even things for fighting with?'

'Don't touch,' his aunt said. And she pointed to the notice – Silence.

Toby understood. The things with names were really people and wanted to talk without being interrupted. Or perhaps people were having their say too often and it was the turn of things who could not otherwise get a word in edgeways? Toby listened carefully, but he could not hear what they were saying.

My trusty sword Excalibur, Durandel, Angurvadel...

and did not the Maori maiden exchange love-gifts with her warrior? Ear-pendants named Kaitangata, Touhungia, Kaukaumatua?

Toby stroked the pendants in his hand. He could feel them growing warm. He had brought them to life. What should he name them, the love-gifts which Evelina had refused because he was not making his way in the world, because he took fits and bit his fingernails and picked his nose and was a drag on society?

What should he name his gifts? He touched his cheek against them, he, Toby, warrior, landlord. Then, 'Get out of my house,' he cried, smashing the doll's tea-set and spilling the dahlia wine and the dock-seed tea. And then he fell down in a fit while his sisters, alarmed, ran crying from the summerhouse, and only Evelina stayed, wearing her ear-drops, comforting him when he woke into the unbelievable secretive marsupial world that breeds and hides the infant Peril until it is strong enough to message the earth (thump with its language) and kill.

VII

THEY STAYED. Like a habit, a penance, a fly-in-the-sealed-room dream, a mnemonic, an out-of-date adjustment like a third eye or flightless wing.

There was no need for them to stay, standing there against the wharf shed, trying to shelter while the rain poured down on them, and Aunt Norma kept wiping her face, shaking out her handkerchief like a flag as if to say, 'Here I am Toby, waiting in the rain with your father for the *Matua* to sail and take you away overseas. My face is blue with the cold, and no doubt your father has caught a chill, but he's stubborn, all the Withers family are stubborn, he has to see you sail away.' She and Uncle Philip (before he went to work) and Toby's father had all said Goodbye.

'Goodbye Toby.'

And Aunt Norma had slipped a five-pound note into his hand – well there are so few currencies between people that one has to use something.

'From Uncle Philip and me,' she said warmly, flushing with pride at her kindness.

And Bob had stood with his face grey as a wing of one of those elderly seagulls that do not apparently go to sea anymore but stay safe on the edge of the wharf – you can see them there any day, in rows, rocking gently in the wind, standing on one foot with their eyes shut.

Bob's lips quivered. 'Take care of yourself, Toby.'

Then he had shaken hands formally with a cold air of dismissal which aroused in Toby the concern and wonder he had felt when his father first decided to shake hands with him instead of kissing him goodbye. He remembered his curiosity then — why was his father shaking hands with him and not kissing him? What had decided the change? His father must have looked at him and thought 'He's grown up. He's too old to be kissed.' Had he noticed something, perhaps, in Toby's face? Or in his eyes? They said that many things showed in the eyes.

'Goodbye Dad.'

And now the occasion was embarrassing, unnecessary and prolonged. Norma and Bob were martyrs in the rain. The ship did not leave for over an hour.

From his position on the crowded deck Toby could see his father stamping his feet and flapping his arms to get warm, and his aunt turning up her coat collar against the wind and rain and huddling into the slight shelter given by the wharf shed. And if Toby moved away from the deck railing or was swept out of sight by a surge of excited passengers, to reappear a few minutes later, searching out the dismal figures waiting resolute, melancholy, he fancied he could plainly discern the reproach in their faces, because he had neglected his vigil. Had he been travelling by train, perhaps from the North to the South Island, they would have said unconcernedly, 'We won't stay here until the train leaves, it's no use hanging around, on a day like this too, you find yourself a seat and get comfortable.'

But this was a voyage, it was a ship for overseas, it was Toby going overseas; an adventure as serious and fraught with peril as birth or death. It was all very well for the Shipping Companies to advertise with glossy posters portraying the comfort and pleasure of life on board ship, but everyone knew it was really a blind, really it was only a blind, a cover-up for the inexorability of the ocean; no one was ever entirely safe at sea. And the Shipping Company proved it by adding to their tickets dire afterthoughts in small print with the words *Hurricane, Act of God, Tempest, War on the High Seas...*

Somewhere on the wharf a Pipe Band began to play *Cock o' the North*.

Bob started to wave his arms; he cupped his hands and shouted through them to Toby. 'Hear the Pipe Band?' he called. 'Hear the Pipe Band?'

Toby wondered what his father was trying to say to him, and thought he looked demented, waving his arms down there and half-dancing. He looked like the little boy Shortie Baker who had wanted to get a film contract from an Australian producer – most of the children in Toby's neighbourhood had ambitions to go to Hollywood – or at least to Australia – and the producer had made him stand on the stage of the local cinema and wave his arms and shout, 'Watch Out, There's dynamite down there!' All the little boys had queued up to shout it. Watch out, there's dynamite down there!

Toby wondered, Could that be what his father was saying? Was he, like Shortie Baker, trying to pass some kind of test where he needed to cry out warnings?

There was danger certainly. Toby shivered. The water lapping the sides of the ship was dark with blood.

Realizing that he could not be understood, Bob turned to Norma.

'I wondered,' he explained, 'if he's noticed the Pipe Band.'

He screwed up his eyes and tried to pick Toby from the rest of the passengers.

'He's not at the other side of the world,' Norma said sharply. 'He's not deaf.'

'Amy used to say his hearing was going.'

Bob talked as if Toby were a piece of machinery with Amy as its only mechanic, sensitive always to secret defects, listening, testing, pronouncing judgment on conditions and prospects; selfishly caring for and handling.

'Yes,' Bob repeated, feeling suddenly lonely because Toby did not seem to be aware of the Pipe Band. 'His hearing is going.'

'It's hard to keep in touch,' he said, straining to catch a glimpse of Toby. 'We should go. It's no use waiting.'

'But we can't *go*. We can't just go and leave him there. His mother – Amy,' Bob said incoherently. He was thinking that if Amy were alive he would be writing her a letter that evening, telling her what time they had arrived at Norma's, describing the weather, what they had eaten and at what time, what Norma and Philip had said to them and what they had said to Norma and Philip, where they had been, whom they had seen, and the cost of everything. Sentences which began, On the Monday... On the Tuesday. Ending with... On the Friday we saw Toby off. It rained. We had shepherd's pie for tea, shepherd's pie and custard. While Norma did the dishes and Philip read the *Star*, I sat by the fire, working a puzzle, undoing two staples. We sat around for a while after that but I was dead tired. Ten p.m. Norma made a cuppa. Ten-thirty off to bed. Slept like a top.

You liar.

On the Friday...

You came in my dreams, your great check felt slippers sailing like arks into the room, and I remembered the day you cut off your long red hair and the children were afraid of you and I could have cried, a First Class Engine-Driver crying! You came in my dreams – 'Where's Toby? What do you mean, Bob, on the Friday you saw Toby off? Where to? Where's he gone?'

'No we can't go and leave him there –'

'But in all this rain –'

'It's not long now. Listen.'

A brass band standing alongside the *Matua* began to

play *Now is the Hour*, and the crowds edged closer to the ship, and streamers were flung and exchanged. Toby found himself tangled in a crimson streamer, and leaning over, he tried to grasp the end of a bright blue one trailing towards him.

'Hey, that's for me,' a voice cried, and a short man with silver hair and a kindly face grabbed the end of the blue streamer as if it were a life-line. He peered down at the wharf.

'My sister's at the other end, if I could find the other end.' He spoke with an Irish accent. 'I've been visiting little old New Zealand.'

He craned his head to find where the streamer ended while Toby searched too down the twisting swaying thread. Yes, there it was, with no one holding it. The end hung free. It was a stray. Someone must have had too many streamers and no one to share them, or the flimsy paper had been encouraged by buffeting winds to escape from restraint, to discard its role of trying to preserve a communication between people whose human custom was to announce farewell before they had ever really met. The sodden splash of blue was trailing in the milky-green tide that busied itself, going out, against the newly painted ship.

'Sheila must have gone,' the Irishman said. 'I've lost her.'

He looked desolate.

Well why don't you throw nylon lines, iron hooks to each other? Streamers are no use; they are made of paper, they break, you lose them and they trail in the sea or wind themselves around rotting posts or are captured in error by people whose faces you recognize only in dreams.

I know. At the edge of the alphabet all streamers are torn or trail into strangeness.

Now is the Hour. The tune swelled and the passengers looked at one another, embarrassed, swamped with wartime memories, angry at the cheap come-hither approach that is always used by national music to waylay and exhibit as public the most private inexplicable loves and loyalties. Now Is The Hour. There was no help for it. Some cried. Farewells were called again and again, aimed, like the streamers, at particular people but falling useless and ragged in the air and on the water. Red in the face the brass and snorted and farted; it was enveloped in streamers. At the other end of the wharf the Pipe Band played

Speed bonny boat like a bird on the wing,
Onward the sailors cry,
Carry the lad that's born to be king
Over the sea to Skye.

Toby was feeling lonely. He laughed. The bagpipes always made him laugh. He looked for someone to share his laughter. Then a sudden gust of loneliness passed through him and left his house empty and dark. He frowned. He looked at the chaos of the ripped-up floorboards and the flapping torn curtains, the broken windows, and through them into the stone-shape of darkness. Ha, he said to himself. Ha.

'There's Sheila,' someone called in his ear.

It was the Irishman. Miserably Toby looked down for Sheila. He saw a thin woman with a sharp nose and a pale freckled face; she was attached by suction-device to a rubbery infant. Sheila.

Speed bonny boat like a bird on the wing,
Onward the sailors cry,

Carry the lad that's born to be king
Over the sea to Skye.

The lad that's born to be king? Why, Toby said to himself,
and was suddenly bashful and made himself delay saying
it, Why, that's me! As if words had arrived (overcoated,
demi-veiled) to embrace the wordless.

'Why, that's me.'

It is difficult to live here on the edge of the alphabet, Toby.
I have tried to find the words for you. I look for advice to
give you. But how can I give you advice when no one will
advise *me*?

I grandly gesture, hook my forefinger to accuse myself,
beckon. A god comes running neat-aproned
but no one will give me advice. Friends?
The antiseptic whites of their eyes show fear.
It is nothing, it is not in any bond. Only the dead
at the centre of our lives are thus detached enough
to write and distribute pamphlets
falling ripe and sad where we parade our loves
autumnal and the new-style lamps lean embarrassed
    by fog,
hindered in their murder of bright blue and green
and rosy blood under the skin. Only the dead have so much
    to give away
for when you die, as I say, old advice flakes from you,
as if you lived with your head in the sky like a tree.
Onward the sailors cry, Carry the lad that's born to be king.

I leave the long land in its turmoil of growth, the islands
dripping with green and blue juices, sweating steam, ejac-
ulating fish-filled urgencies of tide, turning in fever to the

cold compress of snow against the forehead, the white bandage of ice, the blue-bordered handkerchief pressed by Mother Sky upon the wrinkled infant folds of skin, the burning dry bone and mouth

I, Toby, leave to attend my ceremonial crowning.

You old witch, you invading bacterium, you perpetuating mother with black wings and circlet of light, how dare you skip over water and dance over sea to intrude in the secret places of my purple robe!

So I cry. The hills are like soap-sud water, the light is green in the iron drains and the winds attend with whips and lassoes the rodeo of newly branded run-away seas and coasts the mirrors are cut off in midroom and we will never never now go down the spiral stair

it is like this Evelina, I must explain to you, It is like this

Goodbye my father, Dad, locomotive engineer First-Class; the liniment for your back is on the sideboard, the soldering bolt is where you left it, and the hammer and the two-inch nails, the plane, the spirit-level, the awl; you were so jealous of your tools, you would not let your son touch them, you love your tools, you stare at them as men on the first spring day stare in the window of the hardware store – Clayton's – have you seen them, Dad, young men, like myself, though I am thirty-five, with new suits, and hair slicked down, dreaming, their gaze fixed on chisel hammer set-square slide-rule –

once when I was small, Dad, I stood at the wash-house door where you kept your carpenter's tools, and you shouted across the cracked asphalt path where chickweed and clover were sprouting light and airy but three-leafed clover and the chickweed for the pet rabbit to nibble, and you shouted across the path and into the kitchen where my mother stood dark and damp and threaded like a sack of coal my fuel-mother emptying herself to the greedy

64

fires, Where's my vice? you cried, where in the name of heaven is my vice? And I did not understand carpentry, I thought you were shouting for your advice, that you had lost your advice

hammer set-square slide-rule –
Onward the sailors cry

Now you old witch my mother to sneak across the frontier to break the barrier to throw steel hammers upon the deck, to promise to cradle my head in your lap while we flee (you and I) you with your suitcase of Latter Days, your prospect of Peace between Nations. I with my pills, my letter to the doctor overseas explaining that my most urgent need (as needs are judged by our facility to move unembarrassing as cardboard among people who shall not cry out of turn, disturbing the peace, Help him, Love him, minister to him) yes that my most urgent need so judged can be satisfied by bottles of pills swallowed after every meal; my pills. And my Lost Tribe, my Lost Tribe.

You witch-octopus whom I loved, who in the dark distressful ocean manoeuvred for me with your bright tentacles of comfort: (Are you all right, Toby?)

'Dad, Dad, he's going from one into the other, he doesn't recognize me, Dad it's a stupor, his face is blue and swollen, Dad what is it, what has come over us all, get out the dictionary from the bookshelf – the threads of its binding like worm-cotton eating through epigram epigraph but not through that one word — (but it's no reflection on us Dad, even when they say it's in the family) – what do they mean "in the family"?'

the dictionary epicentrum the point at which the earthquake breaks out, do we live there, is that the disturbance or epiphanym epiphyte

hands out of your pockets, Toby, no little boy should put his hands in his pockets, for Onanism is not the name

65

of a beautiful lady upon a white horse, so spit and mark your boots with a cross and tie your laces, and let us love one another for the first heaven and the first earth are passed away and there is no more sea...

Have I said it for you, Toby? You will visit me one day in your voyage – In October? – lemon light, giraffe shadows, children let out of school; lie coloured stones rattling in glass bottles. Against the sky. Snatch and grab of sound.

'We'll go,' Bob said. 'He's disappeared. Probably gone to his cabin.'

'He might have waved us goodbye,' Norma complained.

'He did wave, a kind of wave, with his hand stiff in the air, like royalty.'

'He's getting above himself, going overseas.'

Now there is in Toby's land (and in my own, I, Thora Pattern writing here on a Saturday morning while the light hammers sheets of roofing-iron in the sky and autumn tries the trick of the watering can as if we were thirsty flowers; a sheen upon my withered petals) there is an affliction of dream called Overseas, a suffering of sleep endured by the prophetic, the bored, the retired, and the living who will not admit that it is easier and cheaper to die, die once and for ever and travel as dust. But being dust how can you return and have your name in the paper and your self pointed out in the street as having been 'overseas' and your conversation filled with the names of places you have visited, your words received with wonder, as prophecies: I saw a silk mountain where ants lived in palaces; I saw a stone tide *flowing*; a dislocation of summer, a cajolery of politics sitting sunbathing like pixies while a mushroom cloud grew from their clotted mental dung and darkened the early morning sky; I saw a handout of lucidities, a twist (machine-wrapped, factory-tested) of compromise; I saw a red winter corpuscle, the sun shining before twilight behind the trees on the Common –

How, if you are not Marco Polo or Herodotus?

I, standing in the main street of Waimaru telling the world of my travels, walking majestically up and down between my sandwich board of fantasy.

'Look, there's Bob Withers, you know Bob Withers, his son went overseas, I saw it in the paper, and now I see he has returned from his travels and is giving a lecture at Toc H.'

'Overseas. Just imagine. Things have changed. One time it took six months to get to the other side of the world; scurvy and ship's biscuits; and look at things now, a month of sunbathing and moonlight. Pampered. And look at the foreigners flooding the country on every immigrant ship, la-de-da Pommies and all. And what did Withers talk about at Toc H?'

'Oh the usual. Riding on a London bus, etc. He had photos too – the pigeons in Trafalgar Square.'

'He can take photos of pigeons in his own country.'

'But this is Overseas. Overseas!'

'You're right. Some people are lucky.'

'But you know I went fishing yesterday. I caught a salmon, and just as I was getting my spoons back into the water there was a flash, a giant fish leapt into the air, all colours of the rainbow, larger than a salmon, I've never seen the like –'

'A tall story if you ask me...'

'Tall if you like. But only twenty miles from Waimaru. Let me tell you I wouldn't travel ten thousand miles from home just to pick up a few tall stories, just to stand in a Square and have a few ordinary pigeons go shitting on my bald head. I tell you I'd see wonders you never dreamed of. But it's my own country for me every time.'

'Have it your own way.'

'I will. I know where I stand.'

'Still... overseas...'

'You're right... Overseas.'

An October warned by frost,
the children sucking pink slabs of a glacial earth,
the running stitch of snow in the sky
to mend
birthsprout
the hamster his cheek lined with fat, wordless.
    Conferences
the rusting resorts this October birched with memory
    the switch
from the green trees where birds were plump and sleek
of paradise and ample morning shadows
the day served for the light to feed on
now October scraps of leaves and light
the starved shapes creeping up the evening walls
around corners
the tall skeleton transparent
while sleeps the tortoise his back marked muted mapped
    with boundaries
his underflesh soft for knives ancient spears pen-nibs
    all
objects driving home in lust hate or chance.

The council flats, the wardrobes with equal shelves
    drawers
lined with newspaper and mouse-dirt
Peer's Son Warned
Daughter of Bishop Detained for Questioning

Admits Terror of Relative Pronoun.

Who bided his time for ever in the human brain
as in a nest
who brought forth no young
who cut through cables of hate with a moonstone, one
    springtime,
whose hibernation is patient and normal
whose larder is full.
Despite terror of the relative pronoun marching
    unnamed even in sleep
we have gone back to the gap and the birth, the edge,
    where
some leap in,
others camp on the edge, incomplete with folding
furniture plastic cutlery tea kept hot in polythene towers
    where
bells toll the groove and flies keep their balance;
some shout or coo-ee God, God.

II.

The Lost Traveller's Dream of Speech

'As from today,' Toby lied to himself, 'I am free.'

He remembered the grocers' bills which included at the end the warnings and frightening finalities of expressions like 'as from'. As from... As from Friday... As from next week we regret that we are unable to supply you. The words themselves seemed to have little meaning – why 'as from'? Why not simply *from*?

But it is imperative, for our own survival, that we avoid one another, and what more successful means of avoidance are there than words? Language will keep us safe from human onslaught, will express for us our regret at being unable to supply groceries of love or peace.

As from. Believe me to be. Hoping this finds you as it leaves me.

I have to be careful, Toby thought, because I am going to write a book. As from today.

Do you want words, Toby, in a wheelchair of italics, words forced to their knees, begging pity? Or whole words standing without support, without floodlight, armour, or trumpet, growing like fruit, the ripe result of their own bush or tree in a harmony of climate, caprice, inspired obedience – like apples, Toby, guavas, pawpaws, and railway-line blackberries grey with travellers' dust?

'You cannot even spell your own name, Toby.'

'No more I can.'

'Leave him, Bob. Many of the world's great men could not spell. And some day Toby –'

'Yes. Some day. One of these days. My fits will go. I will marry Evelina –'

'No no Toby, a great man never forgets his mother.'

He dresses her in lace –

'Evelina makes lace –'

'Toby, when you were little I used to make all your clothes, on the sewing-machine in the back room, and although your Aunt Norma criticized the seams and when she visited she always had to help with a cotton block, they were my very own work. If I'd had time, Toby... In my life, if I'd had time –'

Soon they would be far out on the open sea, so-called because people hope through words to penetrate its closed locked and bolted doors. On deck the passengers were still roaming, staring at the receding land with the kind of voracity with which people stare at the face of the dying, in the hope of finding and keeping to themselves alone, if they can, the last explosive discovery which is so often really the handful of fire thrown away at birth, in error or petulance or ignorance, but which they now long to possess no matter how much it consumes them with its flames – will they find it, prying like crows like telescopes into the light-year tapping of death?

The land crackled and died in smoke or cloud, but it kept returning, like a dream resting on the edge of consciousness, troubling, insisting, like cloud or flame, that it be given a shape, an identity, relevance to human desire. Then as if the sea had fumbled the green handful, the land seemed to drop suddenly beyond the horizon while the evil demolishing sea without explicit comment slid and heaved compulsively under the sky; the Pacific sky.

Toby was lying on his bunk, the lower one in the two-berth cabin which he shared with the Irishman, Pat Keenan, who had tangled with him in paper goodbyes.

'Am I fiction then,' Toby wondered. 'Why should I share a cabin with an Irishman?'

He trembled with suspicion and fear. Who was lis-

74

tening, who was recording the secret beating of his blood as it found its way – miraculous, never bored, punctual, blindfolded – through his private body? Was he not still home in Waimaru in his bedroom, with the fir tree shadowing the window and the clubbable magpies in conference there? His mother would come in soon with a cup of tea and a buttered scone, a date scone.

'In your cot already?'

Toby opened his eyes.

'I'm Pat Keenan. Going overseas?'

'Yes. My name is Toby Withers. From Waimaru.'

'Toby. You don't often hear that name now do you?'

'I don't listen to it. If this is a joke –'

'You know what I mean. Feeling sick?'

'No,' Toby said abruptly. He wasn't feeling sick. It gave him satisfaction to know that he was not the type to get seasick. He had always been able to travel on trains, in cars and buses, and people had marvelled, saying Just Fancy; because all had the idea that if Toby took fits his infirmity would leak, as it were, to other aspects of his life and health. It had gone to his brain, hadn't it? they said. It had made him backward at school. Strange then that he was such a good traveller; it didn't seem fair somehow; but perhaps if it came to long distances, like overseas, it would show, it would show in time.

'No, I'm all right,' Toby said.

'You can tell pretty often the ones who have never been around,' Pat said confidently.

Then suddenly he opened his locker, withdrew the little bowl, and was sick in it.

Pat was forty, he said, with a mind to settle down. He had visited his sister in Nelson in the hope of finding himself a wife, not that there was any objection to Irish or English wives but, 'I'm branching out,' Pat said, raising his arms like a tree.

'I'm branching out too,' Toby said. 'It's the only way.'

Pat agreed that it was the only way.

Pat's search for a wife had been unsuccessful. He took out one or two New Zealand girls, he said, to the cinema and the Hop-Pickers' Ball, although he was getting too old for dancing; but there had been drink, he said, homebrew outside in the paddocks, and although he liked a drink or two he preferred it in a civilized way, not out in paddocks with the cows and sheep staring; besides, he said, girls were the same everywhere, too flighty with nothing to think about but sex and all seemed to want only one thing out of life and that was bed bed and more bed. Pat made it known that he occupied his thoughts with other more important topics. He spoke of his insurance policies, he had valuable policies in London where he had worked driving the buses. He had put aside for his future in other ways too. His overseas trip had been carefully planned, nothing had been wasted. Not that he was a skinflint, oh no, he liked to be comfortable because what else could you be with the world as it was? Food and sleep were the thing.

So he went promptly each night to his bunk – he called it a 'cot', and slept if possible with his body facing the north, as facing the north supplied him with the electricity necessary for restful sleep. It seemed to trouble him that he was never sure when he had acquired enough electricity; as a result he often woke looking pale and tired, and as soon as he had washed and shaved he would hurry to the notice board to ascertain the *Matua*'s position, speed, and direction.

Also, his mind was occupied with thoughts of Ireland and its need to 'break away from the domination of Westminster'; he was concerned about the temptations and plight of young Irish girls visiting London; he was shocked by what he called 'the increase in blacks' in London. His voice had a permanent note of urgency; his kewpie tinted face grew more flushed when he spoke. Everything was urgent, everything was in need of attention, he said, of investigation by the authorities.

Ah, the authorities! Pat grew ecstatic when he talked of them. It appeared that he himself was something of an authority. All his life different people, recognizing his talent, had consulted him for advice, requested him as witness to sign documents, care for valuables which no one else could be trusted to handle. This legal and personal ability, Pat said, was a family trait – his brother was a District Attorney in the United States. He himself ought to have been a lawyer, or someone in the police.

'Or I might have been a doctor, Toby. People say I have the qualities for a doctor. I have close friends who are doctors.'

Sometimes Pat offered advice. Many of his sentences began with 'What you want to do when you get to London is to –'. And he tried to be helpful. The first day of lifeboat drill he adjusted Toby's lifebelt and showed him where to go, interpreting the notice on the cabin wall as if it were in a language which he alone could understand. He helped other people too, pointing this way and that and advising, explaining, criticizing. The crew thanked him for his co-operation. He stood with them laughing, talking, apart from the passengers. People remarked that he was a born organizer, and that when the time arrived for concerts and Fancy Dress then Pat Keenan would surely come into his own.

'Come into his own' – that was Pat's anxiety, for you see, however confident, informed, he showed himself to be, he never 'came into his own'. It is a difficult process anyway, rather like entering the parlour of oneself while the spider is waiting. And one's 'own' can so easily be lost! Sometimes at night Pat was seized by anxiety which set him trembling and wondering. Where was his 'own'? Why was it not safe like his wallet and his passport and his insurance policies?

Then he would think, Well why worry. He would smile to himself, confident again, assured. After all, the authorities would see to it; they would have to see to it. Ah, the authorities!

Then he would sigh, and sleep, facing the north, snoring a soft rustling snore like mice in the next cabin.

IX

ONE NIGHT TOBY took a fit. He knew nothing of it until he woke in the morning and Pat leaned down from his bunk.

'What were you doing in the night?'

'What do you mean what was I doing in the night?'

Then Toby knew. His mouth was sore. Packed behind his eyes there was the feel of shredded corned beef, lawnmowers in his ears, and in the far corner of the cabin a geranium with a stinging velvet smell and scratches on its petals flowered from dry stony soil.

Toby remained silent. 'It's my trouble,' he said at last. 'I suffer from some trouble.'

'You mean – you don't mean you're an epileptic?'

'I do have turns, yes.'

Pat was worried. 'But what are you doing travelling by yourself so far away from your home? What do your parents think?'

'I'm doing what I'm doing,' Toby said truculently.

'I've come a long way in spite of my trouble. And it's my business.'

'But what if you take a fit while I'm here, here in the cabin?'

Pat glanced around the cabin as if it were a sacred place. 'Here, in the cabin! I've seen epilepsy before, you know. Don't think I don't know how to handle it. But shouldn't I report it to the authorities?'

'No. It's my business. I've got my passport and my ticket and I'm going overseas –'

'I didn't say you weren't free to travel, but who's looking after you?'

'I look after myself,' Toby answered sulkily.

79

'London's not New Zealand, you know.'

'I didn't say it was, did I?'

'Where will you stay, how will you manage? Look, there's a room being kept for me in Clapham, the land-lady's a friend of mine, there are other rooms in the house, all for men, reasonable, near the Common. I tell you the landlady's a friend of mine.'

Pat could never keep the triumph from his voice when he talked of people who were 'friends of his'. He was like a big-game hunter, proud of the carcasses, but doomed to have no relationship with the living animal.

And how proudly he talked of the police as his friends! They gave him information which the man-in-the-street never dreamed of, they communicated with him in times of crisis, asked for his help. And not the ordinary police either – the C.I.D. Plainclothes detectives. All the author-ities, even landladies were friends with Pat.

'No, London's not New Zealand, Toby. You would be safe in Clapham.'

'You understand,' Toby countered, 'I'm branching out on my own. I'll stay in a cheap hostel.'

'No, no. Cheap places, for layabouts. You come to Clapham.'

How kind he is, Toby thought. He is interested in my welfare. I've misjudged him. He only wants to do what is right. But Pat's right was *so right*! The *only* screwdriv-er to fit in or remove the plaques of wisdom. Yes, Pat is wise, Toby thought. But why is my father wise also? I am a man, thirty-five, branching out on my own. I ought to know.

'Oh, you won't get far on your own.'

Toby did not tell Pat about the book he planned to write in his spare time, though he mentioned his 'spare time' and Pat laughed.

'There's none of that now. It's work work work.' (He pronounced it 'walk walk walk'.)

'It's work work work and home to your cot.'

So it was arranged, in the meantime, that Toby would stay in Clapham. Well, he thought, I can always leave if I don't like it.

'I'm thirty-five,' he said aloud suddenly to his mother who brushed past him, touching his cheek, pretending to be a respectable ghost keeping an eye on him when in reality she was an old witch preparing her brew. Oh no, oh no, Are you all right, Toby, are you managing? Ah, he knew her, how she used to write recipes for the magazines, *New Ways with Lamb*, *New Ways with Roast Beef*. Economically brewing over the kitchen stove. New ways with Death.

I'm a traveller all right, Toby thought. I must go carefully, tread softly, discovering... It is time I wrote my Lost Tribe... but what if I suddenly grow in two, like a carrot or parsnip under the earth?

'You're thirty-five? I'm getting on forty,' Pat said. 'I have to provide for my future, make sure of a pension. There's nothing like freedom, that's one thing about being a bachelor.' Strange, Toby thought, I never considered Pat was a bachelor. He reminds me more of an old maid. But then when you grow older it's hard to tell, your self is so used up that you pick the flowers and weeds on both sides of the creek in order to get your supply; even my mother was growing whiskers on her chin and her chin seemed to lengthen to cast a lean patriarchal shadow; and little hairs, like mould, grew out the side of her face.

'I would have stayed in Ireland,' Pat said, 'but there's no work. You want to go to Ireland someday. If there's any place you want to go it's Ireland, especially the South where you find the real Irish. I'll show you the

81

leprechauns, the little people. You go out at night and see them running about, you can see their little houses too where they sit by the fire and look out of their windows; they're neat, they're clean, there's no vice among them, oh I wish now that I were a little leprechaun, Toby, gathering in the criss-cross twigs for my fire!'

Toby marvelled. He could believe his own fantasies but he found it hard to believe those of other people. Pat Keenan too, with friends in the police, the C.I.D. This information haunted Toby and depressed him. The police were beginning to draw circles around him with stopwatches.

'Do you really believe in leprechauns, Pat?'

'And why not? There's historical proof. If you come to Ireland you can see the little houses in the ground. I'm not the sort of person to have fancies, if that's what you're thinking. I tell you I've seen the leprechauns. Well, another day, Toby.'

X

YES, another day; and people.

People.

The parson's wife who campaigned to give lessons in country dancing. The talented pianist who practised in the morning and caused people to marvel at his virtuosity, and to inspire them with thoughts that... perhaps... perhaps I have it in me; so that when he finished playing others would stroll towards the piano, fingering the keys, scowling angrily – cut off my hands why can't I do what Peter Connington was doing, getting everyone's attention with my skill – why is it thus, why do piano keys consistently refuse? And why in a closed society – ship, room, prison, human heart – is it so necessary to invite the Gods and Goddesses and worship them, touch the hem of their garments? Peter Connington, the God, the pianist – there he sits at the Captain's table. The Captain's table? Awe, envy, tributary pride (I knew his mother's cousin by marriage, they lived two doors away, not two doors away). And ah the clever and beautiful young graduate with her scholarship to Oxford; ah the self-possessed, the compact whose limbs adhere to their sticking-place; the mysterious, the rumoured... claws, teeth, cabin-lairs, the nightly kill, the white dinner-jackets dripping with blood, the smell of death, of devouring; the soft splash, far in the night, when the victims are thrown into the sea...

So it is evening once more, only a few days at sea, and the pattern of people trembles into place, outwardly harmless as a paper lantern, but fixed to the ceiling of desire, greed, longing.

'It's night again. How it goes.'

Pat climbs awkwardly up the ladder to his bunk.

'Did you get some sandwiches for supper? You want to get some, you want to claim your rights, Toby. And after Pitcairn you'll go to the social, to get to know more people? You don't want to be on your own all your life.'

'You don't want to be, you ought to, why don't you...'

'Ah, into my cot again!'

Pat is feeling pleased that Toby may come to stay in Clapham. He feels that he has performed a good deed, rescuing Toby from the perils of London. He enjoys good deeds, giving people happiness, yet it must be the kind of happiness which he has prescribed for them.

You don't want to, you ought to, why don't you.

On the swivel table by Pat's bunk Our Lady stands as a plaster statuette, enfolding her marble-faced baby. She wears a bright blue robe. Pat prays to her every night. She has travelled with him all the way from London to New Zealand. Now he kisses her on the forehead, resting her a moment upon the blankets then restoring her to her place upon the table.

'Goodnight,' he calls to Toby. 'Pitcairn early tomorrow. Sleep well. Only the guilty find it hard to sleep.'

The scales are fallen from my eyes, I no longer see the patched world, the scabbed vision that weeps and is poulticed by blindness. Give benediction on a small note, a ticket of leave peep show, your aquamarine robe your platinum skin your carnation blood my Lady Our Lady and the swans leave by the last train from Paddington or King's Cross.

And Pat dreamed that someone dropped a handful of safety matches which he picked up – he chose one for they were so big they resembled faggots or walking-sticks. He struggled under the weight of the match and the splinters jagged under the skin of his hands pricking blue clots of blood. Now the important thing to do, Pat thought, is to strike the match. But if it is a safety match how can it be struck?

That is why it is called a safety match, a voice told him. It was a leprechaun from its kitchen window, drawing aside the clean muslin curtains and peeping out.

'Conditions are not good under the earth,' it said. 'The damp seeps through, there is a gradual growth of mould over our furniture and our walls and our faces.'

Strike the match, Patrick.
By the light o' the peat fire flame
the light the hill-folk yearn for.
Strike the match Patrick.

'I wish I had wax vestas,' Pat said. 'They strike anywhere. But these are safety. What am I to do if all through my life I have no wax vestas?' Just then Toby appeared with a bundle on his back which contained, he said, 'all his worldly goods'.

'But it's a matchbox,' Pat told him.

'Yes,' Toby said, loosening his bundle and placing it on the ground where the leprechauns came and climbed over it. They wore woollen cardigans full of dropped stitches; one had the face of Our Lady. Pat could not see the Child until he heard it crying and noticed it holding up its hands where the splinters from the match had pierced and drawn blood.

'Suck them, put them in your mouth,' Our Lady told the Child. The Child put its hands to its mouth.

'Aren't you going to strike the match?' Toby asked.

And the leprechauns echoed, 'Aren't you going to strike the match?'

Pat leaned and hauled the match towards the giant box, but before he could strike it, it had changed to a walking stick and he had become an old white-haired man tottering along with the aid of the stick. He was walking in a lonely place, near the edge, among weeds and rusty tin cans and derelict words and people. The matchbox had diminished in size. He picked it up, opened it, and a piece of blue thread was shaken out.

'Enough to hang myself,' he said, 'on Our Lady's Robe.'

Then Pat slept deeper, the dream was gone, and he ventured underground by the dripping rivers and caverns and shining a small torch he tried to tease the glow-worms, the Waitomo glow-worms.

'IT'S PITCAIRN. I've got an invitation to stay. Any time. Any time I happen to be passing.'

Toby spilled an armful of oranges on to his bunk and waited for Pat's expression of admiration and envy, and when Pat did not seem impressed Toby looked surprised, then sympathetic.

'You should have been on deck, Pat. Islanders everywhere. I don't say they wouldn't have invited you – well, you're different, you don't understand them as I do. They're my friends, Pat. They invited me to stay.'

Pat listened curiously, thinking, He goes on deck, he buys fruit, he talks to the Islanders, they give him an invitation to stay, the invitation they give to all the passengers of every liner that passes Pitcairn; and he comes down here as if he were the only one invited. And when in all your life do you 'happen to be passing' Pitcairn? This Toby Withers is simple, no doubt about that; he's not the full pound. He seems to live in a different world, blind and deaf to ordinary goings-on; yet he worries about little things. The cabin door, for instance. What fascinates him about the cabin door? He's been at it for the past few days, playing with the lock, snipping, unsnipping, opening and shutting the door, and all so seriously. It scares me. And the swivel table has lost its swivel, through his playing about with it. Why does he keep touching the furniture as if it had some special meaning for him? Why can't he leave things alone? Can't he understand that things are always better left alone?

Having arranged the fruit in golden battalions on his locker Toby sat down to write his first letter home. Dear Dad, I have been invited to stay on Pitcairn at any time I happen to be passing. We have had calm seas and I have not been sick. I share my cabin with an Irishman who is wanting me to stay in Clapham London SW4. He has been a bus driver but he says, as if I don't know, that I can't get work on the buses because of my trouble. The girls on the ship are a lot of old hags doing country dancing. Remember me to all. What do you suppose Mum would say? Your loving son Toby Withers. P.S. The old car engine down in the shed is mine and I don't want anyone to interfere with it. Just put a piece of sacking over it and leave it because it is mine.

Writing for Toby was an arduous task as if a limbless man were setting out to dance. The act occupied his entire body, creased a frown on his forehead, thrust his tongue out the side of his mouth, forced his fingers to grasp too tightly with the result that the writing was scarcely legible. Blots came, ominously, in strange shapes and clusters; the pen twisted or splayed its nib; the words did not know how to spell themselves but choked their letters together, partnering strangers, refusing conventional and correct marriage; or, solitary, uncertain where to go and what posture to take up. How often had the teacher said to Toby when his spelling was despaired of, 'You carry a picture of the word in your head, Toby. That's how you learn to spell. Look at the word, close your eyes, and you have a picture of it. Spelling is easy, Toby!'

But surely she had reckoned without the individuality and caprice of words and the letters that composed them, their reluctance to appear naked, as it were, in people's minds only to be plucked (the letters like passion-fruit along a trellis) and splashed (their seeds and juice flying) upon a sheet of paper! In his mind Toby saw pictures of words – they allowed him that indulgence – yet when he tried to write them they refused to leave him, would not be uprooted, and the picture of their letters (strung now like flimsy spiderwebs between trees) changed to spider-blots, nothing but blots of ink. Plants, fruit, webs, insects, animals, the words were in turn all of these, yet in the end they became blots, fly-specks (like the dead), mouse-dirt, a mess to be cleaned up. Sometimes Toby felt the words moving in his arms, down his arm into his hand, wriggling like silkworms awaiting their third change of skin before their mouth begins to drip golden silk. He could do nothing to help them. The teacher had never told him that words were like this.

'Look at the word, Toby, close your eyes, and you have a picture of it.'

It was certain that Miss Botting had carried all her words framed and imprisoned, like pictures hanging on a wall, pretty pictures of flowers, trees, spaniels, cats in baskets, cherubs; and none of the spattered secretions of death and decay, nothing which demanded a private lonely interpretation.

After writing his letter Toby felt without energy. He tried to look proudly at his work, but it was no use; yet he did not despair entirely for he was still preoccupied with the invitation to Pitcairn. Perhaps he would find the Lost Tribe at Pitcairn? Perhaps his invitation had been arranged because they knew he was going to write a book and they wanted to help him?

He licked the envelope shut and put it on his locker. I'll go on deck, he thought, and tell them I've accepted the invitation. And I'll invite them home to Waimaru. They can sleep in the bedroom next to mine. We'll get a new mattress instead of that damp doughy one, and I'll fix the sash of the window and move out the old furniture.

He was so wrapped up in these prospects that he forgot to worry over his spelling. And he forgot the time, that it was now long past early morning. He hurried up the stairs. He was not even aware that the ship was moving. He reached the deck and looked about him. Where were the Islanders with their soft voices and friendly smiles, with the fruit pebbled about their feet, their land waiting near, with the morning sun shining on it? The invitations to stay... No one had given Toby so many invitations to stay in all his life. You're welcome. Whenever you happen to be passing.

For a moment Toby could not understand that Pitcairn and the Islanders had disappeared.

'It's a trick,' he shouted, so loudly that people stared and stopped playing their quoits and moving their painted wooden horses from little square to little square.

'It's a trick!'

Time is the trick, to cast you in moments of intensity from the conveyor-belt to the whirlpool below. You are wet with spray from the discarded moments that nobody desires because they are your own (to each his own time) and you stare up at the people in their little boxes or cradles or coffins jerking rhythmically along clackety-clack, being attended and processed, wrapped and delivered by Time. And priced. The cost is too high. And there are rainbows in the air, where the water falls.

Toby, confused now, ran to the deck and stared over. There was no land in sight, only in the distance a dark comma of wave perpetuating the sentence – death sentence – of the ocean.

So Toby found a deckchair and sat in it, his head leaning in his hands. Come and stay with us in Pitcairn. Any time you happen to be passing. Someone had snatched his dream away from him. It had mattered so much. And then writing to Dad and telling him and imagining his face, his surprise when he discovered how well Toby was doing overseas, getting invited to stay, making friends...

Someone spoke to him.

'Feeling seedy? You won't be wanting ice cream then, but here's the beef tea.'

Toby took from the steward's tray the morning cup of beef tea which was dark, dark with carriage-wheels and proclamations of mutiny.

That was it, mutiny.

He would show them. He went to the deck-rail and flung the beef tea over the side, and for a moment it stained the sea; an unhealthy colour, as if something had died in the water.

XII

THEY STOOD against the horizon, holiday blocks of light borne on their shoulders and cast aside. They were powerful red and gold men supervising while the slaves heaved with their picks against the light, hacking the blocks into small stones that showered into the sky, glittering down into the sea. Toby watched them. They were warriors. They drew crossbows towards the sun, seeking a gap in its dazzle. The waves rose and fell, looped with greenstone pendants – Kaitangata, Touhungia, Kaukaumatua –

'How was I born Mum?'

'You came in the baby-ship.'

'The baby-ship? Stopping at ports and unloading, the wharfies on strike, the troops out in their thousands?'

Certainly now I will take action against the Shipping Company for fraud. They have issued a leaflet portraying me in my dinner suit on a moonlit deck surrounded by beautiful women with bare shoulders and breast gullies where the snowberries grow. I will issue a writ for fraud.

I am lonely.

When my ship comes home. That was my mother's life. 'Some day,' she said, pinning her tarnished only brooch to the lapel of her costume coat, 'some day when my ship comes home.' And her perpetually expectant gaze which some attributed to hope and faith and others took for signs of exhaustion disguised as enthusiasm, kept searching, searching the faces of those around her, that is, the faces of strangers, for signs of 'news'.

Meanwhile she wrote little songs on the backs of used envelopes and broke bread in the presence of Christ.

She trickles down inside the lining of my skin, like golden syrup; the witch.

Ah, there is Zoe Bryce, the Midland schoolteacher, spinster, in a low-waisted dress five years out of fashion – she keeps saying it is out of fashion. She sits in the corner of the lounge drinking coffee from her acorn-cup, and talking with her companions whom she describes as 'the girls'. I have heard her. They share the same cabin. Fancy her being a schoolteacher. The teacher read my composition out in front of the class. The Lost Tribe. I have never met a real schoolteacher. Zoe Bryce shares a cabin with those other women...

Yes, Toby, they share a cabin, the women who dress discreetly for dinner. They gaze at the complacent sea, the millionth bait, the torn tissue-paper that is a flying-fish, the stars name-dropping from their circle of light. They gaze. They say, We need on board ship to witness, always to witness. What does the blind man consider, listening near the deck-rail to the waves foredoomed in shape trampling one another with sighs?

Entertain me
land land
another ship
a great white whale
a fleshless mariner
   the daily chart
the quoits, the country dancing on the village green
with the sea looking on in derision;
and the painted wooden horses being moved from little
square to little square, groomed and fed and stabled at
night to fill the empty corners of our sleep.

At sea spend the holiday of your life, laze as you have always dreamed of doing, meet people, meet romance, you, she, alone on the upper deck, you, she, the moon, champagne. Don't let your orbit be deckchairs and sleep and sun. Blink a little closer to the human race. At your peril, Toby said.

So as special arrangement for the solitary ones whose shipboard life had not attained the ideals of the Shipping Company's pamphlet or discovered on the cold sea-slopped deck the described enticements, the Social Committee organized a party one evening in a last attempt to make passengers 'get together'. For it is the rule; human beings must live in clusters, hanging like grapes from the scaffold, or in flocks like sheep in a bleating panic from the hawk.

'Yes,' Toby said. 'I will go to the social.'

He wore his best navy suit and white shirt. Although the *Matua* had long ago entered the tropics and other passengers were changing into light-weight American suits and gay tropical shirts, Toby preferred his usual clothing. He was sensitive to weather – snake-heat and paw-frozen snow – but never cared to flirt or negotiate with it. Other people in their approach to outward weather create what is for them perhaps the only satisfying relationship of their lives – the old maid (Zoe Bryce?) in shorts, nibbled chastely by light tentative breezes; the married who can no longer meet each other because they have lost their passport or mistaken the true boundaries on their map of love, now see them gently open to or shafting the sun, melting downstream in the light all the pooled queries crossword clues and plots devised from birth and the first floating onshore gasp. No more among the anemones and the spiralled shells and the salt encircling weeds. Buffeted. And now see those in bathing-suits who trick the impersonal sunlight into caring for them or punishing them, who lie all day curled about the swimming pool and on the open spaces of deck, providing for their lives, without the responsibility and unpredictability of human love, the secret ingredients of pain and pleasure.

'You'll be hot in those clothes,' Pat warned Toby.

'But they're my best!'

He put brilliantine on his hair and stood by the mirror, fingering the greenstone earrings. Then he went upstairs to the lounge where he was greeted by a floral woman (hothouse-forced, blooming once only) who pinned a card to his lapel.

'You're Orpheus,' she said. 'We have to try to make it a mixture of classical and popular. Now find your mate.'

She had few petals left.

Toby said nothing. He sat in a corner and surveyed the women whose throats were fenced with pearls, and the men, surrounding them, who were choosing their partners and surprised, dismayed, pleased, questioning them to determine their insanity, 'Who are you? Do you know who you are? Do you know who I am?' and when the answers proved negative, falling to the general level of irresponsibility where it is agreed that pearls, after all, are for thieves, that throats are for cutting, that all passengers are adrift in one-class fear on the dark seas of identity.

Orpheus? Toby thought. How can I be expected to know about Orpheus when I left school early because of my fits, when I've never had a proper education, and can't spell? I've read books, yes, but not enough to know about Orpheus. I do not think he is a Hollywood film star. Is he from the Bible? Oh I wish I knew! Perhaps his wife was turned into a pillar of salt? My mother said to me, Never look back and never open forbidden doors and boxes. But was not Orpheus a musician? In a jazz band? On the air? With harp, lute, guitar, organ – oh no, the sun, why the sun and the beasts and the people stopped still, now I remember – the day did not strike and the fire froze with its tongue in mid-air.

And there were willow-trees surely, and an old swamp-hen in bed with a nightcap on. Listening.

The collapsible sea folded up and went home to weep.

Toby listened. He smiled. I'm darned, he said, if I know who Orpheus was and where he lived.

And what about his wife?

But Toby was alone, sitting in the corner, not knowing who to look for, and realizing that he disgraced himself by going to the social; it was a reflection on his ability to get to know people and make friends with them. Reflections were things to disown. It's no reflection on us, his mother used to say.

The passengers who had stayed away were those who had discovered their own companions without the artifice of tickets and labels, but merely with the artifice of themselves and their displayed wares.

Orpheus sat alone in the corner. No one appeared to be in search of him. Tom and Maggie passed, dancing, a mile-wide stream separating them.

'I know them,' Toby thought. 'They are brother and sister.'

He found himself watching the woman he knew as Zoe Bryce, who had been seasick almost before the *Matua* left harbour, even before it had shaken off the yearning dolphins. She had lain, people said, for days in the ship's hospital. She looked pale now, and sometimes closed her eyes. Her hair was brown, snuggled damply to her head in the way that wet leaves cling to surfaces of footpaths and gutters. And who was walking upon her head and what was flowing through it, carrying straw and coins and foam?

She wore her low-waisted dress and her pearls, cultured.

Evelina.

Toby walked over to her and sat down beside her, waiting. She would know the identity of Orpheus. Was she not a schoolteacher?

'Are you my sister?' Toby said.

She looked timidly at him. 'How curious,' she said. 'You're not Mickey Mouse, are you? I'm Minnie Mouse. Of all people! Oh, you're Orpheus, how wonderful!'

She stared at Toby, observing his heavy sunburned features and his blue eyes. She thought he looked like a sailor – oh, a sailor! She turned away and closed her eyes. She was holding very tightly to her handbag as if thieves were near, pickpockets and other evil characters who snip away the handles of your bag when you are not looking, and leave you with only the snipped handles, and your treasure stolen.

'You should be dining or dancing with Eurydice,' Zoe told Toby.

'I can't find her.'

'You know it's like me to be Minnie Mouse, to have been given that label. Has it occurred to you that such placings of identity, you as Orpheus, myself as Minnie Mouse, could only exist in fiction? It doesn't make you afraid, does it, that you are fiction, that you are not really aboard the *Matua* sailing to England, that you exist only in someone's mind, some poor writer who cannot do better than bring forth the conversation of musicians, poets, mice?'

'But mice listen,' Toby said. 'Mice listen in the wall and scratch with their fingernails on the parchment.'

'Parchment? Are you a lawyer?'

'To do with law,' Toby said earnestly. 'Who should be my partner?'

97

'Eurydice.'

'I never had a proper education. I left school early.'

How strange, Zoe thought. I have made a long speech. And tonight I will lie in my bunk and consider the thoughts which, as fiction, I have been encouraged to express. But no one knows. My secret is safe. Is my secret safe?

'I would have liked a proper education.'

'Well you should be dancing with Eurydice.'

Evelina.

'I told you that I cannot find her.'

'She will be in the Underworld then. Some day – did you say your name is Toby Withers? – you will be torn to pieces. But have you seen the passenger list?'

'Yes. They gave me a booklet bound in red and blue with names and photos. The sea crashes against the alphabet, the letters crack and split like icing when the soft sweetness has worn away and only the brittle water-tasting bones remain. What? My left ear causes me some trouble. Did you say the passenger list? I have words sometimes, you know.'

Zoe spoke excitedly. 'Nothing. Nothing. There's a family coming aboard at Panama. You know the ones. Their names are called out and they're never present, they are put down for raffle tickets and lotteries until someone remembers they are not on board, and crosses out their names. A table is set aside for them. Their empty cabins are waiting. Can't you see how the life of the ship revolves round them?'

She leaned towards Toby. 'Do you know,' she said. 'I keep thinking of them, and waiting, waiting. I pass their cabin and look in and see everything prepared and clean, the towels unused hanging over the towel-racks, the space beneath the bunks empty of suitcases. Sometimes

I think that perhaps they have died and the Captain is afraid to tell us; they have been stitched in shrouds – one, two, three, and slipped overboard at midnight. And do you know, when their names are mentioned I've seen the expressions of reverence on people's faces, and I've heard them murmuring, as if they were repeating a prayer, "The family that's coming aboard at Panama. The family that's coming aboard at Panama."'

Zoe stopped speaking. She blushed and smiled.

'Forgive me Mr Withers – Toby – I've had some unusual experiences on board this ship. My whole outlook on life is changed. Something happened –'

For a moment Toby thought she was going to cry. But she smiled, with a kind of pride, and said,

'I've been seasick you know. I'm just out of the ship's hospital, and you know how you feel when you've been ill and are up again out of bed; as if everything is walking through you without your consent, ignoring your flesh and bones; and you hang, helpless, like a bamboo curtain in the doorway of all events and purposes. Forgive me. You're not a sailor are you? What have you to do with the law?'

'Law?' Toby said curiously. 'Nothing to do with law. I'm self-employed –'

'But you said –'

'Should I be dancing with Eurydice?'

'Eurydice.'

'I never had a proper education. I would have known if I'd had a proper education. Things come to me sometimes you know. Just like that. They tell me you're a schoolteacher. Do you have crushed coloured chalks for supper? With ink thick and black poured on for cream? You don't. I always wanted to know.'

'So you're self-employed?'

'Self-employed,' Toby repeated with an air of mystery.

'But don't worry, I've read a few books and I've got my plans. There are mice and lawyers in the lining of my head.'

'They are in my head too,' Zoe told him. 'Well you have to find Eurydice and I have to find Mickey Mouse, and both have vanished. You'd think people would play the game!'

'The game? But they do, they do!'

'Oh to tell the truth I'm tired, I've never felt so tired in my life.'

Toby was losing interest. He wanted to talk more about himself, about Waimaru and Mum and Dad, about his not having a proper education and the fact that he was branching out on his own; about being invited to stay on Pitcairn Island.

'Yes, I'm tired.'

And then Zoe turned away suddenly, blushing with shame. Oh how dare I sit next to this stupid and strange creature and get talking to him about my innermost life! Orpheus indeed! Yet the trouble is, one never knows. Since my secret experience I keep thinking, One never knows, how can one be sure? The labels are switched, stolen or lost, and I am frightened. And the family coming aboard at Panama, how I hate them! How I hate their two empty cabins, side by side, and the times when their names are called and people question and answer with details of them, speaking as if they were gods – our masters, gods. Why can't the ship stay as it is, with the same people, cosily with the same people, and never stop at any port, only have strangers rising now and then from the early morning tide – heaping oranges upon us, jumbling us immodestly, enticing with offers to stay, and us only half out of sleep, fighting a curious curved path through the golden bulwark. As it was that morning, at Pitcairn. They invited me to stay. They came to the ship's hospital and invited me to stay on their island, whenever I happened to be passing. I wanted to tell someone – whom?

Here I am sitting here looking for Mickey Mouse and wearing my low-waisted dress bought at Norton and Stroods; and my best pearls.

'At least, although you're English you don't speak with a la-de-da accent,' Toby said.

'I'm from the Midlands. Or am I? Does it matter? I came to your country for a working holiday. I worked at hotels.'

'If you're a teacher then why don't you teach?' Toby asked reprovingly.

'Well this and that,' Zoe said. 'I've given up teaching.'

'But you must have been teaching for years!'

'Yes. I don't know. I'm tired. Something has happened to me.'

'Minnie Mouse. I used to watch the Mickey Mouse cartoons in the pictures back home. Minnie wore an apron and swept the hearth with a little broom, a broom with a red handle. They were friendly animals then in the pictures. That was before they started making their faces bulge and their teeth show like meat-hooks. You remember?'

Zoe said Yes, she remembered. It was before the killing, she said.

'So you travelled to New Zealand?'

'North and South, yes.'

'Rotorua?'

'Rotorua.'

'The Waitomo caves?'

'Yes.'

'Mt Cook and the Glaciers?'

'Mt Cook, Mt Tasman and the Glaciers. And along Milford track.'

'Down there,' Toby said (soon, he thought, I shall tell her about Waimaru and Mum and Dad and being invited to stay on Pitcairn), 'there's a valley of the notornis, the flightless bird. The land is full of unknown unexplored valleys where you might find' – he smiled secretively – 'where you might find... perhaps...', he hesitated, 'strange tribes, lost tribes.'

He was seized by fear then as he said those words. Supposing Zoe Bryce guessed about the Lost Tribe and stole his idea, wrote about it, had it published when she returned to England... How could he prevent her? So many people, Toby knew, were saying, even now, on deck, in their cabins, in the bar, the lounge, 'I'll write a book about my experiences. Oh I could write a book. One of these days when I get down to it I'll write a book.'

Supposing they decided to write about the Lost Tribe? Well they'd better not, Toby thought, for I've had that idea in my head for years and years and it hurts like an African thorn that has jagged itself in me and festered to bursting point, and it throbs day and night. Is everybody else that way, with thorns in their head? Zoe Bryce? Will Zoe Bryce write about the Lost Tribe?

And now Minnie Mouse who had cancelled her right to take part in modern mythology by tearing up the label pinned to her breast (corsage, flowers my dear, an orchid, violets) was sitting silent, resentful, and feeling a sickness that no water biscuit or 'turn round the deck' would cure. It was not the fluid swilling in the merry-go-round of her ear. It was thoughts, sadnesses, regrets that emerged as numbers, chiming the theme of her intolerable secrets. Thirteen one nineteen twenty twenty-one eighteen two one twenty fifteen eighteen which it did not need a schoolteacher to add to one hundred and forty-eight.

Divide by two, Zoe said to herself.

Seventy-four, the length of my natural life, my code of anguish. The answer must mean something.

I am quite at a loss.

I have been rocketed beyond meaning with two dogs, a white mouse, and specimens of human skin. I take photos of the handkerchief-distance with its corner-snot of cities.

Since it happened I am not myself.

Seventy-four. Not beans or shelled peas but years picked from the ashes, cleaned, dusted, polished, but my voyage tells me that I shall not live so many years.

'I'm seasick again,' Zoe said miserably, and hurried from the lounge to vomit her loneliness in private. Omelettes and wine, you have paid for it haven't you? And buttercups grow and English cathedrals rise from the stiff-backed menus which passengers hoard between leaflets and lavender, in order to be reminded.

For memory is so often a single explosion, like a firework in the face. One is blinded. One scrabbles about with damp matches trying to ignite an empty blackened little column of cardboard.

Toby was alone now. Goodnights were being said elsewhere, and the air was filled with the swift excitements of plots and rumours, wild laughter in other places, decks, cabins – 'other' being the habitual situation of laughter. In the cabin Pat was fast asleep dreaming of his leprechauns or of the complications of adequately sized people who have not yet arrived full circle to shelter in caves or holes in the earth but who journey there by degrees, and will soon scratch the skeleton of sunlight upon the cave wall, bury their mouths in their own fur, while the glaciers in a five-million-year slice go shifting, arranging, blotting with the white sheet the gnarled reptilian writing and the human sound Ug and Oh (with fear) frozen to hoops and triangles in the sky.

Your sleep is secret, Pat. You lie, a giant, in the orchard of sleep; at the slightest stir of sensation or thought you are pelted with ripe or rotten dreams where the codlin moth hangs her milky white curtains of decay.

And now all over the sea the chopped light lay beneath the guillotine of tropical darkness.

'I will sleep on deck,' Toby said, talking to the burnt-out cigarettes in the ash-trays and to the lingering solid smell of people, a smell that after a while shudders out of itself, like a conjuror escaping from a locked box, and vanishes.

Toby took a blanket and pillow from his cabin and lay on deck staring at the sky – he saw it striped with painted rails, heaved and slopped with silver flood and the stars in their courses.

'The stars in their courses,' he said, surprised, and fell asleep.

XIII

ZOE BRYCE did not sleep. Her five cabin-mates were lying gratefully dead in the small cabin which seemed to be
built very close to the engines, or life had been breathed
into it by design, generosity or malice, until blood
surged and throbbed through its walls, its palpitations
were marked and known, and a mistake of immodesty
in its construction had layered in the ceiling a number
of naked pipes criss-crossing and disappearing through
dark-rimmed holes in the wall. As Zoe from her top bunk
considered the pipes and tried to follow the advice of 'going with the motion of the boat' which she could not do
successfully, not being a politician, how she longed for
the power to forbid the compulsive rising and falling, to
strike at the steel wooden and iron evil which could not
progress through the waves without forcing one to adopt
a bowing motion – as if in obeisance – and why should
one submit, why establish the same rhythm as every other passenger? Why move into the same climate of body
and mind and have indistinguishable dog-daisies sprouting in agreement from one's life?

Why, to survive. That is, to die. And love?

Zoe's mind bowed obediently before the movement
of the ship. Yet her body needed the persuasion that she
could not give it. Don't use a pillow, people had said. Keep
the porthole open. Soda water is good. Lie on your back,
flat. Looking at the clouds, the pipes in their courses?

The timbers creak, Zoe said to herself, deriving comfort from the unexpected thought that she lay in a pirate
ship where the battered timbers were talking almost
ceaselessly, as trees do, even when they are dismembered,
mutilated, camouflaged, polished at their knotted knees

or sliced in their bone-shafts, still they speak and make one aware of their silence also, their withdrawal on days of frost, and again their voice of complaint in the heat when they seek to burst from the iron hoops of the sun. Have you heard furniture in the night? Why does the sudden speech of table and wall set your heart beating so fast?

Oh how time passes me by, Zoe said. I am a schoolteacher. Two new methods of spelling, a revolutionary means of teaching arithmetic, a return to the look-say method of reading, and I am lost. My schemes are out of date, my plans fall to pieces in my head. A year in the Antipodes, eleven thousand miles there and back in search of what most people find in the next room or, closer, in the lining of their skin. My feet are not bleeding and bandaged, I do not suffer after long wandering in deserts with the sun gonging its brass doom in my ear and settling like golden flies upon my parched lips. I have no foreign visas or secret papers other than my passport and the photograph of myself caught out in the criminal pursuits of being.

I have a secret. Everything is changed. I try not to leave my fingerprints in foreign places. I have seen the hot springs of Rotorua and the Maori girls dancing in skirts of flax and the men performing their haka. I have seen the glow-worm caves at Waitomo – what did they say the name meant – 'assaulted by water'?; the Southern Lakes; and I have wound myself in the wide glowing ribbon of twilight on the southern coasts – Fort Rose, Waipapa; but all this voyaging over strange seas to find what I shall never possess, it leaves me dizzy, it sets the fluid in spiteful motion in my ear; and I am not any younger; just as well to let the tide of my loneliness flow into the heave of the waves and scatter itself as a foul mixture in this aluminium bowl, this drain which we all carry in our lives, made visible.

Oh the beautiful fences of sparkling wire –!

I stood in one of the small towns waiting for the thinning air to receive the sound of a voice and carry it to me; the telegraph wires were weighed down with plaintive messages, and the monosyllabic wind sang its note of death in the great shuddering trees.

But blue sky. No city smoke like a stole across my shoulder. The pruned air like a stalk with the blooms cut off except the solitary centre bloom of light. Yet how I yearned for the swish of people instead of leaves, and for the sweep of crowds, the only permissible litter, not fined five pounds for being deposited thick and fast just one level above the sewers and the gas mains where the men with iron exclamation marks remove the pavement stone, lean, listen, blanch, and fall crying with their hands about their ears. Who listens without fear to the burgle and runnel of decay?

Reading-readiness. Eleven-plus. The lute-player in an Etruscan tomb.

And I have changed. I must touch the surface. I must encircle what is dead. I must think in this way, shuttled over and under. I, Zoe Bryce, shopping at Norton and Stroods where the counters are polythene-covered, protected, and men's ties striped and spotted swing on their stand in a languid circle. I, Zoe Bryce, on my working tour of New Zealand, spending my day crying out in the white kitchens, Soup two, Roast Beef one, a lady, corned beef one, a gent, to follow!, the rhythm of my demands alive in my mind beside the composite historical cries of my own country – victory, rag-and-bone pleadings, church-music of ice cream, disaster, bring out your dead.

Bring out your dead.

XIV

THERE IS A core we bite into that is no one, seeming nothing, a dream turned out of its dwelling.

O Ihr Zärtlichen...
Step now and then, you gentle-hearted,
into the breath not breathed for you...

Ruined I, Thora Pattern, have come here to rest. For thirty, forty, fifty years under the black hood of time Light has photographed the same face.

So I dreamed.

I dreamed that I shared a world of snow with a black cat and a white tablecloth laid in the kitchen of a strange house, a house on the edge of the alphabet. Travellers came and went, drinking dark medicinal juices and singing 'Aft Forward, Aft Forward'. They wore bow ties made of rats' tail grasses and their eyes were soot-strewn with paspallum.

The cat vanished. The tablecloth melted even while the snow fell. And swinging like bells, staying miraculously in the smoking white air, heavy crimson birds, flightless, compassed the sky.

Moments are shafts of light.

I know there is a moment when sound slips down the torn lining of itself into silence, is carried unheard and secret in its own pocket. But the crimson birds could find no such escape, no means of slipping beyond themselves between the cracks of colour and song to a white undiscovered silence. I stared at them. Their bloodshot eyes loomed upon me. All other powerful winged birds lay frozen. Here before me now is the blue and white tablecloth. Here is the black cat. I spread the tablecloth to catch the bird-cries. I put the cat outside to lap the crimson leavings of light that trickle down the walls of the sky. Now I sleep in the snow and death is a white silent bird beating at the snow.

I hear your thoughts, Zoe. I am here and there, there – here the *Matua*, there – here the room also at the edge of the alphabet, also in South London where the rivermists rise in autumn and the winkle-pickers walk bell hoop and melt and the cars on Sunday morning are polished left hand right hand.

You who are a schoolteacher must know the activities of our infant room. How quickly we learn now to destroy under supervision, to scissor people's eyes out, to make fringes and bracelets of their hearts. We clap in time to the music. No one must be out of tune. We must follow the leader, dance, and at the signal-siren of ring-a-ring-a-rosie we must all fall down (not dead or radioactive) sneezing and blessing one another against our fear. What is your interest, Zoe? The treble chance? The permutation of bakers' boys and zeros?

(*The fascination of what's difficult*
Has dried the sap out of my veins, and rent
Spontaneous joy and natural content
Out of my heart.)

Cherish your interest, pursue your private research. My interest is the maps of roads, underground cables, the terrible hoover that works here upon the stairs, sucking identities into the steel tube so that I watch floating and grasping vainly at the pegs and hooks and niches of air, the people I have known – Toby, Zoe, Pat, and others you do not know yet – and myself, and the creature, the member of the crew who stood apart like a god shaking the mixture of fate and pouring out in that cool room your necessity you touched his sleeve?

Day and night, Zoe, I have walked in the market among the crowds and the cries, Lovely Oranges, Lovely Oranges, while the night-papers exhort *Crucify, Crucify*.

XV

ZOE THOUGHT, Shall I write a book? Everybody is going to write a book. Memoirs on writing-paper, toilet-paper, café wall, pavement, or stone column in a city cemetery where borders of trees provide a tripwire into silence. Shall I write? Shall I engage in private research of identity? For kisses do not seal – the locks fly open, the bands fall apart, the contents are riddled by a secret ray; as the sun himself knows, prowling like a cat-burglar, safe-breaker, among the futile security measures of endowed leaves and mansioned buds.

I had never been kissed before. The literature of the first kiss. Sunday school picnics, park seats, next-door bedrooms, rusted pine-needles beneath weather-rocking trees; street corners, alleys, cinemas; and no word spoken of the last (which is often also the first) coffin-kiss, for by that time it is impossible and undignified to tell.

And between youth and death is that other first kiss which fills one with shame that it should come so late without tenderness or promise. One asks why. I have seen kisses on television, in cinemas, tadpole-tongued in summer parks, on railway stations, and at the doors of houses that swift convenient cipher which in the married provides at once its own familiar profound translation. How was it that I, Zoe Bryce, had never experienced what people are proud to call their 'first kiss'? Or any kiss? Now in the country I have just visited I sometimes watched the sheep, and the dogs on trial, mustering them, and at times the sheep were people, myself one of them, being urged and barked at (but never worried) by the years. And I found myself driven with others of my kind into the end pen, with the gate into the field (they call it *paddock*) shut and my only escape the other unknown track which I did not care to use. Not yet.

And the pen was shared with other women who were unloved, who had never experienced their first kiss but who never mentioned the fact; who spent some part of their dreams in regret, self-pity, secret desire. And the dogs, the barking years, began to neglect us, forgot their training and the medals looped around their necks; they jostled us, attacked us, so that we turned upon one another in the close contaminated pen. And now it is blood and death amongst us, the old maids. Our lives?

We go more often to the Outsize Shop, we buy from advertisements on the back pages of magazines the mail-order 'supports for the fuller figure' and the small round pink hedgehogs called spot-reducers which 'magic away unwanted flesh'. Or, enticing our resentment inwards to permanent board and lodging in our body, we grow thin, are consumed, our breasts limp upon us and furred inside and stale, like empty water bottles in a desert.

And so it would have been for me. Until then.

Until it happened.

A slight progress away from the shame of being unloved. A flesh kiss.

I shall grow old, alone. I was never a successful teacher. When at last I retire from my private research in my bedsitter in London I shall spend my dark afternoons in the cinema among the old age pensioners, paying ninepence admission if I produce my pension book in evidence. And I will sit there holding my umbrella fast against my knee, thinking that I ward off the advances of the dirty old men who are in fact too tired to notice me. And I shall wander in the streets, standing, as old people do, uncertainly at corners and crossings, trying to choose and focus. Lonely, talking to few people I shall pick up comments on the weather, the fog, the traffic, as if I had found gold sovereigns to treasure later in my room, bargaining for them between self and self at an agreeable profit.

Or so I thought.

Now there is an influence working which tells me I shall die by suicide, which chooses what I eat from the menus decorated with buttercups and cathedrals, which pinned upon my low-waisted dress from Norton and Stroods the label Minnie Mouse. Yet before it happened, before the flesh kiss, I was only a Midland schoolteacher who was half asleep always in the classroom, who was forced to seek help from the headmistress on the days when it was impossible to cope, who at night stayed late in the empty room, marking grammar mistakes, circling words and phrases with bitter red pencil...

In the small ward of the ship's hospital Zoe lay – how long ago had it happened? – listening to the soundtrack of an old film, the evening's entertainment of the crew on their deck outside. A woman sang in an undressed voice. Now there was her manager speaking in petty breakfast tones. And now a half-cooked onion-soup of music; musicians like furniture removers trying to wield their instruments through tiny side-doors of the spirit. All the piercing restlessness and vulgarity of unsophisticated sound, of a film shown far from the padded palace of a cinema where the comfortable upholstery, like an ample lap taking a noisy child to tame him absorbs and softens the voices and music. The crew were laughing and talking, not paying attention to the film. 'Go home, my gal,' the manager said.

It was hard for Zoe to move or breathe. The voices pierced her body. Her only need was to sink into the darkness, far, far from omelettes, wine, and buttercups growing on menus. 'You wish to leave the table? At your first meal aboard ship? Why, we have scarcely left harbour. But you have my sympathy. In a few days you'll be striding around like an old salt.'

The used words have their peril. The rust on them (they say) brings tetanus to the wounded life.

The crew bred their own jokes. They laughed. The woman acting in the film, hearing their laughter, began once more to sing her strident song which was followed by worm-taped applause ribboned through the wall, its flat head and fangs in Zoe's ear, while the ship stayed obedient to its course, passionless, riding the waves, and the pirates, one-eyed, flung their lost sight overboard and its dark blue stones made circles in the water.

The engines throbbed, important as fleas' legs under the flea's tiny head, but 'I have no fleas,' Zoe said.

'I am sorry,' the steward had said, 'We cannot serve food in the cabin for fear of cockroaches.'

For fear.

So at school, she thought, there were pudding girls who changed overnight to ice cream licked by the boys on every street corner; but my freckles stayed, the pasty skin, the greasy hair stuck with dripping, oh buttercups and daisies for the dead in cathedrals.

'She is in confinement, labour, the third stage. It should not be long.'

It was almost eight o'clock. Soon the steward would bring Zoe a cup of Horlicks, and the Sister on duty would bring pills for the night, tuck in the bedclothes, say laughingly, 'You'll never want to go to sea again, will you, but you'll soon be up and on deck and by the time we reach Panama' – Then she would soften her voice, as if to confide an important secret, 'There's a family coming aboard at Panama.'

But it was no secret and why did people talk as if it

were, and why should an absent family command such influence?

'I am not interested.'

But my heart beats faster and faster at the mystery.

'Not interested in new passengers? They say so many things, I myself am eager to find out the truth and be at peace. Does the truth bring peace?'

'If it fits in with what you want... Usually it fits in... it has to...'

'Or you don't find it?'

'You haven't the time for looking in unlikely places, you have to have some idea.'

'You mean that when you steer your mind like a crane through the packaged possibilities you only capture, in the end, what in the first place you hold in your heart?'

'Well Miss Bryce you must be getting better, you are talking more... take your pills.'

Yes, Zoe was getting better. But talk of truth was the first sign that *It* was going to happen.

She could wash herself now, and sometimes sit in a chair in the ward or on the crew deck. The passage of time was no longer strewn with buttercupped menus and lit with distorted omelettes hanging like electric bulbs to be switched on and off with each rising and falling of the *Matua*. Yet it was taking so long to be rid of the sickness, and her body was buried by huge stones that had to be shifted inch by inch every time she moved; and for so many days her body had lain flat and folded, printed with trademarks for soup and cream and chicken, like an empty paper bag carrying its own advertisement.

She wished the film would end, the screams and the noise on deck, so that only a swish of quietness and shaded peace lapped the room, only a small quaker-cap of light hung from the ceiling. She wished the steward would bring the Horlicks, and the Sister come with the pills; then sleep, and the waves telling all, in sighs and sea-shells.

Then *It* happened. It was so strange. Someone darted swiftly into the ward – a member of the crew, dark, un-shaven, wearing a striped jersey. A pirate perhaps. He crept towards Zoe. He did not say Hello or Good Evening. With the languor of seasickness, buried under the stones, Zoe lay silently staring. A waiter off duty? One of the men from the kitchen? A stranger come to say goodnight?

Then he stooped suddenly over the bed and kissed Zoe on the lips. She was so astonished that she did not withdraw her mouth, made no protest, and his lips rested upon hers for many seconds when he stood up quickly, looked guiltily about him, and crept from the room.

Now you who were kissed for the first time early in your life before the hair at your temples was beginning to turn grey, before your neck became corrugated sacking and your oval knees like two old tennis-rackets with sagging strings, why, in your earliest life when you were blushed like cherry-blossom and facing each day the glossy side of the light – you may remember the pleasure of saying to yourself, *My First Kiss*, and the need to describe it, to confide in best friends, even in objects like walls and fur-niture. But if your first kiss happens when, like Zoe, you have lived for over thirty years – shall I be honest and say you are nearly forty? – then the best move is silence, no matter how much you long to tell, otherwise people know it never happened to you before; and they wonder, or pity; and children cry after you because children trail kites of seeing that follow the wind and supervise the complete vision spread out in the sky. 'Old Froze-nose never been kissed! Old Froze-nose never been kissed!'

After it happened Zoe had kept her eyes closed. It was important to think, to realize the meaning of the incident, to separate it from the motion of the ship and the gleaming fittings of the ward and the sound of the waves cornered gripping scooped building liquid shells which dissolved, fell apart, or were broken to pieces on faraway shores and became dust in sightless eyes, and sand, warm sand over the eggs placed there in faith, the reptile eggs hatched to new, ancient life.

Tell whom?

My first kiss. A swift dirty deed. Comfort. Self-pity. Horror. And a host of lonely thoughts broke into Zoe's mind, sweeping away the customary furniture, the knick-knacks, the cosy draperies of usual language that for so long had spread their flatulent warmth; like the worn verses in autograph and birthday books –

Whatever is, is right.
Whatever you are be that,
Whatever you are be true,
Straightforwardly act be honest in fact
Be nobody else but you.

And

Never be sharp, never be flat, always be natural.

A member of the crew kissed me, Zoe said to herself. A first kiss from no one to no one, like those cables which swing between mountain peaks and carry nothing.

And then she laughed aloud to think that she had never known, that she had always believed that people were separate with boundaries and fences and scrolled iron gates, Private Road, Trespassers Will Be Prosecuted; that people lived and died in shapes and identities with labels easily recognisable, with names which they clutched, like empty suitcases, on their journey to nowhere.

'Well it is a mistake,' Zoe said smiling. 'I am interested now in traffic lanes, in byways, highways, in the terrible hoover at the top of the stairs, and the way my identity has been sucked in with the others so that in the dust and suffocation of the bag which contains us all I cannot tell my own particles, I am merely wound now with the others in an accumulation of dust – scraps of hair and bone welded in tiny golf-balls of identity to be cracked open, unwound, melting in the fierce heat of being. Something's burning.'

A dirty member of the crew kissed me. Who was he? You see, one is not satisfied with wraiths and breezes, with visiting gods.

Was he myself, my parents, my dream-husband, lover? Zoe wondered. Now I shall never rest until I know. My life has been sucked at last into the whirlpool, made shapeless as water, and here I am trying to carve it as if it were stone; and how beautiful is water which never shows the marks of age and decay!

A dirty member of the crew kissed me and like a creature in a fable, stole my identity, left me naked, in rags; I must make something, quickly, recapture a shape, pin, hook, net the milling ocean – but oh my god!

Zoe touched her lips with her tongue, feeling a soreness there, remembering the splash of notices inside the doors of public lavatories in the city. Venereal Disease is Dangerous. Treatment is Free and Secret. Do not delay. Supposing... was it not a sign when the lips were sore... one never knew with people on board ship... sailing here and there to all countries... the crew mixing with all types of men and women...

It might be different, Zoe thought, if the man were English... brought up, say, in Liverpool or somewhere local but... one never knew with people from abroad... ships take anyone these days. Yet... I used to think this way... I used to be suspicious of foreigners

oh my god hell is local.

Again she touched her lips, aware of the soreness. What would happen if in the few years left to her she had children? They would be born blind, with a yellow crust over their eyes. When she grew older she herself would perhaps become paralyzed, lose her power of speech; her face would be twisted to a permanent grimace, she would have to stay in bed in a tall narrow bed in a back room overlooking someone else's allotment, with the district nurse visiting on Tuesdays to rub her back and feed her with barley soup...

But the children. They mattered most of all. They would be born blind.

Zoe's heart was treadling against her ribs, faster and faster. Again she felt the sore spot on her lips. Gradually, however, her fear diminished, soothed away by the rise and fall of the ship and her need to concentrate on its motion, to assure it in some way that she could not yet explain that she could not help rebelling against it, that the only means of surrender would be death; and death does not transform people into sailors, though it frees them and allows them eternal restlessness, independent of sunlight, wedged among pearls and a dim, flowering ballet of trees.

Calmly now Zoe considered the fact that she had been kissed for the first time in her life by a stranger. Yet who can deny that kisses between those who love are also kisses between strangers? A kiss that was neither a beginning nor an ending, it was isolated from the pattern of Zoe's spinsterish life with its secret desires and dreams and dreads; it was, in a way, a mythological act, as when the gods in the shape of birds or animals or human beings descend from the sky to touch the human maid. It was an act beyond reason. No doubt the sailor had his reasons. No doubt he was startled to find that his prospective evening's pleasure was an exhausted timid woman with greying hair, and cheeks flecked with vein-spots as if tiny arrows had found their mark; and eyes coerced by inward pressure to commit (and instantly regret) fantasies of arson upon areas of human property.

To Zoe the kiss was like a divining rod which twists suddenly and trembles in a desert where no one believed in the existence of water – or of wine.

A dirty member of the crew had walked into the room and kissed her... at a quarter to eight in the evening, fifteen minutes before the steward was expected to bring her Horlicks and the Sister her pills.

And now it was eight o'clock.

The steward appeared with the Horlicks upon a tray. He put the glass on Zoe's locker.

'Thank you.'

I have a secret, she thought. What will it lead to? I am changed. Tomorrow I will ask to get up and eat my lunch in the chair. I must make an effort. Seasickness, they say, is only suggestion. My path is certain now. I even think differently. I am changed, like those people who after the visits of the gods begin to sprout wings (or horns) or give birth to monsters.

I wonder who kissed me? What is he doing now? If I ever have children they will be born blind and deformed. Soon it will be too late. I will lie in my labelled box, divided and arranged in overlapping portions like wrinkled dried fruit... Will I have children some day, or will they always be mere dreams dispensed by absent-minded Gods?

The Sister brought her the pills for the night and she slept.

Some days later Zoe was well enough to return to her cabin where the five other passengers whom she had met only briefly showed the confidence which people like to feel in these matters by declaring that she was 'back to her old self'; as if seasickness had granted her a temporary separation and while she had been lying in the ship's hospital her bunk in the cabin had been occupied by an agreeable social self who had yet been unable to indulge its many pleasures without her.

'Now,' her cabin-mates said, 'You can enjoy life on board ship, get to know people, catch up.'

Their own lives were spent in 'catching up', in grabbing the gossip and rumour which on board ship are forever disappearing around corners, into corridors and closed cabins. The five women were a Norwegian school-teacher who seemed thankful that her slight knowledge of English helped to preserve about her areas of silence and peace which the others did not have the energy or skill to penetrate; two shorthand-typists from the North Island of New Zealand, who had arrived on board wearing identical grey terylene costumes with pleated skirts, and who now spent their time dressing, undressing, and dressing again, never satisfied with what they had chosen to wear at dinner; exchanging pearls and earrings, and brooches and dresses.

'Does this look – right?'

'Not exactly – right.'

In their passion for rightness they began earlier and earlier each evening to dress for dinner. They were fresh-faced buxom girls, brought up in a small dairying town. Often when they lay on their bunks eating chocolate and wondering about their future 'overseas', comparing hopes and prospects, their eyes would show anxiety, misgivings. They would search their wallets then for the photographs which they never tired of showing to each other.

'There's Mum.'

'There's my little brother.'

'This one was taken on the beach last year. Labour Weekend.'

The photographs would comfort them, and once more they would begin their discussion of evening wear. The second sitting, of course, attended by the Captain.

'Have you seen the Captain today?' they would ask each other. 'Have you spoken to the Captain? Did you see who I saw talking to the Captain?'

Oh, the Captain! And to think that the walls seldom collapse and show us people in their underwear, cleaning their teeth with a pin or picking their noses! Oh the magnificent Captain! (His wife, the new child, the lonely hours, the passengers on board crawling sideways like crabs to get to him, to nip him with their wealth and status.) So the walls do collapse, and people are buried in the ashes, and we do find them naked, fossilized in their intimacies. The other two passengers were a blonde, Clara, who spent her time in other people's (men's) cabins, getting drunk, wearing tight pants and sweaters, providing vicarious adventures for the two shorthand-typists and the clerk from Nottingham, Betty, who preferred to be addressed by her wartime name – Tim.

'I was Tim to everybody,' she said.

And then, putting it another way, perhaps in case she had not made it clear how much the wartime name meant to her, that people during the war had known her and been fond of her. 'Everybody in the Army called me Tim.'

She talked often about the War, with nostalgia, as people recall their childhood, a past holiday or a dead love affair. She told of her travels round the world on 'working holidays', showing the photos taken of her with a python around her neck, with a well-grown lion cub standing beside her, with a kingfish in her arms – herself in danger, embracing danger, comparing herself with danger. As in the War.

'People were friendlier in the War.'

Everyone was fond of her in the War. They called her Tim. The women in the cabin were friendly. Clara, who was so seldom present, was made the object of any bitterness or envy. There was speculation about her sex life, the time she spent in men's cabins at night. And wasn't her hair done with a new kind of bleach or with that stuff in a bottle – Light 'N Bright? And her clothes! She had no sense of shame, no modesty to dress like that. Who did she think she was?

In these moments of envy Tim would turn her face to the pillow and think, 'It's all very well to be called Tim, to have one's photograph taken with a python, embracing a python, but –'

And the two shorthand-typists would frown, studying their terylene costume; frown, thinking, 'Did I choose correctly? Is grey really *my* colour?'

When Zoe returned from hospital there was a new interest for everyone in the cabin. It was decided that she needed to be 'drawn out', a process of social economy where one is encouraged to extract and display one's personality in the manner of a small boy drawing out a length of chewing gum.

They supervised Zoe's dressing for dinner. They asked had she nothing but her low-waisted dress from Norton and Stroods and her single string of pearls. They advised her to seek the opportunity while she was on board ship to 'catch a man' so that by the time she returned to England she wouldn't have to continue as a dowdy schoolteacher...

Yes, dowdy.

It's true, Zoe thought. But how little they know!

On Zoe's second day up the vicar's wife came in with an invitation to join the country dancing.

Zoe declined.

'But you must join in you know. And stay on deck as much as possible, in the sea-air. Or would you like a book to read? There's a very nice library...'

'Well what about a swim?' the girls suggested.

'Or come on deck and watch us in the pool, and have your photo taken in front of the rigging.'

Zoe went on deck near the swimming pool. Her clothes seemed to disown her. Her bones felt now brassy and hollow like bells, now flat and massive like the silver head of an axe. She was tired. She could hear people saying as she passed 'She's a mere shadow.' People pointed to her as 'the schoolteacher from the Midlands who was so sick that she had to be moved to the ship's hospital'. Hearing these words so often gave Zoe a flash of identity. She felt a pride which was swift to resent stories of sickness other than her own; for was it not now her province, her claim to fame?

But it seemed that a young woman, mother of two, had been seasick since the ship left harbour, and that she had still not recovered. Besides, the ship's doctor visited her twice a day! Zoe knew a sad waning of her fame. How simple it would have been to stand beneath it for ever, to accept its light as the light shining down upon her from her 'own true self'. It seemed that nothing remained to her now but the secret, the fact of the kiss. An uncouth member of the crew had kissed her. The woman, mother of two (born blind, deformed, with a yellow crust over their eyes?) would not have it all her own way.

My first kiss. Zoe closed her eyes, remembering. She was lying in a deckchair watching the swimmers plunging around the pool – the accomplished, aware of the increased striving for recognition which is a part of life on board ship, wasting no time in blowing bubbles and nose-diving, but settling down at once into their expert crawl or backstroke; the others, making up for their lack of skill by letting everyone see what a 'grand time' they were having – laughing, shouting, playing games with brightly coloured rubber balls; then there were those who did not care to go in the water, who lay submissively on deck undergoing a personal barbecue, slowly turning their flesh in the sun.

And wet footprints everywhere, three-toed, for the monsters had emerged from the sea.

Under the awnings beside the pool people were being served with drinks. Everyone seemed whole and in possession. Even the squeals from the pool were sophisticated and complete, not the ragged sounds of alarm which people make when they are not sure how much of themselves is within and how much has escaped their desperate supervision. As Zoe watched she could see people's lines of behaviour, like wire-netting in the sky, with the sun like a big yellow hen testing its beak on the wire... How strange, Zoe thought. My first kiss has made me see things this way. I never saw people like this before. How completely they are welded, without seams; and goat-bells are ringing wickedly in their eyes!

Then she wondered about the man who had kissed her, if he knew in what way he had transformed her – or perhaps he was only a little boy throwing a firework in the dark or ringing the doorbell of a strange house and running away. Would he appear and speak to her, ask her to share a drink, a meal? And afterwards walk with her on deck and point out the stars to her? Perhaps... would he and she stay together for the remainder of the journey...

Oh how absurd, she thought, I am thirty-seven and already I have... is it so... hot flushes... irregularities, the sort of thing you read about in advertisements... and where are the children who will be born blind and deformed? What have I made in my life, what shape have I formed other than crimson pencil-marks encircling misspelled words? Surely the kiss has some meaning for *him* – oh how I long to believe that it was not a spurt of impulse like a little dog running suddenly on to the grass at the side of the road and weeing, then running on, urged by other smells and places...

Zoe smiled. How vulgar I am, she thought. These yellow flowers on my sunsuit are too large. My neck is like leather. And now they were having their photos taken – she and the two shorthand-typists – by Tim, and being encouraged to smile, for they were all cabin-mates, weren't they, and the photo would be a memory to keep for ever. But these snaps turn brown, go blotchy, coffee-coloured. Zoe was trying her best to smile in a friendly way as a contribution to that pension called Memory which we need to sustain us as we are growing old when, as in childhood, the grass grows too tall, roots are tangled and dry, yet strangely 'the rain it raineth every day'.

'Smile. Good'.

Click. And the moment is snapped off like toffee to be stored wrapped in great panelled jars that reach as high as the sky.

It was then that Zoe noticed one of the waiters with a tray of drinks, bending over a table. He was slight. His face was dark. He was the man who had kissed her. She felt her face go pale and her heart quicken as she remembered the kiss; and with the inaccuracy of emotional focus which is sometimes mistaken for intuition, she imagined that the waiter – for surely he was glancing her way now? – must also be remembering, and thinking of her. She thought, Perhaps he will make a sign to me. It would not matter if they never spoke or got to know each other, if only he made a sign, with his eyes or his hands or a movement of his brow recording some letter from the alphabet of love, as glow-worms passing each other (Zoe thought) twinkle their light to establish the fact that both are glow-worms; only some advanced insect- or animal-signal, some twitch, odour, flash of colour, to frame and make real their shared moment!

With the tray still in his hand the waiter hurried across to a table near Zoe. He glanced at her and her companions. There was no recognition in his gaze. He served the drinks and made his way towards the lounge.

Zoe realized that he did not even remember that he had kissed her.

Again how strange; people's memories on the other side of the wall, other people's darknesses and rings of fire; calling out to them, making primitive signals to ask 'Five yards (say) from your wall in an area three seconds by two seconds have you a small light burning, as I have?'

Calling.

And dancing with rage and pain when there is no answer, when we find that our code of measurement is singular, is not printed in anyone else's heart and cannot ever be shared.

A member of the crew kissed me and changed my life. Forgetfulness of my past ways and days grows now and spreads like a sponge-weed upon the surface of my memory.

So that evening Zoe went to the social. Minnie Mouse. And Toby Withers appeared, quiet enough to be discovered and explored.

XVI

And I, Thora Pattern, living – no!
in a death-free zone
scream of diesel and steam
people walking breathing neighbourhood smoke;
in the market oranges, white grapes splitting
under the supervision of wasps,
new lettuces in green hoop skirts,
old lettuces covered with slime.
A death-free zone.
A West Indian on the top floor
at the window, alone, looking down.
Fires of life in the sky.
The television spire
hung with prayer, lightning, dirty linen;
a man receiving treatment at King's College Hospital
for nails driven through his hands and feet.
The children playing on red scooters,
the young man in winkle-pickers,
the young girl in stiletto heels,
the car shining from its Sunday wash
and the bloodstains all gone
in a death-free zone;
A West Indian on the top floor
at the window opposite with its new cheap curtains,
looking down, alone...

Now fumes rise; no one comes running;
forests are eaten away,
minds are ragged with new patterns of decay;
with the road torn up and no hope of repair
there is no escape anymore to where, they say,

waves of oblivion rise and fall
in peace treaties with the pole and the moon
and the sewage with its shaggy golden mane
is adrift silently on the tides
that cushion the drowned
against all sound
that saturate the room and lace draperies of my ear.

People gape at the hole in the road.
A bomb-crater? Lightning? Whirlwind?
Men build a little house with brazier, and make tea.
But secret spiders are at work weaving milky resilient
    webs
from pipe to rusty pipe. A rat's black
full-stop nose concludes the sentence of destruction.
The traffic is at a standstill. Tales are told
of how many million years ago
the acid was first spilled
out of sleep into waking light –
the acid of memory.

XVII

THE SKY WAS MISTY and green like dirty dishwater. Along the banks of the Canal the alligators hobnailed the mud and shuttered their heads against the sun between years of rare movement. One yawned. His decayed yellow teeth needed a dentist to arrive with a black bag, a tent, a billy, to camp there, and between siestas and the yearly yawns of his patient, apply chisel and hammer, mirror and drill; the sky providing the porcelain; the undersides of steaming leaves the silver – the gold?

Boiled hearts and sandals' wandering eyeballs' vision. People went ashore at Panama. Women bought native skirts, ivory backscratchers, satin pyjamas made in Hong Kong. Men visited clubs and hotels. Lovers, those whose betrothal would be announced after their arrival in London, and those who would tactfully vanish from sight of each other the moment they disembarked, wandered around Cristobal, knowing instinctively which street and byway to follow, as if maps and directions were just another of the enclosures provided with the gift of love. And the lonely ones – the Zoes and Tobys and Pats? From the deck Zoe watched people going ashore. She clenched her fists. There was a tight curling of her toes inside her shoes. Her feet arched and pointed. A quick ink-onk movement made itself felt deep in her loins as she watched the lovers. I know.

Pat who had not been vaccinated because it was against his principles and who therefore was not allowed ashore, warned Toby as he set out alone.

'Be careful. Don't be fleeced.'

Toby was not fleeced. He did not venture far from the ship.

He stood down on the wharf listening to the black people and the white people, side by side and separate yet all warmed by the sun, like stripes in the human shroud hung like an awning over the dead ruined places of understanding.

And the next morning the ship was filled with bird-of-paradise flowers...

The long-awaited family came aboard at Panama. The three – husband, wife, school-boy son – had a marvellous air of completeness, as if they had been hatched overnight fully developed and clothed, and had never known a time when their legs would not carry them or they could not speak their wishes in language that was swiftly understood, or their hands could not hold whatever they sought to grasp. Clearly, they had never lain wheeled in a chromium limousine, snow-suited, be-tasselled, sucking rubber dummies, parked in a six-yard square of front garden for alley cats to meow at and passing children to poke in the face to see if it was true – that babies have eyes like jellies in a bowl, and they slide out, if you scoop them with your finger.

All the other passengers seemed intensely aware of these three perfectly hatched human beings. People spoke to them in respectful tones. Waiters hurried to fetch their orders. It was accepted without the usual malice or envy that they should dine at the Captain's table, that he should conduct them on a special tour of the ship, invite them as guests for cocktails in his cabin.

Mr and Mrs Kala and son, from Panama.

Their arrival seemed to quell a feeling of anarchy and restlessness among the passengers. People made friends who had not before spoken to each other. Eccentricities were regarded with tolerance instead of annoyance. One or two passengers even gratified the vicar's discouraged wife by joining her group for country dancing.

On land one can go to church and speculate on the Second Coming; or watch television and wonder about the results of the Jackpot Quiz; or plan one's week to the climax of Saturday evening when the Pools coupons are checked. Human beings, whether or not they use it intelligently and truthfully, have the innate habit of tomorrow, and on board ship their indulgence in it is encouraged. Although there is no proclamation of a Second Coming there are certain passengers who regard themselves as messengers who move about the deck and the lounge, drawing people aside to impart their news – Next week we are holding a little concert... There's something being organized for tomorrow night... And this news is received earnestly. The two shorthand-typists write it down, each in her large leather-bound book which is printed with a page for each day and has a gold cover inscribed *Diary of My Voyage*.

They write their news as the prophets of old recorded their divine visitations.

And what else must one dream of, on board ship? Of sight of land, the starved cries at the clouded shapes. Of sea-monsters, white whales, wrecks, a mirage. Of the Ancient Mariner.

In these seas the Ancient Mariner has no hope of pursuing his voyage of doom. When he is sighted alone in his craft 'all all alone', the *Matua* steams to rescue him, he is taken aboard, put in the ship's hospital, given a sedative. The passengers talk excitedly among themselves. 'They say he has been without food or water for days. He keeps raving about an albatross. They say he did it for a dare – he was challenged on television; he writes for the Sunday papers. But he is so ancient – have you seen him? Have you seen his eyes and heard his delirium about snow and snakes and curses?'

The Captain radios Southampton. When the ship berths the Mariner will be taken into custody as a prohibited immigrant. He will never see the lighthouse top, the hill, the kirk, the bay 'white with silent light'; the Hermit Good. He will appear before a Southampton Magistrate. They will deport him. Where? May I ask all ships at sea, if you voyage into the path of the Ancient Mariner, even though he may be dying of thirst and burned black by the sun, do not take him aboard, let him reach his own private country, meet the Hermit Good, attend the Wedding Feast. Let him tell his story! Give him paper and pen and ink or a quill a goose or turkey-quill plucked from the silk house of lice, lately warm against wings and jagged by deep snow-filled winds from the North.

Mr and Mrs Kala and son, Panama. He in a light-weight light-coloured suit, Panama hat, she in a tropical sundress, the boy in shorts and gay shirt. Their manner shrewd, friendly. Business people. Rubber, oil, coffee, take your choice. Civilized, quiet, American accent. Drinking the correct wine. Dining at the Captain's table. Easy and easy and affluent, the deep qualms and guilt like poisonous dreams plucked out only at night, in sleep. And are they the Second Coming? Do they signify a new heaven and a new earth, for the first heaven and the first earth are passed away...?

SOMETIMES in the evening now Zoe would put on her Norton and Stroods dress and her pearls and drink an acorn-cup of coffee in the lounge with Toby. When she was sitting with him she was overcome by a shared feeling of heaviness, and had the sensation of trying to thread tiny needles with rope, of wearing gumboots and dancing on thin sheets of glass laid across the sky. The world itself which is ordinarily nimble enough to evade destruction, seemed like one of those toy globes (seas blue, Empires red, countries that long ago before the first kiss of understanding seemed not to 'matter' – a drab grey colour) where the revolving mechanism is broken, and the globe either refuses to move or adopts an irresponsible free-wheeling motion – both annihilations of the dextrous Time whom we rely upon (as the God in the children's hymn) to 'care for us', attaching his ticking emblem to our left wrist to connect with the beating of our heart.

So the world would not function, everything seemed clumsy, bits of the night broke off, like smashed glass and flew into people's eyes; skin was thick; people lumbered like prehistoric monsters. It was the effect of Toby sitting there with that muddled expression in his eyes. When he tried to speak, so often he did not seem able to lever out the words he needed. His tongue seemed to hamper him, to try to prevent him from speaking at all. He seemed to have to contend with so much – tongue, teeth, lips, even after the idea itself had stirred and crawled its way along the silent corridors of his mind, trying to emerge into the light. His conversation was seldom brave or magnificent or unusual. At times he spoke about himself, in a complaining tone. He had not been treated properly all his life; circumstances and people had been against him; he had struggled all the way; but he would show them, by the Lord Harry he would show them. Nor was he going to let people steal his ideas.

'What ideas, Toby?' Zoe asked. He looked suspiciously at her.

'My ideas,' he said, moving the words heavily like masked weights from his mouth. 'I may not have had a good education but I have ideas. I can see my ideas, like those little clouds that float above people's heads in comics, to show they are thinking. For instance I tried to look up *Orpheus* in the ship's library. I said to the officer in charge when he asked "Can I help you?" "Yes, I'd like a book about Orpheus." He said "You mean that story about the Aircraft Carrier, that war story?" And he bumped his fingers along the backs of the books the way we used to bump our hands along the picket fence on the way to school. Yes, I left school early. They said they couldn't teach me. You're a schoolteacher aren't you? The first school I went to there was a teacher who wore dark blue and had a little chain around her neck. She buzzed, as if she were inside a bottle. Just fancy me sitting here on a ship for overseas, talking to a schoolteacher! Where did you say you taught when you were in New Zealand?'

'I didn't teach.'

'But you're a schoolteacher!'

'Not anymore. I worked as a waitress in your country, in a tumbledown wooden hotel where the rats sat on the kitchen table and the floor creaked every time the ships were sailing out of the harbour, the way a shop bell rings in warning when you step across the threshold. And then, in the south, at a large hotel on the corner where the wool-buyers came –'

'Aren't you going to teach again?'

'There's no question anymore.'

'Did you live in the hotel?'

'Yes, on the top floor, in a rabbit hutch with a sloping roof.'

'I bet you saw things out of the window! Did you see across the street?'

'Oh yes, into the buildings across the street. I remember I used to look into the dentist's and see people in the chair. And into the chiropractor's rooms.'

'I've been to a chiropractor. Mr Hibberd. He massaged my spine. He said my spine was the cause of my trouble. Then they said it was my eyes. Then they said I had to eat wholemeal bread and raw carrots. That was when I was very young. If they'd been able to help me I might have stayed at school and had a proper education. Why aren't you going to teach anymore?'

'Nothing much. Something happened. I don't usually tell things to strangers.'

'Like me?'

'Like you. In fact if this thing had never happened to me I should be sitting here not speaking to you at all. My life has been manipulated, Toby. I am a plaster statuette facing a different way now. A force, an incident, has swerved me to face what people call "the light". A reserve of light which has never been used before and is stored out of reach beyond alphabets and lines and sound. If we stretch our blindness far enough we trap the light.'

Oh oh Zoe thought. Oh, who am I, what am I saying to this country bumpkin? He is not even a sheep farmer. How I would have liked to meet a sheep farmer, to marry him and live in an upcountry house whose tall windows faced the mountains! Or how I would like to marry an ambassador, in Turkey... or Persia... or somewhere. Or Len Hewell. Len Hewell... strange that he never spoke more than a few words to me, not even in the teachers' room at morning break. He was always over at the window (why do some people have to get to the window, at any cost?) drinking tea with someone else. Yet I saw him every day. A dirty member of the crew kissed me. Oh what are we, when we can be hurt by people after they have gone from our lives, as if we kept touching the railway line and receiving the vibrations, long after the train has passed?

'My mother would approve of you,' Toby said suddenly. He had said the same thing to Evelina when they were talking together and Toby became excited, as he always did, when he was having what he called 'a serious conversation'. These 'serious conversations' were as close as Toby ever came to people; they gave him the kind of restlessness and trembling which attack people when they must spend all their lives in waiting rooms with the door to the interior never opening, and no one appearing to beckon them inside.

'My mother was a noble woman.'

For a moment he was troubled because he could not get an immediate image of his mother – he saw just part of her face with all her nobility concentrated in her Roman nose. He hoped that in his mind he was not making a mockery of the dead. Her chin, he thought, is like Popeye's chin. Can the dead share laughter?

'My mother was a noble woman,' he repeated.

'But the dead,' Zoe told him, 'have no sense of humour.'

'What do you mean?' Toby said angrily. 'Have you been listening to my thoughts?'

'No, it is just the paper walls,' Zoe said wearily.

Then Toby became curious again. This time he did not call Zoe by her Christian name in case his mother was listening and thought he was being familiar with a stranger. 'What happened, Miss Bryce, that made you give up teaching?' Zoe did not answer. She put her empty coffee cup on the table.

Have we, Toby wondered, been drinking dahlia wine and dock-seed tea? Why do people keep shifting, like lantern slides inserted when no one is looking. Inserted is *my* word. Soon I will write The Lost Tribe. No one is going to steal *my* ideas.

'Nothing much happened,' Zoe answered.

Yet how she longed to tell! Who does one tell when such things happen? Why are there not waiting at every corner of our lives people whose sole purpose is to listen to our story? Then, Zoe thought, I could whisper quickly and fiercely, I have been kissed for the first time in my life, and then hurry past without shame or misgiving.

'Do you like summer houses?' Toby asked. 'I know a song, *Proudly Sweeps the Raincloud O'er the Cliff.*'

'That's a Pacific song. I come from the other side of the world, Toby.'

'I'm always meeting people who come from the other side of the world. Everybody comes from the other side of the world. Haw Haw, it's a good excuse.'

Toby's voice was growing louder. People were beginning to look, and whisper to one another. Zoe blushed, stood up, and moved away, leaving Toby alone in the corner.

'Haw Haw, it's a good excuse,' he was muttering, more quietly. And it is a good excuse, isn't it, to put seas and continents between yourself and someone whose ways are often so strange that they frighten you, make you stop and peer through the cracks in the pavement of your life instead of hurriedly stepping over them and deadening your awareness by a ritual chant of numbers?

IT IS raining and raining and I will die. The buildings topple, slide with the bruised and broken leaves into the earth, folded deep. The yellow glare in the sky is the striped mantle of tigers, licked cool, healed by the darting tongues of frost. Yet winter, age, loneliness, have come leaping with seventy claws unleashed from summer, youth, and the gentle conditions of love, to stripe our lives with death, to set fire to our cage.

How strange! Our ribs blossom. We are muslin and honey. Somewhere the waves touch white foreheads on the sand. The troubled waves try to cope with sewage, oil, orange-peel.

It is raining and raining. The umbrellas open like prayers; safe; ribbed like bats that sing.

It is nine o'clock now. Here is the news.

Pat Keenan is drinking coffee in the lounge with Zoe Bryce.

IF ONLY, Zoe thought, attacked again by seasickness. If only this and that. If only I could watch the sea. How it slides and slops like unset jelly against the sky. There is too much of it, breaking through the portholes of my seeing, flooding behind my eyes, trickling down inside my fleecy-lined skin. What message does the paperchase of white wave tops carry from shore to shore?

And Zoe remembered the seaside holidays of her childhood – Blackpool at first, but later the smaller beaches of the South Coast – Bognor, the tiny Pagham beach where the waves raked tirelessly over the shingle and the dirty brown pebbles, like paupers looking for long-saved hoarded coins, scraping the bottom of the barrel to find them. There the waves did not make you sick, even if you were licking an ice cream cornet with its topknot of swirled chill and sweetness, or burying your face in a cobweb of candyfloss. Crabs and rocks; the polluted wise sea; spotted pebbles rolling like toffees. Rain, a bewitching of rain, and deep sleep as if inside a hazelnut, and waking to surprise lakes fallen tell-tale from the incontinent summer! Fretful children, and old men in Army shorts, making demands on the sea, striking the waves. Then, high in the trees, in another world, the tattered crows' nests hung out for the rag-and-bone autumn.

And the dead, the strangled-with-seaweed, the toiling dead.

I never had memories like this before, Zoe thought. Why has everything changed? Why is it that I remember a dead man who said, 'The soil is shut against me, all is strange under the earth, there is nowhere to settle anymore, no time or place. Tell the Ministry of Defence to equip the living not with bombs but with adhesive – not a cellotape-like love where the supply runs out leaving you to hold the little dry wooden wheel; not a chewing-gum-like peace that is parked under conference tables and forgotten after the juice and flavour are extracted; nor a glue-like memory that stops the mouth of the past while it picks the till for easy treasure; but a new adhesive, a secretion like tears-pus-sweat-semen only invisible, imperishable, for the living to take with them when they die, sticking their final speck of dust, At Home, Received...

'But I warn you,' said the dead man, 'the soil is hostile.' Why, Zoe thought, does that memory return to me? Is it my seasickness? Can what happened in the ship's hospital have transferred another world to me? Was the kiss (as all kisses are) a kind of grafting process? How is it that a dead man has confided in me?

She was sitting in a deckchair on a less crowded part of the deck with Pat and Toby near her. Pat was stretched out, his eyes closed, gently snoring in the simulation of sleep which people like to employ as bait to entice 'the real thing' – the 'real thing', one of the nobles on the cluster of absolutes hanging like legendary berries out of reach in the sky-bush.

Pat was thinking about food – fruit and steaks and salmon. I am getting too much of a paunch, he was thinking. He began to recollect pleasant days fishing and playing golf. He played golf once a year on his holidays. Golf was the good life, it made him feel superior to his fellow workers on the buses if he could mention that he liked a round of golf, while all they could discuss was Saturday afternoon football. Or boxing and parlour games on the telly. I am not dead yet, Pat would say. During his visit to Sheila he had made friends with golfers and fishermen, and once landed three quinnat salmon in one day. There was his photo in the local paper under the odd heading, *Well-known Irish businessman has good catch*. Pat had not quarrelled with the reference to himself as a businessman.

How can one really identify oneself, living so close to the edge of the alphabet?

As Toby sat watching the sea he was thinking of places in the south where the waves came in and went out, came in and went out, clockwork. He was remembering the southernmost beaches – Waipapa, Fort Rose; the Stewart Island Bays – Rakiura, Land of the Glowing Skies. He was remembering the little girl he met there years ago when the family came south for a holiday. She was Nona, dark and bedraggled with shoulders that sloped like folded wings and head thrust forward like a little penguin's head – an Antarctic penguin with a touch of snow on her wings and a serious expression on her face. Yet she did not laugh at him, though they never made friends and their meeting was for one day only – the time he crossed in the ferry with Aunty Marge and his two little sisters who were sick and had to stay miserable and pale on the rug spread on the beach while Aunty Marge explained to people who enquired.

'They've been sick, the two of them, it'll pass off.'

It didn't pass off; it was the beginning of measles. So Toby had played on the sand by himself. It was an unfamiliar beach to him for it was enclosed by dark trees which reached to the water's edge, mysterious, gloomy, enfolding trees never shedding their leaves but seeming always damp and mossgrown with their leaves flashing with water although it was not raining. Other beaches that Toby knew did not contain this forbidding magic circle of trees. They lay arm in arm with brown rivers, with bright blue and pink lupins growing in the sandhills and scattering their flowers in the yellow sand; the sandhills reached far back to the gravel roads where the fir trees made a wind-break around the red-roofed houses. And in those places there were tide-marks of rubbery leaves smelling sour, whiffed with salt in a way that made you point your nose to the wind, like a little dog, and breathe in deeply.

Sometimes the smell would travel far inland, far ahead of the sea-wind, and slap you sharply in the face and sink again deep in your nose. 'Smell the sea-air?' your mother would say.

So that always you arrived at the sea long before you were in sight of it, and always, though you were too small to understand, you paid the penalties of falsely arriving, of robbing moments ahead, hours, tomorrows and storing them side by side with present time. You came, lonely and cheated, to the dreamed-of sea. You struck at the sand, paying it out, with a crumbling stick of driftwood.

So much of Toby's early life was spent in journeys to the sea, in waking almost before the blackbirds, and setting out in a jumble of people in the slow excursion train along the coast; with the soot on the windows and the rising sun shafting the dust in the carriage and the train forever stopping for drinks of water. And then when at last the train arrived at the sea, why didn't it stop at the station? It always decided that halfway between cattle-stops was as far as it would go. Everyone would have to get down on to the railway track and walk, with blackberries scratching at legs and arms, along the edge of the line, over the cattle-stop, and down the road to the sea; on and on with bundles as if everyone meant to walk into the water.

Would the sea have taken them?

The sea is always in a committee, in a hush and murmur of choosing.

Down south where Toby lived the sea was grey or shades of green. At Stewart Island on the day he met Nona the waves were like no other colour he had seen before, a chilling grey that could only be arrived at by chopping up and slicing thin a giant quarry of kingfisher-coloured ice, turning the brilliant side to face the depths, showing to people who picnicked by the sea and to the dark trees that trailed their leaves near the edge, a glinting chill grey which in spite of the sun's warmth (up north a touch of the sun was enough to giddy the water to bright blue) remained grey, flashing only rarely with hidden colour – rarely enough to make you think you had dreamed it, the quick bush-bird wing beating the seafloor.

Nona. Toby thought her father must be a pirate. She looked as if her father were a pirate. She was sitting placidly on the beach and the way she was sitting by herself made it seem that she had people with her, other children. Now Toby knew that you usually sat by yourself when you wanted people to come over to you and say

'Never mind, we forgive you.'

or

'I'm sorry we were nasty, you can come and play with us now and you can be the Chief or the Head Bandit

or the Landlord owning all the houses and turning us out because we haven't paid the rent.'

'Don't stray,' Aunty Marge called to Toby. As if he were a sheep or steer.

He went over to where the little girl was sitting. She had a book by her, open, with leaves and grasses pressed on the pages and neatly labelled.

'Don't hurt my collection,' she warned, because Toby was a small boy and his feet were very near the book, and one kick and the sand would be all over it and in Nona's eyes too, stinging.

144

For a moment Toby was tempted. He wanted to scuff sand at her. He decided not to.

'I won't hurt your collection,' he said. 'Let me see. Why are you doing it?'

'Do you go to school?' Nona asked wistfully.

'I don't. I have it on the wireless, and by correspondence and we're collecting trees and grass and everything that grows. I know all their names. My father told me.'

'Is your father a pirate?'

Nona had never thought of her father as a pirate. The idea excited and frightened her.

'Of course he's a pirate,' she said.

Toby sat down.

'Why,' he asked, 'are you touching them like that as if they were kittens? Our cat had kittens in the washhouse. They were dead and she ate them.'

'We had a possum at our place.'

'We've got a summerhouse with bankshie rose.'

'I've got a playhouse in the trees.'

'You're only a girl,' Toby said doubtfully, because it was at this stage that little girls started to cry, after you had pulled their hair or thrown sand at them. But Nona didn't seem to want to cry. She did not seem to care about the kittens or the summerhouse with bankshie rose. He told her that they had a cellar, that they could crawl under the house, that he had a sledge made from one of the kitchen chairs with the runners greased every day with dripping. Nona did not seem as awed as she might have been.

'Anyway, you don't go to school.'

'No. But I've got a collection.'

She spread the book on her knee and flipped over the pages and the trapped grasses made a rustling sound as if they were still growing on the hills. Toby realized that it was a magnificent collection. How he wished that he had a collection! He had tried to save beetles once, and had sent a beetle in a matchbox to Big Brother Albert of Station 4YA, asking him to give the name of it, but Big Brother Albert had found nothing inside the box when he opened it.

That was a mystery.

But he had grown tired of beetles and stamps and cigarette cards with battleships on them. How he wished he had a collection!

'Do you want to look at it with me?'

Nona smoothed her hand over the brittle leaves and grasses. 'Feather-weed,' she said, in a chanting tone.

'Feathery-weed, pop-kelp, sea-rimu, tree-daisy. These are names. My father told me.'

Her father, Toby thought, was very knowing for a pirate. He wished his own father were a pirate, away at sea instead of coming home every night and frowning and asking him to tip the coal from his workbag into the coal-shed and to look lively with a shovel of coal for the fire; away in the Spanish Main, and coming home at Christmas with flags flying red and gold and blue upon the mast...

And then he wished that he had no mother and father, that he was an orphan picked up out of the sea, and that at home he had a collection, a wonderful collection with the names written in so that he could speak to his collection as if it were people.

'Have you got a father and mother?' he asked suddenly.

Nona was going to laugh and say, 'Of course, I told you.' But she was an astute little girl. She shook her damp brown hair from her eyes and looked cunning. 'I'm not sure, not really,' she said.

Toby was in first, with a shout of pride. 'I'm an orphan, brought out of the sea.'

146

'But you said your name was Toby. Toby's not an orphan's name.'

'People only call me Toby because no one is supposed to know that I'm an orphan.'

Then Nona had smiled at him and screwed up her eyes.

'I can't give you my collection,' she said. 'But – I'll show you my playhouse. Would you like to see my playhouse?'

But just at that moment Aunty Marge put her hand to her mouth and coo-eed Toby, Toby. She sounded fierce. She was a big woman, bunchy, like potatoes, and she filled every room she entered, and now she was beginning to fill the beach although it had no doors or walls or windows.

'Toby, Toby.'

When she strapped she used the thin length of belt taken from round the wheel of the old sewing-machine.

'Toby, Toby.'

Toby went, running fast, and he never saw Nona again. Though he believed he had read somewhere about her being killed, climbing in the Southern Alps, years later.

'Feathery-weed, pop-kelp, sea-rimu, tree-daisy,' he said aloud.

'Were you speaking to me?' Zoe asked.

'No. I was saying names. To myself.'

'It's the first sign,' Pat said, opening his eyes. Whenever there was something to say which other people often said, which was the accepted word or phrase, Pat always felt the compulsion to say it.

It's the first sign. Right every time. Least said soonest mended. Never seek to tell thy love.

Pat had his eye on Zoe. He was not in love with her, but he wanted to control her. I hope, he thought as he closed his eyes again, that she is fancy-free.

XXI

NOW HERDS of cloud, of smoke trample the fine blue tufts of sky. All is panic. Rain streams on the roofs and walls and television aerials, and the hot-headed leaves that drive downward to the gutter and the drains. The chestnut leaf has five fingers. It lies with its palm out-spread. Everywhere is the stampede of death, an outward silence, an inward thunder, and from the city and the peo-ple the dust rises like blackened pollen from the shaken head of an enormous flower.

Here where I live, the child practises the piano in the front room. Her mother, the hairdresser, late at work, helmets a row of clients clogged under the drier; froths the shampoo, smells the shame the secret burning of hair help help... the child's father – eager, soft voiced in a striped suit promises a glory of television, tape recorder, washing-machine, to the tired shopper dizzy with singing commercials.

The child's father sits at the table checking the invoices – the *In Voices*. Soon he will take his luncheon voucher and try to find a seat in the crowded restaurant. His face is pale... the customary word is *city-pale* – city-pale, work-pale, television-pale, birth-pale, deterrent-pale beyond the alphabet nothing has meaning, the letters are brace-lets of the dead.

The upstairs lodger who works in the Electric Com-pany is dreaming while he packs the Christmas lights (quick, light, and there was light, the snappy tinsel crea-tion); he dreams of treble-chance Pools, of the time when he will check the lavender-coloured sheet of paper and discover that he has won eighty thousand pounds. A party at the Dorchester. Job thrown up. Nothing is changed, says factory worker. Enough to live on, a house, says factory worker. Holidays abroad, a car, says factory worker. The graces of living, wining, dining. Advice for those who win the Pools says former factory worker now an occupant of down-and-out hostel in Hammersmith. I did not mean to pass dud cheque says former factory worker at trial.

Do I, Thora Pattern, imagine that I can purchase people out of my fund of loneliness and place them like goldfish in the aquarium of my mind's room and there watch them day and night swimming round and round kept alive by the tidbits which I feed to them? They rise to the surface. Their mouths are open wide. Shall I overfeed them as people do with goldfish? Shall I starve them? Shall I remove their precious element and leave them gasping, stranded? Look, a water-snail clings to the glass like a small sniffly nose against a windowpane.

I am confused here on the outskirts of communication. I have set out on my exploration – I, Thora Pattern, Zoe Bryce, Toby Withers, Pat Keenan, and all the other people I have met or known – even the child at the piano, the lodger upstairs, his friend the other woman lodger...

They work at the same factory. Let there be light. He arrives home. She hangs up his scarf, his coat, touching them, brushing against them as she passes through the door into the kitchen, to wash the vegetables. Her face is flushed... her heavy neck; outsize underwear; her sagging shoulders; her doughnut breasts, her Gothic legs; her bright, lonely hazel eyes.

The spot of excitement on her cheek; her hand unfolding, with love, the blood-stained wrapper of the two chops, setting out the two plates, cups and saucers, the stiff white tablecloth. Beads of moisture on her nose and in the corner of her eyes and on her forehead. The room is hot.

'Do you find the room hot?'

He reads the evening paper. He is waiting for his meal. He knows that she will go on cooking for him, all her life she will prepare his meals, wash the soiled underwear which he sneaks into the bathroom on Thursday evenings, remind him about his new shaving soap, worry that his clothes are not aired; make him cups of tea... all her life, if he asks it. He does not ask.

'Now what I like is to be free, to go for a swirl on the dance floor in that club in Dolphin Square. Now what I like is to be free.'

But at night when he comes home there is sometimes anxiety in his glance.

'The good lady, is she home?' he asks.

They sit eating their meal. They sit hunched, not speaking. Afterwards, if the landlady is out, they go downstairs to watch the telly, the quiz. 'Who died with the word *Calais* engraved on her heart?' 'Whose last words were *Kiss Me Hardy*?'

'I knew that. I could have won fifteen pounds.'

'I knew that too.'

Now tea and cracker biscuits.

'Up early again tomorrow I suppose?'

They go upstairs, say goodnight, exchange a remark like 'It was fun, wasn't it, the quiz, that man winning three hundred pounds?'

'Yes, it was fun wasn't it?'

They go to their separate rooms and close the door.

XXII

TOBY is getting more and more homesick. He is sitting in his deckchair dreaming all the time of his home in Waimaru. He is a pedantic dreamer. He must walk up correct paths, open and close gates, read notices, unlock and lock doors. He must look both ways, even in dreams, when crossing the road. Therefore he begins every journey to Waimaru at the railway station, on the platform among the seagulls that are squabbling over sandwich crusts and sodden left-overs of sugar buns and shreds (first-class, second-class and third) of journeying people. The departure of the train has revealed the sea, a near thin strip of menace pounding loosening the rocks of the wall which the Town Council keeps reinforcing, knowing that in the end the Pacific Ocean will triumph and surge across the railway lines over the engine-sheds and the station platform and the offices and the road and the old Railway Hotel with its hitching-post outside the door, and the railway houses with their staked dahlias in the garden.

It is autumn. The sea will triumph. Toby knows that even at his home two miles away the crashing of the sea is accepted like an undertone of dream in the daily mesmerics of waking life.

Here is the station platform. There is the door to the office of the loco-foreman, and inside, near the desk, the posting-place where Toby's sister (doubling him down on the bike) used to put the timesheets; asking in a breathless voice, 'Please what time is Dad on tomorrow?'

There is the bookstall with its paperbacks – *Sexton Blake*, *True Story*, *Wild West*; the tea-rooms with the girls mopping up the tea from the counter; Miss Edgeworth, the supervisor, who for a short time moved in glory through the Withers family. Some people's lives have the characteristics of a comet. They blaze fulfilled once only or periodically with years between each glory. Such was Miss Edgeworth's life in the Withers family and the street where she lived. For suddenly everyone knew that Miss Edgeworth's mother was dying and that her devoted daughter was caring for her. Yet for years Miss Edgeworth had looked after her mother. Her two sisters had married and gone to live up north. Her brother won an Agricultural Scholarship overseas. Everyone took it for granted that Miss Edgeworth would spend the rest of her life at home with her mother. No one marvelled. No one was impressed by her. People knew her – thin, with spiked gingery hair and thin arms dipped in soapy water; brown skirt; brown jersey. People spoke to her in the butcher's shop and the grocer's and the tea-rooms where she worked. But no one marvelled.

Until her mother was known to be dying.

'After all these years,' everyone said, 'all these years can you credit it?'

Amy Withers who could not resist the precincts of incipient death (at least when their topography was on the level of awareness) offered to help Miss Edgeworth to look after her mother. She took her beef tea and red-currant jelly, insisted on staying to wash and turn and make the dying woman comfortable. Other neighbours gave help. And suddenly Miss Edgeworth was a part of the Withers family. She became a favourite with the children, teaching them new card games, a different Patience and Old Maid and Donkey, and a game called Nine Men's Morris. She talked freely, and told the Withers children stories they had not heard before. She gave their mother a photo for the family album, and wrote in the autograph book,

There's a pleasure in the pathless woods,
There's a rapture on the lonely shore,
There is society where none intrudes
by the deep sea, and music in its roar.

'Oh, Byron!' was Amy's ecstatic remark. 'Or is it John Greenleaf Whittier? Oh, my favourite verses! Oh, Miss Edgeworth!'

'Gloria,' Miss Edgeworth prompted shyly.

Gloria Edgeworth.

Why, it turned out that she had a cousin who lived next door to one of Amy's sisters up north; that she agreed with Bob over the high-handed attitude of the government; that she had one or two articles of clothing that might be made up for the children to wear. 'Not for best of course,' she told them.

Even in the short time that she was free to visit the Withers family, and even while her mother was still dying, Gloria Edgeworth grew quite plump, especially her hands which lost their soapy blue tinge. She could make wonderful shadows with her hands.

'I've never seen the like,' Bob said one night when she had come to tea (her mother had been ordered to hospital) and was amusing the family with shadows made on the dining-room wall.

'You ought to have taken it up, Gloria,' Amy said. 'Just look, Dad, now who else could make wonderful shadows like that?'

Gloria Edgeworth's face was pink with pleasure, her eyes were bright. The children gazed adoringly at her.

A few days later old Mrs Edgeworth had died. The interest and urgency of death which had involved Gloria in the affairs of other people in a way that she had never before been involved, seemed to fade. She retired to herself once more. She no longer visited the Withers family to make shadows on the wall and tell the children stories. She became again just Miss Edgeworth, not Miss Edgeworth whose mother is dying, or Miss Edgeworth who is clever with her hands; just that Miss Edgeworth who works in the refreshment rooms at the station. She did not ever return the book of John Greenleaf Whittier which Amy had lent her. And one day when Amy was turning over the pages of the autograph book and read the verse chosen by Miss Edgeworth and saw her signature beneath it, Gloria Phyllis Edgeworth, she remarked, 'How strange. Come and look at this, Dad! It's hard to believe that we called Miss Edgeworth by her first name!'

'We don't see much of her now,' Bob said, returning to his paper.

'She might have vanished off the face of the earth.'

Which she had – or, rather, from the human sky; a comet appearing only at the season of death.

And no one ever knew what Miss Edgeworth thought as she sat alone at night in her tiny kitchen, reading her newspaper or the *Woman's Magazine* or the *Bedside Book of Happiness*, or something from the lending library – *Saved By Grace, Doom in my Heart, Lydia's Summer*.

Did she sometimes turn and twist her thin hands to make (with the aid of light) a shadow world upon the wall?

And now Toby is walking down the steps of the railway station past the taxi-ranks with their smart new cars – and there is Bill Ribble who keeps pigeons and greyhounds and owns a racing stable out the country. He waits for Toby to hail his taxi, as Toby used to when his mother was with him in the last days of her illness and she had been visiting the doctor for her injection 'to get rid of the water'. For when Toby's mother came away from the doctor's she would wait in Bill Ribble's taxi while Toby hurried into the tea-rooms to get two hot pies for lunch. Bill would enquire after Amy's health. He had not always been her taxi driver. For many years on the rare occasions when they used taxis the Withers family patronized Don Collet of the Blue Band. They never dreamed of hiring anyone else. Until one day, by some mistake, a Red Band Taxi driven by Bill Ribble arrived at the gate. Amy was horrified.

'But you're a Red Band Taxi!' she exclaimed.

Yet in order to keep her appointment she had no choice; she had to let Bill Ribble drive her. All the way down to the doctor she worried at the thought of being driven in a Red Band when it should have been Blue Band. What would Don Collet think of her? She felt like a woman who had been unfaithful to her husband, though she did not know what that felt like – oh no! (And how shocked she had been when that ignoble man who wanted to collaborate with her in writing songs to 'click on the market', he writing the music, she writing the words, had sent her a postcard from his dreary southern town – 'I'll set more than your words to music if you will let me my love.') Immediately, indignantly, secretly flattered, Amy had announced that she was 'breaking all association' with William E. Treat. He was not 'gentlemanly'.

After her first contract with the Red Band Taxis it was easy for her to accept a second and a third, and in the end to send for them as a matter of course; soon the importance of Don Collet and the Blue Band faded; they became with other irrelevant episodes and people, the unhired extras of memory. Now no seismologist or geomorphologist recorded this change from Blue Band to Red Band Taxis, yet it was only another of those frightening perpetual shiftings of relationships which bring immeasurable faults and folds into the human landscape, which help to raise plains into mountains, divert the course of rivers, dry up the seas.

The intensity of the Withers family made every journey a matter of life and death, and gave the man in charge of the journey the status of a god.

Bill Ribble. Yes, he would ask after Amy's health. Then he would forecast the weather, the two weathers – in Waimaru, and in the district referred to as 'out the country' where most menace lay. If people said 'It's snowing out the country' the Waimaru population would shiver, turn up their coat collars, know the influence of hidden deep drifts of snow, and feel the helplessness at being forever commanded by that overlord High-Country Weather who decreed that Waimaru would freeze or burn, that the surrounding rivers should flood or bare their dry rocks to the sun.

Yet little snow ever fell in Waimaru. The last snowfall I remember, Toby is thinking, gazing in his dreaming at Bill Ribble and hearing Bill's voice which seems more like that of a shepherd than a taxi-driver – the last snowfall I remember was in early spring, the year of the War. The war news came on the wireless. My mother cried and prayed. My father told stories he had never told before, beginning 'When I was in the trenches –'. He joined the National Reserve and spent all afternoon polishing his soldier buttons and buckles. I wanted to join the Home Guard because no other unit would have me, and my father said, 'What use will you be?' So they put me among the old men of the Home Guard. It was snowing. It was early spring but it was snowing. There was a map on the kitchen wall – Flag the Movements of the Allied Forces from day to day; tiny red flags on pins being pricked back and forth on the kitchen wall under the photo of Mickey Savage and the plaque made from Australian woods with the words burned into it 'I think that I shall never see a poem lovely as a tree.'

They dug an air-raid shelter over the hill. It snowed. Early spring. The plum trees were out up the path. At the Home Guard they gave me a small black book on fractures and haemorrhages, and told me to study it; there was a diagram of the body with red and blue lines running up and down it. I brewed some beer in the copper in the wash-house and got drunk. It snowed that spring for two days, and the snow stayed long enough to have footmarks on it, of people and birds and cats running in and out of hedges; and to bank in drifts under the fir tree and in the rabbit burrows in the paddock and under the pear tree, nearly in blossom, and the silver birches.

Surprise whitened the world. The shocked violets unfolded, the veined crocuses bloomed, peaked with gold and white. (No statue was built to the snow, Toby. Historians did not come with book and pencil to note the dazzle. I do not think anyone photographed it. There would have been a blank, a scape of nothing. White. Snow. The two words in idiot conjunction, battered against the wall, white snow, white snow, white snow, white snow, as people who are cold, who fear death, flap their hands and arms upon their own body to find warmth.)

Now the moments hanging ripe, transparent, like redcurrants. And Toby goes on, leaving Bill Ribble and his Red Band Taxi, walking in the Main Street that is covered with leaves from the rowan trees. Past the draper's, the saddler's, the Chinese fruit shop where they used to buy specked fruit – 'Threepence worth the specks, please'. Past the grocer's – there is little Starkie Drew.

Who would have thought of him as a grocer? His brother Bluey put up his age and got to the War and was blown to pieces in Libya; lying somewhere in the desert, Bluey Drew who had never even visited the North Island, who had only sailed in a home-made boat up and down the Waimaru creek!

Now past the grain merchants, the stock agent's, the butter factory, the picture theatres, the police station; the roads branching off – the hill to the hospital, the hill to the Town Cemetery; the side road to the rabbit stores, the wheat stores, the bay and the wharf. Now up the long damp road to where Toby's father lives; the high bank on the right with the houses and gardens in the shadow of it not yet rid of the night-dew; on the other side of the street the Town Gardens, the children's playground with its paddling pool, seesaws – rusted; sandpits; the creek where the swans glide. The swans of Waimaru are notorious. The evening paper prints letters demanding the destruction of the swans. Has not a child been dragged into the pool and drowned? Two children? The swans are a sign of evil, they must be destroyed. Is it the fear that mythology will take control, that one day a swan with urgently beating wings will swoop from the sky upon the innocent young girls – the High School or shop girls or the nurses walking down from the hospital? It is too terrible to contemplate, the townspeople think.

The swans are condemned to death. Yet no one takes action against them, they stay gliding over the surface of the pool, diving to the secret depths where the slimy weeds grow, and the rotted vegetation and the bones of kittens and puppies lie, the guilty deposits of night. How beautiful the swans are, how graceful! They will twist the necks of children, they must die.

Toby walks along the road. Now that he is growing older he walks like his father. His shoulders are bowed. People might take him to be an old man. 'Don't stoop, Toby,' Aunt Norma would say if she saw him now.

He walks past the house where Jimmy lives, and there is Jimmy with his plump face and pleased smile, in his neat brown suit, standing outside the gate, as usual, watching the people and the cars go by. Jimmy is a Mongol which means that he has the privilege of belonging to two families – his mother and father who have looked after him since he was born forty years ago; and another family of brothers and sisters whom he has never known yet who resemble him and whose secrets, perhaps, he shares. He has never met Noel who lives near the station in one of the railway houses; but if you stood Jimmy and Noel side by side you would think they were twins; Noel, and the auctioneer's son, Ed, out the North Road, and the little girl Peterson... so many in one family and not all of them living in the same country. No wonder Jimmy smiles wisely as Toby passes. Whether or not he is wise he has the appearance of wisdom and who will really know whether it is wisdom or stupidity? Perhaps it is both, the ultimate melting point of both, and Jimmy and his numerous brothers and sisters are only the instruments who approach the ashes, smiling, without fear, to pluck the final jewels from the fire.

Now Toby arrives at Dorry's house where the pale-faced ragged children are climbing in and out of the front windows that are broken and patched with newspaper. Dorry used to be known as the town prostitute. Mothers would say to their wayward daughters 'You don't want to grow up like Dorry West, downtown on the corners every Friday night.' People shunned her. Then she married and started having babies and meeting other young mothers down at the Plunket Rooms, and people began to like her and talk to her. 'She's like one of us to talk to,' they said.

She appears at the front door. The children clamber about her skirt. She is pale, with lank hair, and when she smiles you can see that she has no top teeth and that the bottom ones are brown with decay. She smiles at Toby and waves to him. People know Toby. They know he takes fits, and has a struggle to earn his living, and that his mother is dead who spent most of her time caring for him and sheltering him.

Toby stops in his walking. That's it, he thinks. My mother is dead. What am I going home for, if I can't find her at home? He is near the house now. There is the little ice cream shop that has not long been opened. It sells groceries too, and saves the long walk into town. Mrs Ford, the shopkeeper, is a gossip. She peeps from behind the lace curtains.

'A little cake of chocolate, Toby. Just a little cake of chocolate.' Why, that is his mother talking to him, telling him what to buy on his way home, a treat for her, his mother. Now on the right is the open paddock – see the clump of autumn puff-balls growing near the fence. Toby kicks at them. The cloud of yellow dust rises. Poison? You will die. You will turn into a dwarf with spotted skin. You will fall asleep for seven years and when you wake you will be changed, you will remember nothing; and you will be blind.

Now on the left is the Bowling Green at the end of Gardens where the retired men and women spend their afternoons. Toby knows that for years his father dreaded retirement because he associated it with playing bowls.

'Bowls,' he used to say contemptuously. 'Retire and play bowls for the rest of my life until I drop dead in my white flannel suit and white hat. No fear!'

Now Toby is at the gate. There is the paddock, the pond. Hear the magpies? Remember Tom and Elizabeth?

When Tom and Elizabeth took the farm
The bracken made their bed,
And Quardle oodle ardle wardle doodle
The magpies said.

Now see the sun wrapped in mothballs, finely waistcoated; the autumn goldfinches swinging on the thistle-tops, the leaves drifting, the old oaks holding fast to their leaves, unwilling even when they are shrivelled and dried to turn them out to the mercy of the wind. The grave is dug. The body is prepared. Mother holds her offspring, refuses to have them buried, entreats the season to let them remain with her, not to send them into the sodden earth. She tries to prove that they still live when she and the whole world know that they are dead; and still she holds their decayed bodies in her giant surging arms.

Turn away and weep. It does not seem to matter that the willow leaves, slim and yellow, sprightly as ever, have swished their way on the surface of the creek to drown or float, forming a wet carpet for the creek-flies to dance on; or that the pine needles fall and rot through the year in their continual private season of death. Only the oak is possessive – or is she merely truthful? At least she keeps and displays her skeletons.

The sheep in the next paddock lift their heads. Their noses and mouths still work at their nibbling. They flock, then scatter in panic, trying to scramble across that part of the paddock where the underground creek flows beneath a bog of bright-green weed, a-flicker with swamphens. The sheep stumbles, its legs folding beneath it; it is trapped in the bog, and it struggles, bleating, and the more it struggles the more saturated and heavy its wool becomes, pulling it in deeper. Toby tries to reach it, to throw a plank across the shallow edges, crawl over it, and rescue the animal, as he has so often done before. But it is too late. The struggling head is now level with the water, and only the upper part of the treacherous fleece is visible. A few more convulsive movements and the sheep has disappeared. Perhaps in five or ten years' time, when with the whim and privilege peculiar to water, the underground creek has changed its course and the area is dry with couch or tussock, the bleached bones of the sheep will be found lying like broken script arranged in cunning disarray by the penstrokes of Time and the furtive corrections, blots, and underlinings of the weather. (Are our words thus, falling fleshed and heavily fleeced from our mouths, and only after a length of time can their true meaning, their gaunt uncluttered bones lie exposed upon the slopes of thought?)

Everywhere in the paddock you stumble across animal skulls and bones; white, grey, splintered, riddled with tiny holes where the maggots once kept house; clean, faithful, secretive remains.

Toby is at the gate now. Shall he go up the path and into the house? What will he find there? What has his father been doing since Toby left for overseas?

One thing, he has mended the clothesline and made a new clothes-prop. Two black work-shirts hang by their tails; jiving now and then in the wind.

The hemlock is tall; its mottled hollow stems reek with an atmosphere of poison and danger. Toby rubs the smell from his eyes.

'Why hasn't Dad cut the hemlock? I left the slasher down the hill, in the shed, before I went overseas.'

Overseas.

The dahlias are in flower. Full of earwigs I'll bet.

At the top of a lone stalk an empty pineapple-tin is balanced, put there to lure the earwigs who in their nut-brown faith believe they are climbing into the sunrusty heart of a dahlia. 'Where is the cat? Where's Fluffy? I haven't seen Fluffy since I went overseas.' She's in the creek no doubt, in a sack with a stone tied around it. Will Dad be home? Oh yes, he will be home sitting by the kitchen fire reading his Sexton Blake or doing a crossword puzzle or listening to the request session on the wireless.

What did Aunt Norma say to him?

'Now mind, Bob, when you're alone in the house don't let yourself go. Letting yourself go is a crime.' (Aunt Norma with her filing cabinet of crime; her simple thumbed favourites, and the sealed ones in the locked drawer that leaves tell-tale marks of blood on her hands when she seeks in the night in the dark to study them.)

Well, yes, it is the same, nothing has changed since I went overseas. Maybe the cat is dead and buried under the holly tree. Maybe a few more grains of my mother which the dead cannot help dropping around the way the children dropped their crumbs in the forest will have been picked up by the birds of Forgetfulness or are buried under an avalanche of hours and days and months. New people, new flowers grow. What cunning has my mother employed to keep her memory within the house that no longer contains her? What offerings does she bring to pay for the privilege of being remembered? What does my father feel now? What does he think about? Tinned oxtail soup? His cramp? Mary Overton dying of cancer? Winter is here soon, the pipes frozen, the windowpanes blurred with frost, the sky still grey and heavy as the season accomplishes the settling-in process of death...

Toby, let no one tell you that death is a slight scarcely visible moment, a crimson seal, coin-size, on the charred envelope of summer – who has stolen the will? Who has drawn up signed and witnessed the will?

No, death enters the house or the city or the island loaded with personal and household goods, clanking pots and pans tied with string, haversack stuffed with bedding and clothing, wallet full of photos; a swagger with a feather in his hat and baked beans in his belly; an outsider, an encumbrance, an ill-mannered visitor who neither asks to be admitted nor obeys when you command him to leave.

It is the clutter of death which is inescapable. Winter or Death; the old comparison; the cruising whale-spouting clouds with their silver undersides, refusing to swim from the sky; the untidy heaps of sodden leaves; dark layabouts of ponds in the shelter of hedges, in the hollows of the paddocks; the determined squatting of water in every ditch and drain; piles of twigs, of fallen branches, trapped thistledown that was never set free to race in the sky; the pronged silence where all sound impales itself and splits into flying icicles that pierce the ears and fall deep in echoing wells of grey light; the chilled reserve of a house where a terrifying unwelcome guest shows no inclination to leave.

Now Toby is at the back door. Over the short rope clothesline that sags with black and grey work-socks and ragged underpants pegged by their tapes, he peers through the window at the armchair in the corner by the fire. It used to be *Grandad's Chair*. While Grandad Withers was alive and for long after his death, the direction of objects lost or found was described by reference to *Grandad's Chair* – 'I left it near *Grandad's Chair*. I tell you it's under *Grandad's Chair*.'

But there is a family of secret rats. They wear the fur of habit. They destroy with their sharp teeth. They are Change, Time, Forgetfulness, who invade first for a few minutes, then for hours; finally they stay. You may wish to be rid them, to sprinkle in your mind the succulent high-priced poison which, the advertisements claim, these rats love and search out and swallow, retiring to die a pain-less death. You may think that Time or Change will not trouble you while you store a packet of this poison in your heart.

Well, suddenly, no one knew when, but with the aid of time and change and with the familiar frightening shift of identity, *Grandad's Chair* became *The armchair in the corner.* Then it became *Dad's Chair.*

Toby looks through the window at *Dad's Chair.*

He sees his mother standing in the room wearing her faded pink interlock nightie with the old-woman wiping stain down the front.

'I've brought your chocolate, he says.

'It's no use, Toby,' she answers. 'I'm dead. I don't eat chocolate. Where are my clothes? Where's my nice na-vy-blue costume, and the new slippers? The flex of the electric blanket needs mending. I hope your father doesn't sleep without switching it off at night.'

Toby feels jealous. There she is worrying about Dad. You would think he could never look after himself the way she worries.

'But your father won't need the blanket,' Amy contin-ues. 'He's dead. We're all dead, Toby. Death is separation by wall and water and world. Where have you been, Toby? I've come a long way looking for you. I'm a moral woman but I had to bribe and steal and blackmail to get out of the grave and see you. There's barbed wire every-where. Why is there barbed wire laid around the house, it's all down the path and around the cherry tree and the elder tree.'

She wants pity, Toby thinks. She wants me to say, 'You'll be tired Mum. Sit down and I'll make a cup of tea.'

'No don't say it Toby. I was warned when I died that if I wanted to visit you it would be at my own risk. That clause is always put in the contract. You still love me don't you Toby? You remember me? You haven't married any of those flighty Waimaru girls? And have you written about the Lost Tribe? Remember when you were a little boy and the teacher read out your composition in front of the class and everyone admired you and forgot that you took fits – your fits, Toby, tell me about them, do they still trouble you? And you've gone overseas. Why have you gone overseas?'

She vanishes. The house is quiet. So that's home, Toby thinks. My father dead too. But he hears the clock ticking on the kitchen mantelpiece. Who winds the clock then? Someone must wind the clock!

And now his father opens the back door and peers out. 'Well come on in, come and tell me about being overseas. Have you written your Lost Tribe? Still got your fine fancy ideas?'

'Overseas,' Toby murmured.

'What did you say?' Pat opened his eyes and yawned.

'Nothing,' Toby said. 'Overseas.'

XXIII

Now the ship will never move. It is bogged with memories promises hazards and labour-saving last testaments. A white cobweb growth enfolds the engines. The Captain is prepared to lower the lifeboats, send up flares, watch his *Matua* slowly sinking off the Bay of Biscay. The seaflowers and weeds in the sea-gardens prepare to receive the wreck. The fish are singing, the fish who never turned off the power or paid the bill. Mould grows like fur on the faces of the passengers. Their eyes diminish to rat-size. Their tiny pink feet patter restlessly along the deck.

Rumours of sunlight move in gentle currents through the hollow skulls of the drowned. Will the *Matua* sink to lie forever in these liquid palaces of the drowned?

In the minds of all passengers the sea and its buzzing vastness (have you noticed the persistent tiny noise of immensity as it sucks poison and honey at your elbow?) have laid the maggot-thought of death, which wriggles alive with black-blotted eyes, feeding on the flesh of thought. No, no, the ship will not sink, the devoured passengers tell one another. Not even the calamities mentioned in heavy (but small) print in our Shipping Company tickets will stop the ship from reaching harbour. We are civilized, modern, we have all amenities. The Captain was decorated during the War. He has medals, and letters after his name. Everything is calm, people are clothed and fed and employed, governments sit in leather chairs and carry briefcases to and from tall buildings. We are safe. How safe we are! There is no War.

Yet how is it that one keeps moving in and out of wars as on the sea one moves through differing depths revealed by shades of blue and green; one moves through colours of – death? Oh no. Tropical sky. Two on an island. There is nothing but the sky. We are glazed people. There is no death by drowning or suffocation or disease. There is no pain. There is only the near sea washing the sides of our newly painted ship. There is no distant sea.

But as the ship approaches harbour troubling thoughts rise once more to the surface, float in all their ugliness and vulgarity, like drowned bodies; they demand to be retrieved, identified, labelled, put in cold storage until a suitable top-hatted moment crowned with flowers may bear them to a place of permanent burial. Permanent? Discounting the archaeological zeal of dreams and memories which uncover the deepest graves. Burning then – shall we cremate the recovered bodies of our thoughts and scatter them in a ceremony of solemn faces to what is called 'the four winds' – the four corners? I know of people who have cremated their thoughts, paying high fees; who have rented a niche in the wall of their minds, as a token resting place, and then scattered the ashes into the 'four winds'; the same ashes have returned to them, volcanic and burning, like pellets of shot flung in their face and their eyes, blinding them for the rest of their life.

So when the ship approaches land and the bright waves become more like choppy grey ruffs on the neck of a worn-out lion, and the drowned ideas loom like discarded vegetables upon the surface, be careful how you bury the so-called dead, and where you bury them. Just as well when you disembark to tie your dead with brown paper and string or put them in a polythene bag, and on the corner of the next street (it is always the next street) drop them in the litterbox with its warning notice on the outside – 'Do you care for your city?'

Do you care for your city?

Toby says: I have no city. There is Waimaru my home

168

town that will soon peel like weathered paint from my memory, my glossed-with-overseas memory. Well I never thought of that before; it is a warning to write my Lost Tribe. Waimaru is my town; the cause of everything, my mother used to say. The cause of my fits too.

'Oh if only we'd stayed down south Bob in the railway house by the railway line, and the kiddies going to the District High, and you fishing on Saturday afternoons in the Mimihau. And the broad beans growing in a row beside the potatoes and the cabbages, and the black-currant bush in the corner by the fence. Coming north to Waimaru has been the cause of everything, Bob.'

Waimaru. Toby rehearses it. The quarries, factories, tree-lined streets; the timber-yards with their stacks of pine and totara; the new sweet factory – Toby starts with pride to think that he can buy a packet of paper lollies and read on the packet *Made in Waimaru*. He thinks to himself, I know the factory, it's out the North Road, past the Boys' High, on the right, near the Hall of Memories where the boys used to assemble on Armistice Day to sing

O Valiant Hearts Who to Your Glory Came
Through Dust of Conflict and Through Battle Flame
Tranquil You Lie Your Knightly Virtue Proved,
Your Memory Hallowed by the Land You Love,

That was the soldiers. Dad said they all got medals to keep them quiet. I never went to the Boys' High. I never had a cap and tie and monogram. Yes, they sang *O Valiant Hearts Who to Your Glory Came*; you could hear them all over Waimaru. In the park there is a statue of a soldier from the First World War; he is turning green; when royalty came the mayor had the soldier cleaned and polished with Brasso; like a tea-urn; or fire-tongs; he hasn't any eyes of course, statues don't have eyes.

What's my father saying to me now? 'Get two hot pies from Mauger's, not from Webb's, and bring them down to the shed for my lunch.'

I've just been to Waimaru. I'll not stay there. I went down to a Toc H. meeting but they didn't want me there. When I was a little boy I used to go to Christian Endeavour where we sang 'Jesus Wants me for a sunbeam, I'll be a sunbeam for Jesus'. We were in groups called Sunbeams, but the big boys pitched into me. Then I joined the Wolf Cubs but my fits held me back. When I was older I went to Lodge, then I joined Mum's church, because I have to join something don't I? My doctor in Waimaru was a good man, too outspoken for the Hospital Board. He complained about conditions and lost his job, and he lives now on the wild West Coast with a mining lantern on his forehead, admitting people to his visions.

That proves I must write my Lost Tribe. In London I'll branch out on my own.

Do you care for your city? The houses, the hills, the people; the newspapers; the births, deaths.

Pat says, 'My city is London, but I'm from Ireland, the real Ireland.'

'I'm going to London too,' says Zoe.

(What do I mean, running, running, choked with kisses or striped boiled sweets; no sound; I will find you in doorways and attics and sprinkle sawdust in your eyes.)

'Where will you stay?' Pat asks. 'Toby is staying with me, aren't you, Toby?'

Toby trembles with anger. 'I'll remind you that my aim in life is to be independent. I've work to do, secret work.'

He is shouting now, causing the other passengers to turn and stare once again at the man who 'shouts for no reason' as if he were in the bush or the mountains trying to make contact with rescuers and not able to take the usual course of escape, following creeks to the sea or trusting the sun around corners.

'I'll not stay in Clapham.'

My mother was saying only a moment ago that Clapham will be the cause of everything.

'I'll branch out on my own.'

I am a jeweller. I have a high-powered magnifying glass strapped to my left eye.

Pat is offended. After all his plans. He has written to the landlady and knows that her answer will be, 'You're welcome,' for has he not redecorated her house, bought her a new striped sunblind, fixed the new carpet and the stair-rods?

He turns to Zoe. 'Have you somewhere to stay then? What about Clapham?'

(I am not domesticated. I cannot call household remedies by their initials. When people say to me, 'Put some BRL on it' (my chilblains, my insect-bite), I stare at them without understanding, then as I realize that they mean Bolton's Ready Liniment, I say primly, deploring (and envying) the approach to life which brings an enforced intimacy with the contents of a bathroom cabinet, 'Oh you mean Bolton's Ready Liniment?' 'Yes,' they say. 'BRL.' I close my eyes in horror. I who have been kissed only once in my life shall never learn to flirt not even with the letters of a popular liniment!)

'Yes, there's a room in Clapham for you, seeing Toby won't take it.'

'Yes, well since I have no family and am not returning to teaching –'

Pat needs desperately to recruit people.

'No, I'll not teach –'

'You ought to. You don't want to throw it up like that, a

good profession with good money.'

He fusses constantly over his pension expectations, his insurance policies, crouching over them in an attitude of incubation, turning them, settling them, keeping out the cold air of poverty and pensionless old age.

'I shall be engaged in private research,' Zoe tells him.

'Secret work? Private work? What are you and Toby up to? Why not get a safe job, a clean job? You could go as a secretary, easy. They're crying out for secretaries.'

'I don't want to be cried out for.'

'See it my way. Regular hours, clean work, good pay – you can practically state your own wage packet.'

'No,' says Zoe. Her face is flushed. Beetles with shuttered backs are crawling on her skin.

Shall I go to London? Am I betraying my Midland background by going to London? They say everybody goes there and is buried and unlike the usual dead is not provided with a ghost. I shall go to London. Betray what? My first kiss was isolated, detached, like a bloom which had parted from the stem and which I found lying un-identified and picked up without special responsibility to take to my own dwelling, to graft upon my life; to plant in my special plot, press the soil around its bruised neck, wait for it to revive and bloom again – as we used to do with the sooted flower-heads that we picked through the railings and laid in the frosted earth of our city allotment. My first kiss. A god glancing by.

'It's in the mind.'

'It's in the ear.'

'At the base of the brain, size of a pea.'

Oh my Lord Omelette and Parsley but I was kissed scrambled egg I was kissed

kissed buttercup and cathedral for the first time in my life.

It will not happen again.

'I know it,' Pat was saying. 'It's a large room at the back with a table and a gas fire and a comfortable bed. It's not far from the Common where you can sit in the summer. You'll wish you had taken my advice, Toby.'

'Isn't it funny, the three of us here?'

It is so dark. I wish I could escape from the sea. Where will I stay? Does it matter? How lonely I will be standing on the station – Victoria, Waterloo, Paddington – with the high walls rising like ribs around me, enclosing me. Here is the family who came aboard at Panama; mysterious, foreign, privileged no longer. They were to walk like gods among us. Well that is finished now. The marvel of them has faded. They have been with us always. They are the same as we are. He has his moments of greed, of fear, of irreverent thoughts, longings. She has her vanity, the sharp note her voice acquires when she is alarmed – a squawk like a hen disturbed from her perch. Their son whines, complains. Their posture alternates between a quick brace and glance round and an unselfconscious slump, mouth open, piggish, magazines (not explosives) upon the eyes, toad-feet in pools. They have become a part of us. How could we have believed in their glory, how could we have dreamed of their victorious march up the gangway to the tune of our dread, our envy and worship?

He blows his nose. He does not seem to have a clean handkerchief every day. Why? Surely he can afford it. He glances at what he has blown...

It is London soon. In a last attempt to establish their identities by discarding them the passengers parade in fancy dress. London? The streets are paved with prostitutes, artists, one-legged trumpeters, wet newspapers that slyly wrap themselves around the passers-by who do not struggle except to jag holes for eyes and peer out through a face of headlines *Famous Personality Murdered Peer's Adultery Singer Killed in Crash All the Luck of the Pools.*

'Ah, Clapham,' Pat says. 'Clapham is all right but the tone is going down.'

'The tone?'

'The blacks. The blacks and other foreigners taking all the jobs and houses and the money. You have to steer clear of the foreigners.'

Yes, steer clear of the foreigners, the strange arrivals, the secret gods who blow their nose high in the sky in a cloud and glance at what they have blown.

The foreigners, the creators, the mail-order gods who advertise their glory from tomorrow's warehouse and then arrive (demanding cash on delivery) as poor products for wonder.

It rained. The ropes were wet (Toby particularly noticed the ropes). Wanting to be independent, saying goodbye to Zoe and Pat, Toby climbed alone into the English train that was wide and self-satisfied with bitten scenery on the walls and soccer nets above, and a cobweb land muffled him across the face. Where are you taking me, the world owes me a good deal, owed much, owed much, higgledy-piggledy tribal higgledy-piggledy tribal.

Toby's companions were two Dutchmen seeing England for the first time, gazing into the wet and the mist at the wild supplicating arms of the television aerials H H Help and the interlocked bricks in the arm-in-arm houses, and the soot-spattered little back gardens.

I have journeyed, it seems, from winter to winter.

'So this is your England. It doesn't impress me.'

Toby, indignant, disowned the landscape. 'It's not *my* England.'

'Well, whoever it belongs to, it doesn't impress me.'

Deadly. The scaffold stations. The cheated faces. The change of echo under the bridges. The sky crowding down close like grey pastry being pressed around a ten-penny steak and kidney pie that has been cooked once then warmed up, fouled by great black squawking birds with ragged wings that lean forward in the sky like clergymen striving for a pittance. Cry warning, a racketing shudder, a slowing-down, time to think, to draw out the meaning like necessary matter from an unclean wound.

No 'when daffodils begin to peer'. It is a primrose memory that has rotted in the darkness.

III.

THE SILVER FOREST

XXIV

THIS IS London, Toby, London calling in the Overseas
Service of the B.B.C. Here is the News. You have just
heard the chimes of Big Ben filling the small kitchen of
your home at Waimaru and now you are going to hear
plum-in-the-mouth announcers from the other side of
the world. 'So this is England. It doesn't impress me. Give
me Amsterdam.'

Give me, give me, I need a city up my sleeve like a
performing mouse to distract me, to care for, to cage and
feed and give toys to. Will I have Wellington? The houses nearly toppling from the cliffs, the damp switchback
streets where my aunt kept a tiered boarding-house like a
grandstand overlooking the win-and-place involvements
of the city; streets of moss and fern, and the sun poured
like fresh barley-sugar twisting in and out of the native
trees, setting golden upon the roofs and walls. 'You may
have Amsterdam.'

So this is London.

Toby was cunning, arrogant. He refused to pay the por-
ter who took his luggage to the taxi. Why should I? I'm
entitled to it. He watched closely while the taxi-driver
adjusted the meter; the city was a breeding-ground for
sharks. Who were those loiterers watching him being
driven away? No doubt they would jump into a fast car
and follow him, and as soon as he arrived at the Young
Men's Hostel and got out of the taxi, he would be set upon
with coshes, flick-knives, bicycle chains, razors and left
scarred for life... Gradually he relaxed and the tremen-
dous thudding of his heart slowed down to a city slicker's
amble and he gazed dreamily out at the red sandwiched

buses and the blind city workers in their dark clothes, tapping and stabbing their way, with the aid of umbrellas, to an important funeral. When he arrived at the Young Men's Hostel he scrutinized the coins given him as change by the taxi-driver, and he would have liked to spin them on the pavement to detect if they were counterfeit.

'What's up?' the driver said.

Toby put the coins in his pocket. 'Nothing.'

He heard his mother say Trust in the Lord Toby and you will never go astray in the city.

The Lord was tall and serious with a heavy fist which he thumped upon the world when he became angry. He lived in a house in the sky. He had a study with a filing cabinet where he stayed up late at night reading and marking and classifying; licking his fingers as he turned the pages.

His house had dungeons where the guilty were chained against the walls while larks in cages sang to tease them. The Lord smoked tobacco that was a dark colour, like camel-dirt. He worked crossword puzzles, using peo- ple for clues down and across; he fished in rivers, eating loaves left behind by his son, of whom he was jealous, for many people loved his son for his kindness and his proclamations of peace. But 'Vengeance is mine,' said the Lord.

Toby was afraid of him.

In the small room at the hostel, the only one vacant, Toby stood by the basin, looking at himself in the mirror and turning the cold water on and off. He drank some of it. It tasted like soot.

He felt himself in a dangling situation. He had arrived in London, certainly. Yet –

He went out and bought a newspaper and came back

and sat on the narrow bed, reading. He read that some-one who signed himself *Dorian* could now reveal in con-fidence that Lady Craig from Kensington would shortly become engaged to the Hon. Somebody who was on the board of directors of a well-known firm. He read of parties; the important people were named in heavy type – *Freddie Collins, Nigel Wallace, Lady Julia Wedgewood-Norton; Nubia Fenton; Peregrine Holman...* All the names so cosily together it made Toby's heart beat faster and gave him a feeling of gratitude and importance that Dorian should thus confide in him those items which, after all, he had plainly been told 'in confidence'. At the same time Toby felt unreal, as if the pages of the newspaper were the walls of a sound-proofed room which allowed only acceptable commotions to filter through it. *Actress Shot. Singer Accused. Busmen Say No. Dog Stops Traffic. Amelia, Six, Entertains.*

Still, it was somewhere to go, somewhere to belong, a newspaper hostel where you sat cosily round the fire with the Lords and Ladies and Artists and Writers and Television Personalities; eating crumpets and discussing the murder and adultery in the next room.

Well, I am in London, Toby thought. I've got the ad-dresses of people to look up. But I have to find a job and a cheaper place before I settle to write my book. I'll go and see what life is like in London.

He went out, along Oxford Street. All the black um-brellas. It rained and rained and one by one they opened in the streets and shone wet and their gleam, Toby thought, was like the soaking fur of the black cat that had strayed and died and been rained on and they found it un-der the holly tree with the water still pouring on it and its body stiff and arched and the flesh decayed already from around its mouth so that its teeth showed in a snarl.

The street was gloomy. Toby felt tired and old. Something had burst in the sky and left a yellow stain.

People kept stopping him and asking the way. When he told them at great length, expecting them to be pleased and interested, that he had just arrived from New Zealand, they did not seem impressed. Sometimes they murmured, 'Really? That's somewhere in Australia isn't it?' Or they said in a dazed way, 'New Zealand? I've got a brother who emigrated to Australia.'

Toby stopped outside a joke shop and looked in the window at the disguises and tricks – false noses, wigs, beards, rubber food, stink bombs, squeaking cushions. He felt himself growing excited. He had always liked tricks, he had always wanted to work magic on people.

Be the life of the party. Astonish your friends. Astonish your friends!

Which party? Which friends?

'Be your age,' his father said.

But Toby took no notice of his father for this was London and no one was going to order him about and treat him like a child; he was in London, he was going to write his Lost Tribe; he would show them. He experimented in imagination with the tricks displayed, offering people plastic scrambled or poached eggs, drawing their attention to fake ink-blots on their tablecloths. 'Haw Haw.'

That was his laugh. He threw back his head and rocked his body to and fro. He was glad to be in London.

'Haw Haw.'

He went into the shop and bought a cigarette lighter in the shape of a small pistol. You see, you pointed it at people, threatening to kill them, and they threw up their hands in surrender or stepped back in fear, whereupon you pulled the trigger, a spurt of flame appeared, and you casually lit a cigarette. Toby thought it was a wonderful toy to possess. He longed to try it out.

He tried it. He walked into the bank where some of his money had been transferred (enough to keep him until he found a job, and to pay his return fare). He signed a withdrawal slip and presented it to the clerk. Then suddenly, while the clerk was checking the signature, Toby drew out his little gun and pointed it at the man's heart. He stayed a moment or two with the gun poised. He stared with glee at the white face and frightened eyes before him. Then he pulled the trigger, the little flame burned on top of the gun, and Toby lit a cigarette. He was smiling, as he used to smile when he brought Fluffy inside to tease the budgerigar.

'You did that deliberately,' the clerk said, echoing Toby's father.

Toby smiled. It had pleased him, and made him feel powerful to see the clerk's face turn so pale.

I must try this again, he thought. I like London. Nobody is going to cheat me or steal my ideas.

But after a time, after a long walking up and down and jostling and pushing; and the metal faces of the people, and the wire people in windows, with sweaters stretched on them and their breasts prodding the window; and the speckled rain falling, and that yellow stuff running out of the sky; and Toby was lost, inside and out. Until he saw that he was following the same route as a bus which had the words *Piccadilly Circus* displayed in front. *Piccadilly Circus.*

Toby had never been to a circus in his life. He remembered, with bitterness, the time each year when the circus came to Waimaru and the Big Top was put up in the park next to the Middle School, and everyone in the world went inside to see the circus; that is, everyone except those who could afford only the sixpenny zoo, open in the afternoon, where dirty animals with matted hair sprawled on straw at the far end of painted cages, and the children, when the attendants were not looking, poked sticks through the bars to wake up the sleepy smelly lion who lay, eternally satisfied, like a huge doctored cat – surely he was no relation to the lions in *Tarzan*? What had changed him?

Secretly, of course, through his half-closed revengeful eyes, the royal lion was gazing at the people and thinking, surely these are not human beings. What has changed them? But when Toby went to the Zoo he never liked to watch the lion. He liked to stand by the creek, in the open, where the elephant was chained; he liked to get as close as he could and count the elephant's toenails, and stroke its inscribed body and look at its queer behind.

How he longed to see a real circus! He had heard of *Piccadilly Circus*. It was famous everywhere. Also, he had noticed other buses going in the direction of other circuses. London was full of circuses.

I shall be kept busy, Toby thought.

He found his way at last to Piccadilly, to a corner which throbbed with lights which seemed at first to be the Crown Jewels only they said *Bovril Bovril*.

Toby went up to one of the policemen.

'Piccadilly Circus? I want to get to Piccadilly Circus.'

'You're right. You're there now. This is Piccadilly Circus. There's the Circus Underground over there.'

'The Circus Underground?'

'That's right. Piccadilly Circus.'

Toby was mystified. The circus must be somewhere, he thought. How can I be there without knowing? Perhaps I'll stand on the corner and watch where this bus goes. It says *Piccadilly Circus*. I'll know that wherever it stops is the Circus.

He watched the bus turn the corner and, still in sight, come towards him, going in the opposite direction. Now that was strange. With a feeling of dismay he read across the front of the bus *Cricklewood*.

It took him a long time to realize, and even then he did not believe it, that there was no circus, not underground or anywhere.

Next he saw a notice outside a cinema: *Commissionaire Wanted*. He put on his best manners and applied for the job. He got it.

XXV

Two days later from a basement room in Kentish Town which he had found to share with two Irishmen, Mike and John, Toby set out for his job in Piccadilly, and if you had passed by the cinema that day you would have seen a burly commissionaire in uniform, Toby Withers, standing in the foyer near the door. Looking bored. For Pat Keenan was right. It was work, all work. And the hardest work was to stand around switching your face on and off from welcoming (to patrons) to threatening (to suspicious characters). Toby thought everyone seemed a suspicious character, therefore he was inclined to retain his threatening expression. The senior attendant ticked him off.

'Withers,' he said. 'Look more like a commissionaire. Upright (you stoop). Smile, bow, and clean the cigarette ends out of the flowerpots.'

'It's the cleaner's work.'

'You're not here to idle you know. This is the West End.'

Late at night after he finished work at the Wonderland Cinema Toby would have dinner in Kentish Town at Tom's Midnight Snack Bar. Mince Pie and chips or two veg. Or Giant Toad and two veg. And apple tart in a deluge of pus-coloured liquid called custard. Then he would go home to the basement room which was squalid and dark with its three beds and their potent-smelling bedclothes, placed against three of the walls, and the other wall occupied by the kitchen arrangements, including a rusted gas stove with splayed grey legs, toes pointed, as if it were caught in the act of dancing a minuet. There was a sink with cold water lured out through a length of hosepipe. The one window, which was glued with dried paint and would not open, gave a view of the pavement and the lower half of passers-by. A door led out to a tiny coalhouse and another door from there led to a small yard where, the landlady told Mike and John and Toby, the coalman could tip the coal without having to enter the house. And that was an advantage wasn't it?

The landlady was anxious to list many advantages, naming them in a tone of joyous discovery, particularly when they lay jewelled in the adversity of things that would not work. 'The bath is out of order, but the drain is being seen to.' 'There is a knack in pulling the lavatory chain. It works all right if you put your hand on top of the cistern, press heavily for a few seconds (at the same time pulling the chain), then remove your hand quickly. See? Well I can't seem to manage it now but I used to be able to, when I lived on the premises.'

'Living on the premises' seemed to have the advantage of automatically conferring power.

After two weeks as Commissionaire Toby found that his job was making him too tired. He had no one to talk to. Mike and John came home late at night, often drunk, and went at once to bed, sometimes without undressing. They worked as street-sweepers during the day, shuffling the leaves and newspapers along behind a wide wet broom, scooping the muck into their small cart. They wished they had never left Ireland. In the morning they were away early and Toby's only communication with them was a remark about the weather or the Football Pools, and the task, when they had gone, of finding somewhere to empty the tea-leaves from the shared teapot. He had planned to spend his few free hours in the morning writing his book. But he did not feel like writing it. He kept thinking about the cinema and the way he was ordered about and told to smarten up. 'It's all the same,' he said to himself. 'Class, class. I won't go opening doors for anybody and everybody.'

He longed to write a letter home to his mother, Dear Mum, the job is getting me down. I have a kind of swelling on my left arm, it's blue on the outside, and I think I ought to get compensation for it. Here in my job they expect you to be at everybody's beck and call.

And how he longed for a reply from his mother, Dear Toby, I hope you are watching your food and getting the right nourishment. I think you ought to go to the doctor and have your arm seen to. You shouldn't be at work with an arm like that.

Another thing, the mornings were growing darker and darker and at night a terrible yellow glare swelled like a blister in the sky casting its shadow on the buildings and the streets and the people's faces. The streetlights were switched on in the afternoon and the buses lit. People walking had wreaths of smoke or fog rising about them; they looked like people sleep-walking in hell. Their faces were pale, some of the women had pink hair and scooped-out mauve eyes, ragged old men with matted beards lopped up and down with sandwich boards which announced in dangerous letters *Railway Lost Property Great Railway Sale.*

'I might get something cheap,' Toby thought.

So one morning he rode early into town and before work he visited the shop where the Great Railway Sale was being held. The tight-packed window looked gluttonous and seedy, a swallower of bits and pieces of travellers who had not been able to cope with their clutter of possessions – their loves, their memories, their desires, and the armour they wore and the weapons they carried – umbrellas, suitcases, briefcases, raincoats, cabin trunks. Toby had an idea that inside the shop there would be a store of human leavings which the company dared not display in the window. It appalled him to think that perhaps when people made a journey and parts of them were lost, the Railway Company was there to seize the stray pieces, renovate them, offer them for sale – *Great Railway Sale*.

The price was up too. Someone was making a profit from the desperate people who used a railway train as their material confessional.

Toby stared fascinated in the window. He was overcome by a feeling of dampness which seemed to spread through his body, adding weight to his clothing which became clogged and stiff with a green mould growing in its alleys and ridges. He felt saturated with a sense of poverty and loneliness. Someone had robbed him. Everything belonged to him. Those were his suitcases with the threadbare tapes, the weave showing like crossword puzzles where the words have not been filled in. The red price tickets perked at him, like signalling lips. Then he felt as if he were going to fall. His hand was shaking, the movement gradually extending up his arm. He held fast to his hand (as his mother had taught him when she believed this was a way of 'stopping it') while his head turned slowly as if to address something or someone directly behind him. The whites of his eyes showed as his head turned. But the attack was kind to him and as sometimes happened he did not fall unconscious. After a while the shaking ceased and his questing head became still. He felt that he wanted to cry. He always cried when the fit was over, sobbing and sobbing in an abandon of loneliness. He most needed his mother now. He always needed her when he woke from a fit; he needed her warmth and softness and her sour work-smell, like potato-peelings. He sighed and shook with a few sobs, but no tears came.

He looked once more at the window of the *Great Railway Sale Lost Property*, then he walked slowly and dreamily along the road to the Wonderland Cinema. His head ached. His arm was worrying him. He centred his feeling upon his arm. He knew that his mother would tell him to have it seen to, that he shouldn't leave it, the way it was puffing up and going blue.

He was late for work.

'It's not good enough,' the manager said. 'We've had complaints, too, about your talking to patrons. The tone of the cinema has to be kept up. You're in the West End you know. Smarten yourself up.'

'I'll not have any of that talk from you. I'm my own boss. So this is what you call English democracy. I'll not go bowing and scraping in front of fancy toffs like you. We don't do that where I come from.'

'You colonials are all alike. Sorry, Withers, your reference from the mayor of your home town – how do you say it? – is all right but we have among our patrons some very important people.'

'Well I'm finishing now and you can stick the Wonderland Cinema.'

I've got my rights, Toby thought, as he walked to catch the bus to Kentish Town. The anger was slowly flowing from him like an electric current that has been earthed. He wished his arm would stop aching, and he wished that the sky had not grown so dark. It was not yet noon but he had the impression that already people were hurrying home to escape from the looming darkness. He rode on the crowded bus to Kentish Town. He went to his basement room and switched on the light. No light came. The house was in darkness.

He climbed the stairs, exploring, and knocked on the door where he knew a woman and her little girl lived and were home during the day. The woman opened the door a few inches. There was a flickering glow inside from a candle.

'Hello. You're from downstairs? It's a nuisance about the light, isn't it? The electric people have turned it off because the landlord hasn't paid the bill. I don't know where he lives because I just pay the rent when he comes each week, him or his wife. They're on the phone but I can't get through to them myself. It's urgent for me, the light I mean, though I suppose it's darker downstairs where you are. Pitch dark.'

She opened the door wider and Toby saw a small cluttered room where a thin child sat nursing a doll on an unmade bed. In a corner of the room there was a table littered with tiny plastic or plaster animals, paints and brushes. The woman saw Toby glancing at them.

'You see I paint their faces. They're made at the factory, but someone has to put in their eyes and the looks on their faces, and I have to have light to see by. Can't you do something about getting the light turned on?'

Toby was doubtful. 'I'll ring up, if you like.'

Then he held out his arm, rolling up his sleeve.

'Look at my arm.'

'It looks bad.'

'I'm going to have it seen to. I'm off work.'

'There's a doctor round the corner, two doors on the left. I was on the panel myself three weeks ago. I'll give you the number to ring about the light. We have to have the light. I'm behindhand as it is today, with the days being so dark now and there's been no summer this year. I hope it's not going to be a winter like after the war.'

Although the woman seemed eager for someone to talk to, she did not invite Toby in. It appeared that she lived in the room with her little girl and earned her living by doing 'homework' from the factory and sometimes by sewing, but her machine had broken and you had to have the right kind of electric machine before they trusted you with sewing, and if the man from the electric kept turning off the power it wasn't much use was it?

'So I work with these.' She indicated the tiny plastic animals and people. Even from where he stood Toby could see that most of the figures were without eyes or individual faces.

'Yes, the work's piling up,' the woman said. 'Only sixteen eyes this morning, and half the number of mouths and cheeks and the pay is robbery.'

'You'll ruin your sight,' Toby said.

He wanted her to invite him in for a cup of tea. He could see a kettle steaming on a small gas ring in the corner. He longed to have someone to talk to, to tell about the way the manager had fired him, or rather the way he had given his notice, and how he had come to London to be independent and to see something of the world, and to do important secret work; his arm too, to have advice about his arm.

'So you'll ring up the landlord? He might listen to you.'

She was a plump woman whose pallor seemed closely associated with cunning and economy as if she herself were as responsible for tinting her cheeks as she was for painting the faces of the miniature people and animals. She seemed to have decided that she couldn't afford to use too much paint. Her little girl was pale too, with straw-coloured hair that had not been combed, and with the ragged look that belongs to children who play in the streets till late, under the nightmare light of the streetlamps.

The woman's eyes were brown, speckled like raisins.

'I'll see about the light,' Toby said. His head was aching.

Why didn't she ask him in for a cup of tea?

She gave him the phone number. He went at once to the phone box at the corner and rang the landlord who answered, 'Don't worry, we'll have the light turned on at once, it's a little matter that slipped my memory.'

'We have to be able to find our way around,' Toby said sharply.

He returned to the house. He stood on the steps outside, in a dream, scarcely aware of his thoughts or surroundings; then he went inside and as he walked along the corridor past the woman's room he saw the light suddenly switched on, and heard her exclaim, as if she had solved a mystery which had baffled her for too long, 'It's the light! It's the light!'

In his room Toby sat on the sagging bed. A damp smell that came from the lower world seeped through the room. He lit the gas oven and opened the door, to get warm. His arm hurt. Who could he tell about his arm and losing his job? Why was there no one to tell? He phrased in his mind a letter to his mother, Dear Mum, My arm is bad now and I must go to the doctor to have it seen to. I have given up my job at the cinema. The power was turned off today because the old skinflint didn't pay the bill but I jolly well reminded him. Wouldn't I like to be home now on the sofa.

He sat, brooding and lonely, encumbered with himself, while the warmth from the oven slowly filled the room with a smell of burned biscuits and bacon. He thought about his book which seemed so strange and far away now, as if he had dreamed it. Only the day before, he had bought an exercise book from Woolworths and a new HB pencil with a perfect point, and had sat down early to write his book. *The Lost Tribe*, he had written, in slow careful writing. Then he had stopped, seized by fear. Perhaps that was his book, just that, three words, nothing else, no chapters or sections or descriptions of people. Could that be so, only three words? What about all his dreams, the composition he had written at school; the teacher reading it out in front of the class; his mother saying, 'Some day you'll write a book, Toby.' And all the times he had said, 'Wait till I write my book,' and his father had scoffed, and his mother had defended him, had even defended his poor spelling and the fact that he hadn't had much education in writing books. 'Don't worry, Toby will write his book. Remember his composition, and the teacher reading it out in front of the class?'

After writing the three precious words, Toby had shut the exercise book and put it carefully away, with the sharp pencil beside it. The pencil had a tiny rubber attached to the top. Toby liked this, and he had made squiggles on the table, rubbing them out with the rubber. Of course a pencil like that meant that you couldn't put the end in your mouth, but you had to give up something to have a rubber always ready. Yet it didn't rub out ink, not ordinary or ball point. Well, if you wanted to buy a special rubber which rubbed out ink...

So Toby had put his book away. I'll start *The Lost Tribe* some other time. It's my idea. No one is going to steal it.

He got up from the bed, turned off the gas in the oven, and made himself ready to go out to the doctor. He was just twisting the rusty key in the door when he remembered again about the Lost Tribe. 'I must write it. It's *my* book.'

Then, satisfied that he had at least given it a thought, as a parent gets rid of a complaining child by offering it a sweet, he turned his attention to his arm. Perhaps the poison in it was spreading?

I wonder, he said to himself as he went up the stairs,

what has happened to Zoe Bryce and Pat Keenan and the rest of them?

Yes, the poison would spread and clutter up his system if he did not go immediately to the doctor.

XXVI

MRS CRANE, the landlady of The Elms, Clapham SW4 stared suspiciously at Zoe when Pat introduced her.

'I thought it was a man you were bringing. You know I don't have women staying.'

'Oh now Ma, you can trust me. Zoe's quiet. She's going to get a job in the neighbourhood. She's been a school-teacher,' he added with pride.

At that, Mrs Crane smiled at Zoe. She was middle aged with grey hair, a pale plump face, with flesh hanging in a shelf under her chin. Her bosom was rising and circular, and combined with the hissing of her breath, made a sound like two pancakes cooking. Her dress was neat, a grey woollen material with a frill, like an oyster-skirt, at the neck.

'I'm the daughter of a vicar myself,' she confided to Zoe. 'I would never have dreamed of keeping tenants because I was brought up to be a lady, but when you're a widow... and now Pat here has brought you to stay... I usually take only men, they're less bother you know, qui-eter... not hanging up washing and getting hair down the plughole in the bathroom...'

She spoke as if Zoe were an exception because Pat, whom she liked, had invited her. Besides, Zoe had been a schoolteacher.

'I see what you mean, Mrs Crane. I'm from the Mid-lands, originally.'

'I thought you sounded like it. My daughter's living up near the Lake District. Her husband is with one of those new army projects. They are miles from anywhere. My daughter doesn't like it. But I must go. Pat will show you your room Miss –'

'Zoe Bryce. Zoe.'

'You show her Pat, and explain things. I'm late for my meeting. I'll see you later about the rent.'

Then she was gone, after returning to her kitchen and calling, 'Goodbye Chummy Chummy Chummy.'

'Her cat,' Pat said. 'Remember to make a fuss of her cat if you see it. It's a fat old thing and puts hair everywhere but you'd better stroke it when you see it and talk to it or Ma will find some excuse to turn you out. Ma and I get on well together.'

He was leading Zoe up the carpeted stairs. He pointed to the room off the landing.

'A Welsh chap lives there. Queer bird.'

He pointed to the next room. 'The chap in there works for the Oxygen Company. Public School Boy. Queer bird.'

The door of the next room was open. Pat walked in.

'This is your room, see? Gas fire. Big window. Comfy bed. I'll leave you now for I have to get in to Victoria and see about my job. How about coming downstairs first for a cup of tea? You wouldn't like to come with me to Victoria – there's an agency I know. They can fix you up with an office job anywhere in London. They're crying out for secretaries.'

'But I don't want to be a secretary.'

'But they're crying out for them. What will you do, then? You've thrown up teaching. If you take my advice you'll go back to it. Surely you're not going down on your hands and knees scrubbing doorsteps?'

'I'll find a job on my own. Just enough to keep me.'

'You only have to ask me you know. Come into Victoria with me and we'll fix you up as a ten pound a week secretary. Come on downstairs and I'll make tea. Ma's out. We've got the place to ourselves.'

People talking, talking, possessing, arranging.

Zoe went downstairs and sat in Pat's room in a trough-like floral armchair with a linen cover draped across the back to protect the upholstery. Zoe was tired, train-sick, bus-sick, seasick and dizzy. She leaned against the antimacassar. Where could one stop in the practice of putting linen covers upon furniture? One could drape the entire chair, all the tables, sofas, even the walls with washable removable linen coverings so as not to have the furniture rimmed with tidemarks where human heads and arms and legs had rested. But it was the head that was dangerous, landladies were at war with the human head because more than any other part of the body it stained, it oozed against the wallpaper if you leaned there, and against the beds and chairs. Dark stains. An unclean substance in the head.

Pat was setting out cups and saucers and biscuits. 'I feel as if I've never been away. While I was across the sea I often thought of this brand of biscuit. Digestive. They're digestive. The factory's not far away. You want to get a job there, yes, there's the place for you, doing light clerical work. You'll like Clapham. There's the Common. I often go walking on the Common. But it's a bed of vice.'

He flushed with anger. 'All those young girls, it's disgusting. There's no decency left. They come to London and the next minute they're on the streets. I work a lot with the police at night when I'm driving the buses. I see what goes on. The Irish girls need protecting too. I belong to a society that rescues them from temptation. It's the blacks that have helped to bring the morals down.'

The flush of anger – or jealousy – spread to his neck.

'Black men going out with white women!' he said furiously. 'And foreigners crowding the country from left and right.'

'But you're not from England yourself,' Zoe said mildly.

'That's different. I'm from Ireland, the real Ireland. We've been under the domination of Britain for long enough. I'm from the real part of Ireland.'

His eyes grew dreamy. 'Ireland is the only place.'

XXVII

I KNOW YOU Zoe Bryce. I can see you arranging your belongings in your room, testing the gas to see if it leaks, in case it kills you in the night; opening and shutting the window that looks upon the back yard and garden (trying to correlate the efficiency of your life with that of the furniture which surrounds you?) arranging your books, lying on the bed, resisting the temptation to masturbate, counting the blankets and studying their labels to see if they are *Pure Wool* (in which case you feel warm at once) or *Wool Mixture* (when you shiver with anticipated cold although you would never have noticed the difference if you had not studied the labels); trying the lock on the bedroom door; walking from corner to corner of the room, claiming the intangible part of it which you cannot test, having no unit of measurement for it, then stopping in the middle of the room, listening.

You are right, Zoe. The ship creaks. It is the sea outside whose mysterious talent it is to strike a note of tragedy from a limited range of complaint.

The Ugly Duckling who became a swan was not really the loneliest among ducklings. The loneliest was the true duckling who felt himself to be a stranger in his own family. His story has not been written in the fairy-tale. Few suspected his condition – for after all he was living with his own species in his native square of farmyard. Wasn't he, wasn't she, Zoe?

Yes, you have been kissed. What does it mean now? You have changed from the Midland schoolteacher with just enough confidence to face your class day after day, with your routine life in your flat, your occasional terrifying dreams of the War, of the time you came home and found that the house you lived in was gone, smashed to pieces – the dust was still rising, remember how you felt suddenly sealed all over, like those containers which are made with such a quality of containing that they have no corners or seams, no outlets? You could touch nothing. The road was flooded, with great holes in it, and water squirting up from a giant hidden deep in the earth with the Romans. People with false noses gaped at you. People enfolded you while you cried.

You realize now, don't you Zoe, that it is a luxury to have someone enfolding you while you cry?

So you have been kissed. So you have changed. What are your plans now?

'If you start at half-past seven in the morning, clean out the sitting-room, do the corridors and your share of the bedrooms, you ought to finish by eleven. You have lunch here at eleven. But you are... well-spoken... why do you want a job here as a cleaner?'

'I'm doing private research.'

But on the cold foggy mornings it was hard work taking out the perilous fly-away ashes from the sitting-room fire, trying to sweep them from the carpet with an old-fashioned carpet-sweeper choked with hair and fluff and bone-splinters fallen like threads from the woven and frayed students; and then sliding along the corridor trying to polish while people walked up and down saying, 'You don't mind if I walk here, do you?' and Zoe smiling and answering, 'No that's quite all right.'

I'm Zoe Bryce doing private research which means that I clean in a student hostel until eleven o'clock every morning when I sit with the others round the conference table with our thick slices of bread and margarine and our mugs of tea, and we talk about the War, the War, the bombs, the raids, the lootings, the bodies that were never recovered – the general and universal War which some-times like a sea invading a private inlet engulfs one of us, and, receding, leaves a tide-mark of personal encounter which is described again and again, measured, explored, with all the beachcombing resources of memory. Our conference centres on the War.

And on the telly. We are the derelict people whose only hope of work now is a cleaning job in office or fac-tory or hostel. Some of us have had nervous breakdowns and cannot return to our former occupations. We are the unmarried mothers, the retired prostitutes, the obsessed, the 'mentally backward', the widows, the separated, those who have been kissed once in their life, on board ship, and are now engaged in 'private research', preparing to create flesh or idea, for the childhood fantasy that kisses make babies is, like many other fantasies, a fly-over, dual-carriageway, to truth.

Zoe's job did not last long. 'I am leaving,' she said. 'My re-search work forces me to leave.'

They said it was nice having her, they were sorry to say goodbye. 'Come and visit me,' Milly said, giving Zoe a piece of paper with her address on it, but when Zoe was getting off the bus she put the paper, in mistake for her ticket, in the litter bin. Come and visit me. I get so lonely in the evenings. But Zoe had only the bus ticket in her hand and there was no name or address upon it, only a confusion of numbers which she had once used, with other children, to tell her fortune, her lucky days, the man she would marry and the number of children she would have.

Winter. The curtains drawn completely in the sky and the smell of death on the hands of the people who touch each other in the night. The late sun, seen through mist on the far side of the Common; little dogs, wet and black, out walking on the rubbed brown grass; the West Indians, stricken with cold, shrunk in their cheap baggy suits, standing on the grille above the Underground, warming their feet; below, the harpy scream and hiss of warm air, the whine, the hurtle of trains through the tiled catacombs, past the cave-paintings of corsets, milk drinks, cough cures; the winter need to go home towards the light; the lonely people huddled by the shop windows – by the confectioner's, the late-trading stores and the smoky pub with its treacle-coloured furniture; the dead sliding by in tall cars manned by rosy-faced attendants; the wet clay heaped like a new grave around the filled entrance to the old bomb shelters; the children's cries in the grounds of the Council Flats, sharp cries rising like metal hooks against the walls of the buildings, jagging the pot-bellied sky; charcoal to burn in all the little houses built over holes in the road.

Hands to warm; fists to shake in the dark winter; touch me, the pity and comfort of skin.

XXVIII

ZOE WAS walking alone in Hyde Park near Speaker's Corner when she met Toby. At first she did not recognize him. She saw only a heavily built man dressed in a new cheap suit with the coat too long and the trousers ballooning at the knees, the sort of clothes which marked him as one of the lonely people – like the coloured outcasts and the tramps grazing like fretful sheep in the parks and along the embankment, and those who appeared each night to claim a cubicle in the down-and-out hostels. Toby recognized Zoe at once, and smiled and came towards her. There was no surprise in his expression. It was almost as if they had arranged to meet there. As he came closer she saw that he was eager to talk and already the words were queuing to get out. But he spoke slowly, as always,

'I've been cheated,' he said. 'I bought some bananas from that barrow-boy and he nipped them on and off the scales. He didn't give the weight a chance to settle. Cheats.'

Toby possessed the whole world. He moved in it as if it were his private estate. One word from him and the tenants would be evicted and no mercy shown them. Even now you could see him turning and frowning upon people as if considering the fate which he had prepared for them. This obstinate conviction of his own power had driven him ten thousand miles across the world, to visit other lands, to walk in them as the rightful king, to force people to realize that Toby Withers was no ordinary epileptic whom people could put out of sight in an institution, or turn from and abandon when his fits became an embarrassment to them.

Since Toby had been in London, the doctor who was providing his pills had told him about a Society for

Epileptics where the sufferers met and talked to one another, worked out their problems, regained their sense of proportion... or so the doctor said, adding fatuously, 'You're all human beings you know; not epileptics, just human beings.'

Toby was not so sure of that. He declined to join the Society. Besides, there was his secret, his writing of the Lost Tribe. He had not yet begun it but he would, he would in time. Sometimes at night he heard his mother's voice saying to him, 'Remember, Toby, Napoleon was an epileptic, many great men and leaders, Toby, had your trouble. Great and good men, Toby.'

'Am I good?'

'*You're* good, Toby. You would never turn your mother into the streets would you? And you'll look after your parents in their old age?'

Dad! Dad!

Toby remembered the dark bitter faces when his father's family had gathered to consider who would 'take' his father's mother who was old and querulous and dying. She had a knotted stick; her bloomers were dark purple and her shape stayed in them, like a watch-dog, when she took them off and hung them on the end of the bed. She said, 'I'll go ben the room. Dinna fash yuirsel.'

In the end Toby's mother 'took' her, and his father's family, the sisters and brothers, relieved, kissed one another and Amy and said, 'Amy's naturally good. She's the religious one.'

Then they hurried away to their homes while their mother, from her wheelchair, considered her new but not unfamiliar surroundings, and the meanings which would begin now to penetrate them, like vapours rising from a house that is built upon a well of death.

205

'Yes, cheated,' Toby said. 'By a barrow-boy. I've seen the police move him along too.'

For a while it was his sole topic of conversation. Then he told Zoe about his arm and his being off work, and his job at the Wonderland Cinema. Then he asked Zoe about her own life, but did not wait for an answer.

He waved his arm about him. 'Hyde Park,' he said. Anyone could tell that he owned Hyde Park, that he alone knew its acreage and boundaries. They walked past the speakers who were shouting into the bitterly cold foggy air about the urgent need for contraception, licensed brothels, nuclear disarmament, National Health Euthanasia, transistors and Hi-Fi equipment in coffins. A man walked up and down with the placard *Prepare to Meet Thy God*. The dampness wound itself like a corkscrew into the people; their voices, trapped, looped the loop and fell to the earth. The fog hung like bubbles of perspiration in the air. Someone said it was going to snow. Snow before Christmas. There had never been a winter like this one; it was like the year after the War, the queues, the shortages, no electric power. Within living memory it had never been so cold so early, or so dark. A pale man with a knife was cutting a trapdoor into the rapidly thickening fog; he disappeared through it; one heard his cries. An old man with a reap-hook was harvesting the fog, hacking at the stiff yellow bushes that tumbled around him showering him with smoky pollen. And there, once more, was the stain in the sky, and the red haze from the sun. The burned fingers of the light probed the leaves and the people, turning their separate layers for closer scrutiny.

'Prepare to Meet Thy God,' the shabby man with intensely blue eyes shouted at intervals, not sure that the message on his placard was being put across to the crowd who wandered listlessly from one speaker to the next, hoping for violent news of other human beings – a fight, a riot, a moment when the speaker would be unable to answer a question put to him, would be forced to admit his ignorance – anything to prove that the essence of people had not been rubbed off, absorbed, in a world draped with antimacassars of fog.

On the edge of the crowd an old woman in long skirts, a black scarf over her head, was commanding a set of paper dolls to dance upon the pavement. They danced, they bowed, they joined hands with one another, all on receiving softly spoken orders from the old woman. No one could understand how she had achieved such power over them. They danced and danced. Now they were moving on to the grass verge, still dancing, their pink paper legs high in the air. The woman was fast selling one doll after another, hastily packing them and murmuring to the buyer, *Instructions Enclosed*. Soon they were all sold. The woman sat down suddenly, in a collapsing way, like one of her paper dolls. Then she got up and disappeared outside the park gate. One or two people who had bought her dolls were already trying them out, commanding them in self-conscious tones, and looking foolish when they stayed still and dead, refusing to dance. How was it done? The fog, magnetism, the atom bomb? The sky sagged, undone, split, cloud and stuffing bursting from it. Someone remarked that it was going to snow. Separate untainted flakes falling, merging, massed in filth and sludge upon the pavements, in doorways, in the angles of roofs, on windowsills; the dirty democracy of snow.

Toby told Zoe of his room in Kentish Town. He was going to tell her about the Lost Tribe but he thought, I'll wait. They parted then. They had scarcely spoken to each other. They had merely walked with the crowd from one speaker to the next, and any communication they achieved was got from secret mirrors trained upon other people and reflecting upon themselves. It is only when other people are the sun that such communication is dangerous, reducing one's companion to ashes.

They made no plans for meeting again, although Zoe gave Toby her address and directions for reaching it, and a map of the neighbourhood. He put the map in his pocket. He liked maps. Sometimes he sat alone in his room and traced the map of London, journeying his finger many times over every street; and then satisfied and tired, with aching muscles, with grit and smoke stinging his eyes, he would lie down on the bed, pull the eiderdown over him, and sleep.

If he slept in his clothes the question next morning was how to uncrease them and tidy them; not that he cared very much; but they were new, got from the market where the suit had been flipping back and forth with a vivid label around its neck, *Reduced, Sale Price*. A man with rolled shirtsleeves, as if selling were a task requiring physical prowess and stamina, had urged Toby to buy the suit without delay. When Toby hesitated, wondering whether he was being rooked, the man waved his arms recklessly towards a row of suits limp upon their narrow hangers.

'Anyone you like, the same price, anyone at all, cut-price.'

Toby chose a suit and bought it, scowling at the market dealer to show that the decision was made without any surrender to high-pressure salesmanship.

And now the problem was how to wash his clothes. Toby had never lived by himself. At first when he stayed in his room he left his dirty socks at the end of the bed, under the bedclothes, and stuffed his shirts into the drawer that was his share of the dressing-table. But one Saturday morning Toby saw Mike and John going away somewhere with a bag of washing. They were going to the laundry, they said. Or you could go to the laundrette, and put things in a washing-machine, but that meant you had to iron them. The laundry was best, quite cheap.

The idea of a laundry excited Toby. He at once decided to take his dirty clothes there too. And now each week when he called for them and presented his ticket his heart beat fast with excitement as he hurried back to his room, untied the parcel, and was confronted by his shirts and singlets all pressed and neat, neater than his mother had ever pressed them, for she had usually been fuddled with the heat of the kitchen and having to watch things cooking on the stove, so that when she began to iron Toby's shirts (even his best one which he wore for visiting Evelina) she had put creases in the back while she was ironing the front, and then, turning to the back, had ironed new creases into the front. Toby did not mind very much unless he was visiting Evelina, but he had heard his father shout in anger 'What's the meaning of this, creases in my shirt?'

So he had copied his father, 'Mum, my shirt's creased. How do you expect me to wear a shirt like this?' And now here they were, ironed, with no creases; ironed by no one he would ever see. Neat, in brown paper, paid for. No one, hot and anxious, rubbing the soot from the old flat iron on to a piece of last night's newspaper, or sniffing to catch a suspicion of scorch in the new electric iron which Toby's father had won by sending in a question for a radio quiz.

'Name the fifth wonder of the world.'

'Why the fifth wonder, Bob?'

'I've worked it out, Mum. Two and two are four, half of two is one, four and one make five.'

'I see,' Amy said, mystified. Her husband was superstitious and did not believe in putting shoes on the table, walking under ladders, opening umbrellas in the house, admitting anyone but a dark-haired visitor when the clock had struck twelve on New Year's Eve.

'The Fifth Wonder. It says the Mausoleum at Halicarnassus.' Bob had found the Wonders named in a battered Household Encyclopaedia which also gave information about furniture, leeches, persons of rank, destruction of vermin, and the number of eggs laid by a queen bee.

In a way Toby was afraid to think that the laundry had such power to abolish his mother and her ironing-board and the electric iron and the wet cloth with the scorch marks on it, and the time, late evening, with his father finished his dinner and asleep in the chair, the room warm with the smell of ironing, the clothes folded between newspapers on the rack above the stove... How could the laundry abolish these when his own dreams could not be rid of them, when his mother persisted in advising him, warning him, appearing to him at night and talking of the Lost Tribe and the Latter Days, quoting *Nation shall not lift up sword against Nation, neither shall they learn war anymore*, then beginning to cry and begging Toby to remember her always, and never to spatter her clothes with mud when he passed in his fine coach.

Toby's Saturday morning visit to the laundry was one of the most exciting times of the week. When he arrived at eight-thirty at the Daisy-Fresh, and the woman opened the door to him, he always looked about him with an air of anticipation. Then after he had surrendered his dirty clothes and taken his clean bundle, he was reluctant to leave and stood gazing dreamily about him at the racks of dry-cleaned clothes hanging in the resigned way characteristic of worn clothes that have been persuasively tortured to receive at any time, day or night, the same human shape. He looked at the floor littered with brown paper parcels sometimes split at the sides to show the pressed, tightly packed linen. Short dark-faced men arrived in the grimy van with its daisy emblem growing across the doors. For these were not the main premises of the Daisy-Fresh. They were elsewhere at a place referred to as 'the centre'.

Toby shivered with excitement when he heard people mention 'the Centre'.

'Has it not come back from the *centre*?' someone would ask.

'It's still at the *centre*.'

'There's been some delay at the *centre*.'

For although the notice in the window asserted, *In By Saturday Out By Tuesday*, it was not always so; clothes kept being mislaid, detained at 'the centre'.

The word ran on and on in Toby's mind, alarming him. What was its mystery? Was there a mystery?

He put the fresh neutered clothes against his cheek. They gave him no comfort. Words were running on and on in his head – laundries, lost property, circuses, buses and their destinations – High Wycombe, Peckham Rye, Tooting Bec and Tooting Bdy – did that mean Tooting Body? Tooting Body.

And his arm was still hurting. The doctor told him it was septic, it would heal in time. He asked Toby if he had taken any fits. Then he said, 'Have you got your card?'

Toby had no card.

'You must have a card,' the doctor said. He looked tired. He had white marks down his temples, like the chalk-marks which officials put on cargo in transit.

XXIX

LIFE-LINES of Toby Withers, Zoe Bryce, Pat Keenan, and others whom I have not yet named. Life-line, umbilical cord, fishing-line, trip-wire, strangling rope.

It is Sunday.

The newspapers have been flipped through the letter-box. In double beds husbands and wives were unfolding the memoirs of call-girl and General. Children practise their music – *Raindrops, Auld Lang Syne*; motorcycles burst to life bucking and charging up the street. Late risers cough their foggy morning coughs. The mist catches in the throat, they say. They say, they say. Everywhere people are saying, explaining, attributing causes, stockpiling their habitual deterrent against the mystery. The still Sunday morning seizes the noise of footsteps, cars, scooters; magnifies, muffles; the world treads on cotton-wool and leaves, in the head and under the feet; the bus stops are deserted. Bells. Jets. The H-Bomb rocking to sleep in its nursery.

The child cries on and on. A Sunday morning cry, knowing that for once in the week its mother is near to attend to it. The day is patched with long silences between moment and moment which, like the silences between the communication of people, give rise to dread; as if the time itself held a reserve of opinion too terrible to express. In the cracks of the silence the people's voices grow like bright feverish weeds whose stalks are hollow and whose shallow roots are separated from the earth (or water) with one tug of a hand or breeze; now and again people's voices disappear in the gaps that open with the continual shock of Time; the world walks then aghast and dumb, back and forth in the streets of the cities. Reptiles waiting in doorways seize the limbs of passers-by – a leg, a hand, a male tripod balancing its charmed brew. The people walk on, unaware of their loss, realizing only a sudden longing for ease, simplicity, lightness, with numbers flying swiftly in their head, proclaiming that at last two and two make four. Their Sunday loss is hushed up. Everything is hushed up.

On bombed sites, on corners, in adventure playgrounds, the scarfed light walks in a Sunday haze of burning.

XXX

WHO ARE the Lost Tribe, Toby? Why do they lie hidden in your mind, like beetles under a stone? Are they beetles under a stone? Are they worms in the hollow eyes of the dead?

They live, he says, behind a mountain approached through a secret pass.

And where, in the world?

'In the South.'

Toby is serious, intense. Why is his face sunburned as if he had spent long hours in the paddocks burning off the gorse and tussock? His eyebrows are brown and singed, like gorse-twigs. His walk is a clamber as if in each step he surmounted obstacles of which other people have no knowledge. What is he doing in London except, as landlord, to survey a corner of his estate, to complain bitterly against the way his tenants are treating him, to issue eviction orders if necessary?

In the lonely evenings when he crouches over the gas oven, trying to get warm, he regrets his journey from New Zealand. He wishes that he were – up Central? He remembers his last visit up Central where the raspberry farms border the river, where the matagouri, the 'spiked plant that does not cry' grows on the hills among the snow-grass; and the loitering mountains, responsive only to Time's occasional *Move on There*, hinder the passing flocks of cloud.

Up Central. Toby thought, once, that you climbed a ladder to get there.

His last visit was purposeful and mercenary. The river was being diverted, they were building a power station, and for several hours of one day only the riverbed would be empty. You know the river? – that it is filled not only with snow, salmon, drowned cattle and sheep, but with gold; its bed, they say, is solid gold. Therefore on that one day people from all over the country came up Central to claim their share of treasure, and during the few hours when the riverbed was drained, they wandered up and down, stumbling over bleached bones of cattle and sheep, and hawk-formations of trees uprooted by storm and flood; up and down, urgently, stooping to gather and sift the silt in the hope of finding a few twinkling grains of gold.

Who said the riverbed was solid gold?

It was luck, that's all it was. Some found a few grains, others found nothing. Yet the fever of searching persisted even after the warning came that the water was rising in the river and the first trickling streams began to flow in the gashes of shingle. And still the crowd (including Toby) stayed on the riverbed in the hope of finding their treasure – you know, the treasure that will 'set you up for life', that will conceal effectively, until the last moment, your breaking-down for death.

The water was beginning to flow more swiftly. Warnings were given. Abuse was shouted.

'It's a free country. Can't you let a man find his share of gold?'

Still they scooped and washed and scooped and washed. In valley, from all the campfires on the banks of the river where the tea-billies hung on their twigs boiling, you could see and smell the smoke from the burning manuka, sniffed-at and longed-for. One by one the crowd left the riverbed and prepared to enjoy their cups of tea. But there was one man who had arrived in a smart car from the city, bringing his wife and family and picnicking, not like a genuine prospector of the eighteen-sixties, but in the modern way with portable chairs, tables, a wicker basket with cutlery arranged neatly inside the lid. This man stayed on the riverbed long after the others had left.

'A moment longer,' he called out. 'It's the opportunity of a lifetime.'

And it was too, for death.

The water sneaked higher and higher, cutting off his path to the bank, and he was swept downstream, and they saw his arms waving in conflict with the water which, foaming at the mouth now at having its privacy invaded, its secrets probed and trampled, showed no mercy, none of the gentle lapping caresses that belong to the moods of water, nor any of the pauses and ponderings when it holds the crinkling shadow of the sky and the trees and the sheen of tussock; but rabid, swirling, it carried the drowning man past the picnickers and out of sight.

Why?

He was too greedy, some said. Others blamed his city manners, his smart car, his wicker basket with the shining cutlery neatly arranged inside the lid.

They never found his body. Bodies are not recovered at once from the mountain rivers; only, occasionally, they appear miles downstream, washed ashore or floating. The water has no means of knowing that they are human. If it knew would it show compassion? The bodies float, unsightly, and equal with sheep, cattle, trees; they lie abandoned upon the shingle beside the bones of sheep and the horns and skulls of cattle, and the river-snags – creatures of dream, branches of willow dressed fantastically in bunched wool, wads of cattle-hair, dull-red, demon-snatched.

Often Toby remembered the time he walked on the riverbed, and how afterwards with the rest of the crowd he tried to find somewhere to fix the blame for the man's drowning. For blame must be apportioned carefully, like a legacy.

He died because he was a stranger, a foreigner from up north where the climate is sub-tropical and people go half-naked in the sun and grow oranges in their gardens; he died because he was different, because he and his family had set up their camp apart, had not joined in and made cobbers with everyone. He died (they said intensely) because of his face and his ways and his wicker basket with the shining cutlery arranged neatly inside the lid. How else could they find meaning for his death?

Toby wished that his mother had been there that day. She would have known the reason – wouldn't she? At least she would have seen Toby walking on the riverbed and drawn from his actions a strange and wonderful meaning. For had not Christ walked upon the water?

Toby was always jealous of his mother's regard for Christ. Her association with Him had been personal. She would defend Him against criticism in the same way that she defended Toby when his father taunted him for his slowness, his childishness. Toby resented his mother's dream that the Second Coming would occur in her home, in the kitchen of the house at Waimaru. In Amy's mind Christ appeared conventionally as a swagger wandering up to the door and asking for food and shelter; telling how the people in the other houses had set their dogs on him or threatened to call the police – this was Amy's dream, in spite of the fact that swaggers didn't appear anymore, they were a race that died with the goldfields. And the dogs in the street were not watchdogs and would have rushed to any stranger to lick his face; and all the people in the street, even mean old Mrs Crouch, would have given freely from their larder, and more than a crust of bread, too, perhaps a piece of cream sponge or a macaroon that had won first prize in the local show!

But what pride Toby would have felt if only his mother had known that he had walked on the riverbed! But the old witch was dead, wasn't she, and the slimy jam jars stood empty over her grave, and the space of Waimaru stone in the tall monument topped by a yellowing moss-grown angel with hawk's wings, still awaited the lettering, the biographical précis which people rely upon, as if it were secretly magnetized, to attract from the flesh of the living the iron spikes that are the memory of the dead. Lettering was costly. And although Amy Withers in her lifetime had not made many demands upon money or space, it was Bob's conviction that she deserved a verse of at least four lines; that he owed her the importance of the complete words 'born' and 'died' instead of the parsimonious reticence of b full stop, d full stop.

Toby felt so lonely; for his mother, for tussock, bracken, a decent-sized mountain with its own light, not having to cadge it from a meanly flickering sun that squibbed and fretted like something bought at a Fire-Sale. And sometimes, huddling in his bed, Toby did not feel like a human being. He felt more like an insect – a beetle, a bed-bug, a spider. Sometimes he was surprised to find himself scratching at the 'wool-mixture' blankets which he had bought for himself at the Surplus Stores along the road, as if his hands were paws, no longer fulfilling the function of human hands. The squalor did not worry him. He accepted it – the dishes unwashed day after day, the accumulating mound of tea leaves, the empty milk bottles which the milkman refused to collect, saying they were not his brand of bottle, they belonged to another dairy firm; yet when Toby hailed the other milkman passing in his whining float, he too refused to collect the bottles.

'They're all against me,' Toby thought. 'They're all out

to nark me. How can I write my Lost Tribe when they're all trying to put me off it? Mike and John too, the way they come home drunk and swearing every night, when I get down to writing my book I'm going to tell them straight that they're interfering with my work, that I've got my destiny to think about. It's the Irish in them, the way they go on,' Toby thought. 'The Irish are all alike. For you have to collect and label the forces of violence and fear, haven't you, in order to deal with them. For there is always an enemy. Drink, women, the blacks, the government, the council, the neighbours, the people up north, the people down south – help yourself, shoplift from the supermarket of fear.'

Other times when Toby felt homesick he would put his hand in his suit pocket where he kept the addresses of people to 'look up', to 'get in touch with'. One evening when he was tired of picking his sore arm and of turning the blank pages of the exercise book where he planned to write about the Lost Tribe, when he was feeling lonely and cold, he wrote a short letter to a Mrs Wells whose address had been given to him by Mr Smart the butcher. 'It's my aunt. She'll be pleased to see you, to put you up and show you around.'

Toby wrote that he had come 'all the way from New Zealand' and that her nephew, a butcher in Waimaru, had given her address and could he visit her some time? A few days later Mrs Wells replied that she would be pleased to see Toby and would let him know when it would be convenient for her. Toby did not hear from her again.

From another address given him by the Horton family the reply came that there must be some mistake, that they (the Knights of Reading) had never heard of the Hortons, and as far as they knew they had no relations in New Zealand or Australia.

Then there was the address of Zoe Bryce, The Elms, Clapham, SW4.

Toby put on his best suit, including the watch-chain with the greenstone earrings, oiled his hair, and journeyed through tunnels to Clapham. A small man with grey hair came to the door and told him Zoe Bryce (if he meant the new woman in the room near the bathroom) was out, at work, and did not come home until past twelve at night.

'And Pat Keenan?'

'The Irishman? He's at work too.'

'I'll call again,' Toby said, and retreated through tunnels (darker this time) to Kentish Town. He did not know why he had gone to visit Zoe. He could not talk to her about himself, about his trouble and his book, and his mother who seemed to sneak in and stiffen and sharpen his shapes of memory in the way frost invades and makes rigid the clothes that have been hanging all night under the sky. Yet Toby liked to be with Zoe, even if he could not speak to her. He was lonely and incomplete, like a house with one wall torn away. He used people, strangers or friends, to keep out the draught. 'You'll catch a chill, Toby,' his mother used to tell him.

With one wall of himself torn away he could feel the wind blowing permanently from the continent of ice. So he needed people – people or stones or woven rushes and flax. Addresses on paper are too flimsy a contact with people. Words are worse, especially if one lives at the edge of the alphabet; yet words may sometimes act like invisible ink, revealing nothing when they are spoken or written, yet days or years afterwards, when they are breathed on or warmed by a flame or the friction of time, they often emerge stark and black with meaning and message, like telegraph wires against a clear sky.

But it is people, their shape, their presence, that are bulwark, bunghole, asbestos wall. For the wind blows from fire, as well as from ice.

XXXI

WINTER will last for ever.

The house at Clapham is clean and polished. The heavy furniture wears its dark bulky smell around it like a skirt of thick material. White clots of smell, clean, like invisible drops of shaving soap, are clustered in the passages upstairs leading to the bathroom where the pervading atmosphere is of men – newly shaved; grapes of sweat crushed beneath armpits; a purple sour smell heavy with swatted houseflies; and the faded dust of lavender-heads floating from Zoe's lavender talcum powder.

The house smells of sooty ambush, of the enemy. Winter will last for ever.

Ma Crane is sitting by her electric fire which has been manufactured to resemble heaps of coal burning like rosebuds. Her room is small, decorated with seascapes and landscapes and a bowl of waxed pears. Chummy is sitting on the cushion nearby. Tonight is not the night for Ma's visit to the Whist Drive at the Ladies' Conservative Association. She feels restless. She cannot settle to read her magazine. The nerves in her legs are 'playing up' – she has had advice about them from her doctor, and tablets to take. She has glanced through the Church Magazine and studied the picture of the new curate and the names of those born christened married buried. She has taken up her knitting and put it down again – the cardigan in blue moss stitch for her granddaughter in the Lake District.

Perhaps, Ma thinks, I will go to the front room and play the piano. She used to be a Church Organist in the days before her widowhood.

'No, I'll not play the piano.'

'Or will I? Am I in the mood?'

She tickles Chummy under his chin. Chummy Chummy, you are the only one I can trust – did you like your coley?

The doorbell rings.

There's someone at the door. Someone for me?

She peeps from the room and sees Toby turn away and wonders what his name is, where he lives, why he has called. She wonders about her lodgers – the ex-Public School Boy who works at the Oxygen Company; a clean well-spoken boy but secretive, secretive; the Welshman with the limp – he's had only one letter in about six months, perhaps his mail is addressed elsewhere?; Pat Keenan – a kind-hearted, willing nature – but why did he bring the new woman, Zoe Bryce?

Ma Crane wonders about Zoe. She feels that men are so much easier to deal with, they seem to be able to stay, like ornaments, where you put them, and not to be changing their rooms around, moving the bed from the window to the wall and back again to the window as the mood overtakes them; women seem to have a quality of dispersal, they seem to linger in corridors and rooms even when they are not present; they spill themselves, like powder; and they spill powder, too, and hang wet washing, and stay half the evening in the bathroom.

Men know their place.

They do not sneak downstairs to get the letters as soon as the postman comes in the morning, in fact, they do not seem to care about their letters, often leaving them for days propped up on the sideboard in the corridor so that the postmark can be clearly studied and one can learn a few details about the correspondence of one's tenants.

And this Ma Crane likes to do. When she hears the letters falling through the letterbox on to the carpet she immediately opens her door and goes to pick them up.

It annoys her that Zoe Bryce is sometimes first to reach them. Who, she wonders, writes letters to Zoe Bryce? Why is she not living in the Midlands if she came originally from there? Who is her family? Why is she working now as an usherette in the Palace Cinema along the High Street if she is trained as a schoolteacher? And what is the 'private research' she talks about?

Is it a cover-up for something – illegal, immoral...?

The burning rosebuds, a cover-up for coal, a cover-up for electricity, cast a red glare in the room and on Ma's pale face as she considers the problem of Zoe. It is not really nice to have usherettes in the house; they are low types; one reads about them in the local press – the ones who are caught. Yet Zoe seems 'well-spoken', and when she is asked she is always willing to bring home a pound of coley for Chummy.

I wish summer were here, Ma thinks. I would take my deckchair and a cushion and a magazine and go and sit in the sun on the Common and watch the little boys sailing their boats. And now I will play the piano. I knew I was in the mood to play the piano.

She goes to the front room which is also her bedroom and soon the chords of *Jerusalem* are sounding through the house. If you listen at the door you can hear Ma singing in a soft voice, a little breathlessly,

And did those feet in ancient time
walk upon England's mountains green...

Bring me my bow of burning gold...

XXXII

In the Circle of the Palace Cinema Zoe is directing the cosily furred and muffled people to their seats. She wears a tight maroon uniform with a gold-embroidered monogram on the pocket (*The staff, to be successful, must have a sense of identity, of belonging* – Director of the Chain of Palace Cinemas in the *Cinemagoer's Journal*).

Zoe is glad the day is not Sunday, the day of the louts. They confuse her. She cannot cope with them, and when they start to whistle and stamp and talk in loud voices she panics and sends for the manager. The arrogance of their lovemaking in the back row produces in her the same kind of alarm which people feel at the prospect of obscure insects or animals who hardly know what they are about, persevering to become the dominant race on earth: that is, the alarm of people when faced with a younger generation. The lovemakers threaten the survival of others by refusing to accommodate anything but their own survival. They cling to each other, tossing the rest of the world over the cliff (or the torn rickety seat) into darkness.

Zoe is afraid. She is alone. She senses that the battle is no longer by means of horns and hoofs, mailed hide, brandished weapons, cradled bombs; the onslaught is with overpowering love and hate. She breathes quickly, Why can't I survive too? Why can't I fit another human being and lock my feeling, powerful and protected, in the enclosure? Why need I be threatened all my life by seeing people together, arm in arm, close, excluding me?

Now all the patrons are shown to their seats. The manager, Mr Beanman, after standing smiling in the foyer, has returned to his office upstairs where he sits behind his desk attending to correspondence and preparing future publicity campaigns. He is a small man, going bald, with a chubby body and pale face. He knows that he is not as young as many of the other managers in the chain of Palace Cinemas, therefore he attends very carefully to his publicity planning – the visits of film stars, the preparation of gimmicks for each film – next week for *My Life With a Tiger*, he is bringing a caged tiger into the foyer. He hopes his plan will earn the approval of the Head Office. It worries him that they keep referring, not directly to his age, but to 'the number of younger managers with energy and initiative'. Mr Beanman likes the Palace to be known as a 'family cinema'. He encourages the patrons and the staff to look upon him as a fatherly person. He takes an interest in the private life of each usherette, giving advice where he thinks it is needed, and warnings when the advice is too late or has failed.

Sometimes in the evenings when he sneaks into a back row of the Circle he is troubled by a vague sadness at the sight of so many empty seats, the out-of-date faded plush curtains, the scratched gold-painted plaster pillars, the cherubs set in their bubble-blowing poses in the roof, the polythene ferns sprouting along the footlights; it all seems to him like a bad dream, or a dream where the scenery is second hand – rusted, tawdry, exposed to its own deceit, like a pier in winter exposed to the mercy of its last patron who is without mercy – the corroding sea. Now the advertisements begin – the cigarette-seduction on the lonely beach, the kneeling-in-prayer for the bedroom suite on Easy Terms; the clothes, the schemes, the ecstasies aroused by soap, central heating, chocolates in rainbow wrappings; the holidays, the evasions, postponements, dreams, desires, shifty compromise...

Somewhere along the darkened aisles Zoe walks up and down with her lit tray of ice cream, drinks-on-a-stick, salted nuts, trying to tempt the audience. For it is the duty of the usherettes to hawk refreshments. Zoe is not a good saleswoman. Groping in her ten-shilling float for change she often makes mistakes in arithmetic, returning half-crowns for two-shilling pieces and feeling only slight dismay in the pampering darkness. Later, however, in the brightly lit cell next to the lavatory, the girls will surrender their trays and count their money in front of Kath, the supervisor, of whom people say, to quell their doubts, 'She's human underneath.'

Mortified, confused, Zoe looks in her purse for extra sixpences to add to her float before it is her turn to face Kath. But Kath is quick.

'It's not good enough Zoe. You'll have to improve.'

Mr Beanman will have to know about it.

How Zoe longs to be able to accept Kath's reprimands and to reply swiftly, self-confidently! How does one acquire in oneself the substance of usherettes which makes them bold, carefree, in command of the situation? And how does one get a dignity so that one can stand upon it, taking the advice so often given? For Netta, one of the usherettes, bullies Zoe, orders her about, 'Go down that aisle, go up that aisle, Do this, Do that.' The others remark, 'She has no right to, face up to her, stand on your dignity, Zoe!'

What use is it if you have been kissed once in your life yet cannot stand on your dignity, cannot even locate it or recognize it or claim it? Is it a carpet, a stair, a platform, a pirate plank? Is it another human being, dead or alive? While Zoe is working at the Palace she is searching everywhere for her elusive dignity.

Netta is fat. Her fatness worries her, and she has sent for a rubber corset to be delivered in a plain wrapper. She wears the corset each morning to work and by noon when she finds it is no longer comfortable, she takes it off and hangs it in her locker, giving a relieved sigh, 'It was killing me.' It is flesh-coloured and has tiny holes like a cribbage board.

It is no surprise to the others when one day a police-woman calls to take Netta into custody. Zoe is grateful to be free of her. She wishes that the device of getting rid of people as soon as one desires it could be used more often and not remain the prerogative of dreams and fiction. And then she realizes that this is just what has happened. The sea of dream is trickling through the hole in the wall and is rising to flood all waking life.

Then I will strike, Zoe thinks. I will strike down people and terrors and hawks that keep flying in my eyes; and I will strike into being (for the purpose of my life now is to create) the crystal tower, and in people's minds the weather-vane at the top of the tower turning, turning to point the direction of love.

I have been kissed. So Netta was a shoplifter in secret? I too have shoplifted from Norton and Stroods where I have been made dizzy from seeing the tight circular cheeses snug in their aluminium foil; the looped brace-lets of flecked sausages; among the jewellery the pearls (cultured) and necklaces glittering, but swinging like bicycle chains out of delinquent artificiality to raise weals and spurts of oil from my skin... and finger-nail brooches; haberdashery, so many buttons, clips, domes, on cards, in packets... like worm-casts... and polythene flowers, 'fair pledges of a fruitful factory' with which the poet must learn to play games even more forlorn than the pet-al-communion of impermanence; food, flowers, clothes – the attentive, abundant yet excluding world of things where the poet can no longer, in a mood of loneliness, drop in for a cosy cut-price pathetic fallacy.

How many other people are shoplifting and not aware of it?

So the usherettes come and go – to prison or clubs or the film studios for 'tests'; and those who stay become gnarled, hard-faced, quick and practised in their duties – tearing the tickets, reporting the hooligans, keeping order, claiming the two free tickets each week, achieving record sales of drinks on sticks, ice creams, salted nuts; subscribing to the weekly gamble on the football pools; year after year until the day they resign and the remainder of the staff is called together to smile on the stairs of the foyer while the manager presents the gold watch bracelet tea-set coffee-set and the reporters and photographers arrive from the *South London Star. Fifteen Years at the Palace. Staff Farewell.* It is records like this, Mr Beanman told us, that make one feel proud to be manager of the Palace.

The Palace.

Late at night, ankle-deep in sweet-cartons and ice cream wrappers, Zoe walks with the others up and down between the rows of seats searching for things of value – handbags, watches, overcoats... and in the lavatories for newborn babies in carrier-bags, for dying women, and other conventional cinema leavings. Windows, doors are locked. The usherettes go home.

Does anyone wait behind?

Only Mr Sands who lurks always to seize his opportunity to embrace and destroy. Mr Sands is Fire. His name is the code-word which the staff must use in order to avoid panic at the first suspicion of smoke or flame, when they must flash their secret message across the screen, 'Mr Sands would like to see the manager immediately. Mr Sands is waiting in the upstairs foyer, in the projection room.'

Dear Mr Sands among the cherubs the velvet curtains

embroidered with butterflies, the coloured signed portraits of 'stars' (men, women, horses, dogs), hear me as I, Zoe Bryce, lie in my Clapham bed waiting for sleep. I have journeyed home in the lit half-empty bus with the drunks and the night-workers from the biscuit factory. I got off at the corner of The Elms near the tobacconist's where the advertisements for last Sunday's newspapers *Memoirs Exclusive Memoirs* flap against the boards in the freezing air, and my eyes were stinging with memoirs, all those lucky dips in sawdust blowing from the desert. And I walked along The Elms to Ma Crane's house.

Everyone is in bed. Ma Crane's light is out. Pat's light is out – he goes to bed early so as to be up in time for work. The other men in the house? I do not know. Their rooms are dark and quiet in the nightly rehearsal for death – now, they say, to death, a few hours at a time and we shall grow accustomed to you and to the void screen where now dreams play cops and robbers with our daily lives.

Dear Mr Sands I have here only a small syllable of your warmth – my hot water bottle which I filled from the kettle on the gas ring, over the hearth. My bottle is at my feet. Soon I shall move it to my back, or embrace it with my arms, upon my breast, and all night the shape and nature of it will be moulded to the whims of my dreaming which will spring up like jack-in-the-boxes released by the hand of sleep.

I have turned off the gas taps on the hearth, very carefully, for I know that accidents can happen, with gas leaking and people being found unconscious in their beds by the landlady who becomes suspicious when the morning's milk or mail has not been collected. 'Are you in, Zoe? Zoe! Miss Bryce!'

I smell gas. I thought I smelt gas.

I have got up twice to make sure I have turned the taps,

for I have had one kiss sneaked upon me in the dark and it is not yet time for my last kiss to settle upon my lips and seal my flowing, like ice forming upon water. I think it will be soon, but not yet... I have to make something. Mr Sands, I am confused. I am not brave enough to sacrifice myself by blocking the flood of dream; I am no Dutch-boy keeping out the sea.

Yes, I journeyed to New Zealand. Yes, I saw the Hot Springs, the glaciers, the Southern Lakes, and I passed through the town that Toby speaks of – is it Waimaru? – a flash of trees, corrugated iron, timberyards, and a dejected sea in a thin green dress sitting upon the hearth waiting for the tide to come home.

And I went on tours in buses north and south. Beautiful New Zealand, they said to me. 'What do you think of God's Own Country?'

I stood in the dining-rooms of the hotels at my five-table station, smiling, smiling, Yes soup three and Roast Beef to Follow, while the rich woolbuyers put their hands in their pockets and shelled out the tips.

I went to an Art Gallery where heavy paintings hung burdened with paint, like a conscience, and prison doors swung shutting out the mountains, and boats upturned upon the beaches were never set adrift into discovery.

Yet there were giants walking up and down Wellington city. I remember them now. I turned my head to watch them pass. And the whole land lay flushed, its past flaking from it like dead skin, in a fever of tomorrow.

'Why don't you stay?' they said to me. 'Beautiful New Zealand.'

'The Apple and Pear Marketing Board smiles at you. The Fernleaf Butter, the Cheddar Cheese wait in your larder; the cattle and sheep are driven on time to the sale-yards and the slaughterhouse. You need never want.

What is the meaning of hunger?'

Dear Mr Sands, I lived my life early in the valley, jostling against people, craning my neck to see over the heads of people and seeing nothing but heads hair dandruff pink-veined old-men's heads, Friday-night Saturday-morning permed hair, people's faces close up like sandhills and fields planted in rows of green and burned yellow where the crops failed. But I said, Hoist me up to see over. And I floated in the air to the mountain. But Mr Sands, what am I thinking of? I should have returned to my teaching job in the Midlands. I cycled, you know, every morning, with a wicker basket strapped to the handlebars and my books in it and my sandwiches. On wintry mornings I wore my woollen scarf from Norton and Stroods; it wraps over my head like a hood and crosses in front.

In all my years in the Midlands no one kissed me. I am no sleeping beauty. Princes do not struggle through forests of thorn to reach me where I lie rose-red snow-white in my glass coffin. The only person who ever struggled towards me was a dirty seaman who had probably been drinking. He changed my life, Mr Sands.

Oh yes, I have had my dreams – shall I tell you why in the first place I made my journey to New Zealand? Sometimes I remember him – Mr Hewell – who taught the eleven-plus class. I scarcely noticed him until one morning I met him outside the school gates. It was spring. The sky flowed blue as water and the snapping winter cries of people had vanished from the air; instead, voices undulated, expanded, cushioned by sunlight. I was wheeling my bicycle through the school gates when Mr Hewell (Len) arrived in his car. For some reason he seemed delighted to see me. I do not know why – it was absurd of me to take it to heart – after all it was spring and there was a clump of crocuses just inside the gates – tiny green spears down their leaves – and flowering currant – its unmistakable invading smell robs one of breath. 'Oh Miss Bryce, Oh!'

I was so moved, so excited, and the sky kept flowing and I was flowing, and water is never alone is it, nothing ever divides water, not knives or walls or fences. 'Oh Mr Hewell, I didn't see you!'

We talked. We had never talked before, not conversationally. Oh how absurd it was that I should have been so overcome! It was simply a trick inclusion of springtime, more or less like one of those cardboard toys which the manufacturers include in their golden breakfast cereals to give pleasure to all, to keep up the price, to dull the suspicion that one is really getting short measure. Yes, my fantasy love affair was a trick, delivered only to me. He was married. He had no interest in me. How I hated his marriedness! And what was the use of playing Schubert's 'Secret Love' over and over to myself in my flat at night? Therefore I adopted the conventional line of action – I went for a journey abroad. The usual fictional escape. If I had been a man and had brought disgrace on my family I would have emigrated. Or if I had been a promising elder son I should have gone quite naturally to service in India.

I fell in love and went abroad to the place which has been in fashion lately – New Zealand. And here I live in Clapham, working on 'private research'. Oh Mr Sands, I am afraid. The wall of dream is punctured like a sieve and the strange other world pours in upon me in a way that never happened before. I am concerned with an intensity of making – yet I make nothing. The kiss is the core of my life. It is my meaning, my tiny precious berry from the one branch of a huge tree in a forest where the trees are numberless. I need to walk in that forest, Mr Sands.

I need to build a house, a tower, under and through the silver leaves into the sky.

I lie here in my Clapham bedsitter. I clutch a rubber hot water bottle to my breast. I am surrounded by layers of loneliness. The house remains quiet. What is Pat dreaming of? Reporting prostitutes to the police, driving his eighty-eight bus, listening to Radio Luxembourg, eating his chocolate Digestive biscuits, doing odd repairing jobs for Ma Crane? I would be a fool to imagine that his dreams are occupied with everyday concerns which are only the daytime convenient notes providing his secret personal music – tuneless jingle or symphony. I have no means of telling the nature of his dreams. Even he passes them by as strangers when he meets them in waking life.

Sometimes I walk with Pat on the Common. And one day I walked alone in Soho and I met an artist, or a man who labels himself as an artist – Peter Heron. He sat in a coffee-bar with other artists, and words moved like spiders from their mouths, forming a white web in the centre of the room to trap the paintings which they wanted to paint but could not, could not. Peter has my address. He will visit me in summer, whether I am alive or dead.

And one day, Mr Sands, I met Toby Withers in Hyde Park. We are brother and sister, in narrow alleyways.

I am afraid. What shall I consider? Shall I find my way by tapping myself like a white stick against the solid furniture of living which exists by general belief and agreement? Or shall I guide myself through private shadows and risk the darkness falling away beneath me? Meanwhile, Mr Sands, facts. My hot water bottle, my chilblains, my tomato soup, my job at the Palace where Princes are unknown, my evasive replies – I'm engaged in private research, private research. My nights, my desires, discomforts, my intensities of making nothing. Dear Mr

Sands, other people in other ages have addressed themselves to the God of Fire. May I not do so as well? Does it matter that your name can be found in any telephone directory, that you inhabit a tawdry Palace, waited upon by plaster cherubs?

XXXIII

WHEN THE advertisements for lung syrup, influenza vaccine, bronchial mixtures began to be printed in small spaces at the back pages of newspapers instead of in half-page centre clamourings; when the first outdoor crocuses and daffodils appeared in the stalls in the markets; when the city business men began to walk the remaining few yards over Waterloo Bridge instead of waiting in the steaming buses; when the dead old trees along the Embankment, in the groves and on the Commons put forth green tongues of leaf to the brash inspection of newly qualified light; when winds that before blew in armies of ice now separated one from the other, some going warm ways, others maintaining a companionship with snow or melting suddenly in death, so that people meeting them exclaimed, 'Why, it's summer before it's spring'; or 'Well, it's winter still, winter is never finished'; when the children brought into the streets their scooters and roller-skates and bows and arrows and once more engaged in gun battles behind parked cars and in the courts of the Council Flats – why, then it was fair to say, as far as one can catch the seasons by the sleeve to identify them, that spring had arrived. Yet as usual the season was more talked of and dreamed of than in evidence. Certainly, leaves fountained from black boles, and park flowers, leaning east, nodded on their sap-filled stems, and men gazed in the windows of the hardware stores, dazzled by axes, spades, shovels, gleaming electric precision tools; and women lingered by the green and yellow-clad shop-models posed (uneasily, vulnerably) on the neon-lit polythene lawns. Yet in the city each clue to the season has to be valued personally. Far away from the comforting symbols of lambs, flowering fields, freshly peeled sky, one is inclined to think that many of the clues are bogus, that convenient alterations have been made to identification papers, passports; that the tourist season while openly displaying its gifts of life has failed to declare the packages of death cleverly sewn inside the green and yellow seams of its new overcoat.

· Spring is the treacherous season.

People dying inexplicably. The suicides in the river, not committed, like the summer suicide, under the claw-hammer of light which twists from their socket, dangling for public inspection, the integrating private forms of love and death; nor like the winter suicide; the sacrificial communion with wasted leaves, and light lying with its cold cheek turned to the earth, remembering Persephone; but after long winter broodings a death accomplished in sudden plunges and passions, as if the tiger had leaned on its paws all night, considering its victim, and made its final leap in the morning when the sun comes to touch and warm the south wall.

Yet death is not so defenceless. It fights against being caught. And the season has vanished before it has begun. It is a dream, a trick of the drowned, a contamination of blossom hawked by bees, those pattering door-to-door salesmen with their suitcases full of poisoned honey.

And so soon it is summer, and the coloured people smile, waiting outside the Labour Exchange, and the little boys sail their toy boats on the pond at the edge of the Common, and the pensioners once again come out of doors, cross the Common, and play their meditated games of chess and draughts in the bird-spattered shelter, near the bandstand.

Ma Crane hangs up her striped awning at the front door, over the porch, to stop the sun from fading the newly painted black door with its pink panels. Her kitchen has been painted too, and her bathroom and lavatory, in rose and green, and she has provided herself with what she calls (with prompting from the advertisements) 'a treat' – coloured toilet paper to match the paint. At first she did not quite like the idea of buying toilet paper which was not white, but she soon overcame her fastidiousness, when the salesman assured her that 'everything matches nowadays'. Which was true, everything matched. There were nests of tables, suites of furniture, families of knives and forks in a canteen of cutlery – all things were insured against loneliness by man, the most lonely.

'Ah, I like salads,' Pat said.

Summer made him light-hearted – one of the statements we put forth who are confused by so many causes dangling like powerful chains out of the sky, for us to swing upon (or hang ourselves) glittering with reason and explanation above the dark riddled seas of behaviour.

Oh yes, it was summer that made Pat gay. He whistled and sang in the bath. He smiled more often. He seemed less intense in his condemnation of prostitutes, 'blacks', foreigners, bus-passengers, and – usherettes.

'You shouldn't be working as an usherette,' he said again and again to Zoe. 'It's degrading. Look at the types you meet.'

They would often have tea together, provided by Pat – salad, tinned salmon or ham, a one-and-sixpenny apple pie, all of which Pat devoured with a concentration which seemed to extend the frame of reference of his meal. He was eating not only salmon, salad and apple pie, but more unorthodox fare such as people, habits, perplexities, decisions: and enjoying them, asking for more.

For Pat, eating was a safe occupation. One need not

be ashamed of it. It was not like love. And Pat was filled with love, he existed for it as a lighthouse exists for light, yet when he came to train the beams of his love upon that part of the world around him which he desired for himself, he formed, out of some topographical fantasy, a landscape of canals, of deep slits of prejudice where his love could not penetrate; a bizarre land- and seascape which he could not possess. Swans flew there, and leprechauns kept their neat clean houses, and Our Lady in a blue silk dress watched over everything; but there were few human beings unless Pat himself could plant them there, digging holes for them in the earth where they lived helpless to fend for themselves, relying (Pat knew and rejoiced) upon his devoted care.

He loved the swans.

In the long summer evenings when the light, refusing to go home (but where is home?) played ring-a-rosie on the edge of the sky, that is, on the edge of the Common for our world clamps down upon us and there are no perpetual horizons, Pat used to walk with Zoe to the concrete-bordered lake in the centre of the Common where the swans lived. He would talk to her about them. His voice would be gentle. He would point out the ragged grassy island with its one guardian leaning tree where he knew the swans were hatching.

'I've come here every year,' he said. 'I've watched them every year. And do you know when I was away over the sea and people were asking, What is it you miss on the other side of the world, I thought, The swans, but I did not say the swans, Zoe, I said, why, the people, my holidays at the Isle of Wight, my county in Ireland. But it was the swans I missed. They're brave birds, Zoe.'

He confessed one evening that he did not know what he would do without the swans – one of those frightening

confessions which only make the confessor more vulner-
able, which should never be uttered, yet which one over-
hears in crowds, on corners, in cafés, as if people cannot
help proclaiming their bonds of desperation.

'I don't know what I'd do without the telly.' 'I don't
know what I'd do without – my husband, my lover, my
wife, my friends. My swans.'

Be careful, take warning, the professional eavesdrop-
per with the giant shears that reach from sky to earth and
below and above is a sleepless creature; he works day
and night; threads, ropes, wires, iron bands are defenceless against him, are snipped like spiderwebs, like rob-
in-bones... the power is cut off, the house is dark, death
looks through the jagged windows.

On the day the swans hatched Pat could not contain
his joy. He danced a jig and was out of breath. I am over
forty, he thought. I shouldn't stay too long driving the buses. Why don't these details leave me alone? Oh, they're
like the story that my sister read me one time when I was
so high – fairies came upon the little boy: it said, 'They
poked him with their long fingers crying, "Look you,
Look you!"'

'See the swans,' Pat cried, forgetting for a moment the
pestering details of his age and work, 'look, the cygnets
after her, and him on guard, and see the little one on her
back, under her feathers, just peeping out! Where's the
bread, Zoe, quick!'

He scattered the crusts and crumbs and the swans
came near gliding, white Viking ships in Arctic splen-
dour, their paddling feet tinted with the shadows of the
midnight sun, their hooded eyes uneasy, watchful; while
the cygnets darted back and forth in swift damp handfuls.

'There are five,' Pat said. 'One two three four five.'

'There was a story,' Zoe mused, 'of the seven brothers

240

who changed to swans. And their little sister – Elise.'

'Maybe there was a story, maybe,' Pat said in sudden irritation.

The next evening when they walked on the Common and Pat counted the swans there were four. 'They always go like this. Children stone them, dogs kill them.'

A week later there were three, then two, then none, not even the mother and father.

'It always happens like this. I don't know why I forgot that it always happens like this – funny, when I was thinking of it when I was away I remembered the little ones growing up and them all flying away together. Funny isn't it, remembering? Well either they get killed or they fly away. The old ones will be back again next year – you don't realize the time passes do you, and I'm too old to emigrate and get a job, except for driving; too old for the police or security work; doesn't the lake here look deserted? But it's some sort of training that I needed, if only I'd had some sort of training while I was younger. Children nowadays are vicious. If I could get my hands on the little devils who stoned the swans! What does the swan mean? It is aloof, sour, a snow-convention, an annual pageant of suspicious probing with a little bag of crusts on the Common. It is Elise, Leda, any changeful God. What is the evil dream that wounds it like the snapping teeth, the pitched stone round and smooth from the hands of innocence? Explain the white evil.'

Call my longing in question yet I dream of people. I, Thora Pattern, dream of all people who turn in their sleep and moan, apprehensive of death.

Zoe was asleep. The swans were circling in her head, the cruel swans, a denial of night brandished in snow-filled wings that gripped the white flowing evil, made substance of it, evil looking in the mirror –

XXXIV

PAT AND ZOE came less often now to the lake and its island where the sun's burning and withering had exposed
the empty nest-clumps spattered with droppings. The
trees leaned now as guardian over nothing but sparrows,
and stones flung by little boys who still beat fiercely at the
island as at a target set by their own existence and the lapping of their blood against their artificial lives.

'See,' Pat said, pointing. 'That's where the nest was, see
the track they made down to the water.'

But gradually he forgot about the swans, or he no
longer mentioned them, he talked instead of his summer
holidays which, he explained, were 'coming up'. It was the
Isle of Wight for him, he said. He could play golf there
and stay at a hotel where he knew the proprietor and his
wife. And then there was his doctor friend, 'a fine chap',
and his wife and children. They always invited him to sail
with them in their yacht. He had snaps of a few summers
ago, he said. He drew them from his wallet and showed
them to Zoe. 'There's me, and there's my doctor friend,
and there's his wife and their two children, Graham and
Leila. They're good friends of mine. I told you he was a
doctor, didn't I? In the evening we have dinner and drinks
together. Now that's the sort of life for me, Zoe. That's
why I worry about what you're doing – a cinema's not the
place for you.'

He reminded her, also, that the time would come when
she would need a pension. He repeated that he was providing well for himself in the future, he had insurance
policies which would mature (and in maturing turn upon
him, tear him to pieces?) at the right time, and other funds
'tucked away' in the Bank and National Savings. And all

that was in spite of what he had used in his visit to Sheila in New Zealand!

'Yes, the most important thing in the world is to lay a little by.'

(And the swans?)

'We have to invest in security. Not like that Toby Withers. Did you ever see anyone so foolish about his own future?'

How Pat longed for Zoe and Toby to take his advice, to leave their jobs and 'invest' in something 'safe and clean'. He knew that Toby was living in a squalid room and not getting 'proper meals'; that he was suffering from outbreaks of poison, like tribal fighting, in areas of his body. 'With a life like that it's to be expected. He won't listen to me. Why don't you tell him, Zoe, that it's not the life for him? And you, working as an usherette when you could be a schoolteacher!'

He said the word 'schoolteacher' with the same reverence that he used for saying 'doctor', 'police', 'authorities'. 'There are jobs going at over ten pounds a week for people like you. And anyways,' he concluded, like a salesman who has at last found a price-ticket, scarlet, dangerous, to attach to his entire wares, 'people today think of nothing but sex.'

Zoe blushed. He meant her, of course. He had seen the book on her shelf.

'Yes, nothing but sex,' he repeated.

Now one day when Zoe had been tormented with fear that she had caught some terrible disease from her kiss (she would lie in bed at night cataloguing the gifts it had brought her, making divisions of good and evil, as princesses do on their birthday when they suspect the intentions of so many lavish godmothers) she visited a shop in

Charing Cross Road, a 'personal chemist's' which sold 'informative books'. 'I will buy one,' Zoe thought, 'and find out. For she was innocent, ignorant and afraid.'

A small dark man at the counter said that he preferred her to come within to the private waiting room. Timidly Zoe entered. There was a couch in one corner, with a blanket on it, and a pillow. Zoe trembled. She refused to sit down but stood near the door ready to make a hurried escape.

The salesman reappeared. 'Now what can I do for you?'

'Oh,' Zoe said, 'oh, a friend of mine is getting married and would like a book of instruction and hygiene.'

'You mean an encyclopaedia of sex?'

'Yes, something like that.'

'We have just the thing. Stay here and I'll bring it to you.'

He was away a few moments and returned with a large profusely illustrated book which he put on the table before her, flipping over some of the pages and exclaiming at the book's value whenever a coloured illustration appeared.

'It's just the thing, Madam. It says everything, in a delicate way. Three hundred illustrations, over one thousand items. Thirty shillings.'

Zoe made some pretence of studying the book, turning the pages, examining the strength of the binding, the publication date, the publisher's name; and some of the illustrations which were intimate and unmistakable. Zoe blushed. 'Well,' she said, 'of course my friend is aware of the facts of the human body and so on...'

'You want something more sophisticated? This deals with everything, Madam. Even Eastern Customs.'

'I'll take it,' Zoe said, hurriedly, giving him the thirty shillings and walking out quickly past the trusses and sheaths and jellies and the counter-display of the latest volume, *The Kiss, Its Meaning and Value*.

That means me, Zoe thought. I can go to an Art Gallery and study the Kiss and its revelation in sculpture. I can come here and buy the facts of it. I am afraid. There are too many dimensions. There are fires leaping up from all corners of the city, fires started by a dirty little rat who chews a wooden matchhead that someone has thrown away as worthless, incapable of flame.

'Yes,' Pat was saying, 'I've seen the book on your shelf, Zoe. I can see it now from where I am sitting drinking my tea. To tell the truth I've had a quick look at it. It's not the kind of book you should ever read. It's not good for the maid to see, either. And Ma Crane would faint if she knew.'

'I don't read it, not often,' Zoe said.

When she had read it she had locked the door, closed the window, drawn the curtains, and even then suffered an uncomfortable thudding of her heart in case someone should knock at the door. Usually she kept the book locked in a suitcase, but she had grown careless.

She defended her reading of it.

'It's useful,' she said. 'People think that everybody knows everything these days but there are some people who never know, who are afraid to know. This book has complete diagrams of the human body. It's surprising the number of people who don't know their own body.'

(Will you organize the expedition for next spring? We shall need supplies of course, transport...)

Zoe went to the shelf, withdrew the encyclopaedia, and brought it over to Pat, opening it at the diagram of a woman.

'There,' she said. As if it had been all her own work.

Pat shut his eyes. 'I refuse to look,' he said.

He opened his eyes, glancing quickly at the page. He glanced again, tracing the complications of the inset diagrams and the letters, arrows, numbers. 'Good Lord!' he cried in amazement. 'A woman's not like that! Not like that!'

Pat's face was white. 'Put that book away,' he said. 'And steer clear of sex. Have nothing to do with it. That sort of knowledge is for the priest and married people.'

Zoe returned the book to her shelf. Pat was sitting tensely on the edge of the chair. He began to talk vehemently about evil books, paperbacks with naked women on them; about the prostitutes on the Common and the young Irish girls going astray; about the vice of Soho; about his need to go back to Ireland one day. Ireland was a wonderful shade of green, oh wonderful, he said. He described it. He described the polished horses at the fairs, the leprechauns darting in and out of their houses in the earth, the lakes and mountains of what he called the 'real' Ireland – that part of a country which we cherish most because it is most illusory, and we admit this by referring to it as 'real' – the 'real' Ireland, Russia, Spain, Denmark, France.

Ireland, Pat said then, had many great men, poets, artists, statesmen. Also, Ireland had swans – 'real' swans, not the sickly oil-smothered birds that you see swimming on the Thames. 'White birds,' Pat said. 'White. It's a pure colour, Zoe. The colour of purity.'

They drank tea, in silence then, and Pat said goodnight, I'm off to my cot, and he went downstairs. The house was silent. Outside, the stoned swans with blood pouring from them, staining their feathers, beat at the window-pane to get in. But Zoe had shut the window tightly. For Ma Crane had said there were thieves about who climbed over the back fences and tried the windows of the houses. The night was hot, inflated; the blood trickled down outside the windowpane and the hooded evil eyes of the swans pressed against the glass. 'Help,' they cried.

But they were suspicious and sad and hungry, and after a while their beating stopped, and they fell to the earth, to Ma's back garden, under the clothesline near the rose-pink lavatory and the anemone border.

In the morning there was no blood or stain. The swans had vanished.

XXXV

YOUR WORK is getting you down, Zoe, Pat said.

(How strange, she thought. He reminds me of my father.) She wanted to scream at him 'But I was kissed aboard the *Matua*. I am Zoe Bryce engaged in private re-search. I wear my pearls and my low-waisted dress from Norton and Stroods. I –'

No, she could not tell him about the few desperate years that were left for her to bear children. Ha Ha they say among trumpets and thieves and novelettes – 'she turned', 'she blanched', her heart did this and that, the words preserved in amber too deep for recovery.

They were few desperate years indeed. She was grow-ing thinner. Something was stealing from her the very shape which made her a woman; the marsupial years had given birth to a creature which had crawled to nourish itself at Zoe's virgin body, and finding no food there, it had begun to devour her breasts themselves and now they hung out of shape like rusty hoops with no hand to care for them and spin them along the golden highways; they were the twisted mouthpiece of dead clarinets which no one played; they were broken water-jugs left empty on the edge of the well; they were weed-grown riverbeds with no memory of a river.

If only, Zoe thought, I were an old maid whose body swells and foams with its longing! But I am changed to a step-ladder, a bony triangle where the hands meet in prayer, a heap of thin twigs among the salt plants on a hill exposed to the sea, where people pass me by, intent only on gathering the first spring asparagus.

It is so strange that I think this way, but I have been kissed. I must stay young, I must make something, I must bear a child.

Now there was a film at the Palace, an Italian film which Zoe saw fifteen times. She wondered if perhaps she should go to Italy, for did not women stay younger there, was there not some tradition of it? And men there were gallant, flashingly handsome, with names like Gino, Mario?

Gino! Mario! Zoe cried for them in her sleep.

But although she collected a few brochures from travel agents she did not go to Italy. She began a campaign to keep herself young. She patronized the shops which sold Health Foods. She bought packets of Wheat Germ which she sprinkled on her cornflakes. She ate brown sugar, brown bread, and at night she drank a cordial which was claimed to be full of 'natural juices'. She acquired a passion for things which she (and the pamphlets from the Health Shop) described as 'natural, unadulterated'. She went to the Town Hall to a lecture entitled *Compost; Foods and Purity*, but during the lecture a young man sitting next to her murmured thoughtfully, '*Love has pitched his mansion in the place of excrement.*'

Zoe frowned at him. She did not go again to the Town Hall. Next, deciding suddenly to spend her free time knitting, she bought wool which the assistant assured her was 'straight from the sheep', and with this she made herself a cardigan which she did not wear for although the wool was undoubtedly pure, scarcely contaminated by man, the smell that lingered about it was unpleasant; if you wore your overcoat as long as sheep, without changing, it too might smell unpleasant.

Next, Zoe bought some fine white wool and inventing her own pattern she knitted, in great secrecy, a tiny dress in shell-stitch, with loops of ribbon at the waist, to fit a newborn baby. Who would she give it to? she wondered. She had no relatives, except for an uncle up north. It is one of the hardest things to believe, that some people have no relatives, not in law, and are quite alone.

'But you must have an aunt, a cousin,' they say, making a quick snapshot tally of their own parents, friends, children, wives, husbands... 'You must have somebody,' they say, who, in fact, if they considered their snapshots more closely, would discover that they too had nobody.

Zoe folded the tiny dress, wrapped it in moth balls, and locked it in her suitcase.

She began often to wander up and down the streets, but the publicity of the summer light distressed her, its beams forever compared her with those among whom she walked, those who seemed to possess the evidence of being loved. Sometimes she met Toby who was also living a confused life. He had a job as a street-sweeper. He trundled along with his little cart and brooms disposing of the social snow, the city flakes that fell endlessly from man's winter need – the need to buy little packets, tear them open, empty them, get comfort from them, discard them. Toby also walked in a dream. Once he told Zoe of his idea of the Lost Tribe. 'You will be murdered if you steal it,' he said.

Zoe believed him.

He talked of seeing a publisher, of publisher's advances, translation rights, photographs for the *Press*. 'Someday I'll get down to writing it, someday I'll write my story of the Lost Tribe.'

He referred to his poisoned arm which he described as 'breaking out' as if it were a convict imprisoned in his body.

He showed Zoe the eardrops on his watch-chain. 'Greenstone. These belong to Evelina Festing who is *my girl*.'

Sometimes they went together to the cinema or walked

in the parks or visited the Museums which overcame Toby with a strange terror. He would shout in the Museums. 'To see if they heard,' he explained. 'To make them come alive. They're holding out on us, Zoe. They're scared to face us. These old mammoths, why do they bother to put them together if they've nothing to say to us, why don't they speak and warn us before it's too late?'

Ma Crane told both Pat and Zoe that she preferred them not to entertain in her house someone who earned his living sweeping the streets. 'Not that I've anything against sweeping the streets, but there's something about this Mr Withers that worries me. His arm is bandaged, too – it isn't anything, is it, that we could catch? After all... infection...'

It is most necessary not to be infected, particularly when one is raging with an ungovernable outbreak of light and life and contamination of love.

Zoe agreed with Ma Crane. 'I hadn't considered it that way,' she said. 'He's had it a long time now, almost ever since he came to London. We certainly don't want to be exposed to anything.'

'Well,' Ma Crane replied, 'the men in this house are all doing clean work, clean brain work.'

Brains, of course, are spotless, polished, snow-white without a trace of thought.

Ma Crane was so proud of her lodgers, especially of the Public School man who worked at the Oxygen Company. It was a day of distress for her when the tradesman called to collect the hair-drier because Lee Simpson (but he's an ex-Public School boy!) had failed to keep up with instalments, and another tradesman called for the stair-carpet which Lee Simpson had bought on easy terms and sold. Ma Crane almost fainted when Lee Simpson was taken away in a police van.

He was tried in court and found guilty and sent to prison, and one morning Ma, embarrassed and indignant, received through the post a visiting card to Brixton Prison. The prisoner, Lee Simpson.

'Tear it up,' Pat advised her. 'I'd tear it up if I were you. He doesn't deserve to be visited. He's got his due.'

Pat was invariably pleased (as we all are) when people at last got their 'due'. But what an upsetting time that was for Ma Crane! She was so much in need of comfort that she invited Pat and Zoe into her private kitchen where she offered them tea and fancy cakes on her best china and told them of her experiences since she had begun to let rooms – of men 'seemingly respectable' who had stayed under false names and kept questionable hours, of one man who had vanished without paying the rent, and of another (here she glanced at Pat and her eyes sprouted a tiny apprehension), 'He lived in your room, Pat, next to mine. He used to entice little boys off the street. Oh, the experiences I've had!'

'And now,' Ma Crane exclaimed, stroking Chummy and trying to tempt him to a piece of cake ('sometimes he likes it, sometimes he doesn't – it all depends'), 'And now to get a pass to visit Lee Simpson in prison!'

'I'd tear it up,' Pat advised again. 'I'll tear it if you don't.'

Zoe thought, I'd like to visit him. If he worked in the Oxygen Company he was probably fighting for his life anyway. I'd like to visit him. Elizabeth Fry. He was young, fair-haired. Now that I think of it he looked like Rupert Brooke, like the photo in the volume of poems that I had years ago and used to prop on the bedside table. Rupert Brooke. His chin was resting in his hands. I think his eyes were grey. He was such a clean poet walking among words. He always wore gumboots and a mackintosh when he crossed the marshes of the drowned, treading carefully on the overgrowth of bitter blossomless words, so that when he arrived at the other side he was clean and unharmed and he always took care to remove the reminding layers of squalor from his smart ebony boots.

No, Lee Simpson was different. How I should like to visit him in prison and talk with him through – is it a grille? When I talk to anyone now I am talking through a grille; it would be an aspect of truth to have it there, visible, for once...

'Yes, I'll tear it for you, Ma!'

Pat glanced at Zoe as if he were speaking for her also. Then as if she were performing a sacrificial rite which entailed the preliminary ceremony of tea and fancy cakes on best china, Ma Crane went to the sideboard and returned with the prison pass which she tore to tiny pieces dropping them like crumbs into a saucer in the centre of the table.

Would the swans fly down and seize them?

'There,' Ma Crane said, half-grunting the word as if she were accomplishing a physical release.

'I was sick and in prison and ye visited me...' Zoe was seized with a sudden fear about the identity of Lee Simpson... for no one really *knew*, for people were all the time being extended, distorted, merged, melted... like pictures on a television set when the tube is broken or worn out and no one will repair or replace it; the silver tube was set now in the sky or in one's own head; it did not matter where. Who was really in prison for succumbing to easy terms? Was it Ma Crane, Pat Keenan, Toby Withers, Zoe Bryce? And the pass? Who was issuing passes which stated that people could visit and communicate with one another... did they know about the kiss on board the *Matua*, the seaman that night...?

Ma Crane had finished her ceremony in her kitchen. Pat and Zoe got up to leave.

'My brother is a District Attorney in the United States,' Pat reminded Ma as testimony that he was not likely to entice little boys off the street.

So the matter closed, as matters do, like quicksands over their victim, and a little notice was put in the window of the tobacconist's at the corner announcing a vacancy, single room, for a respectable gentleman, professional or business preferred, out all day.

XXXVI

Summer stayed on but was not new anymore. The haunches of the park were bald, rubbed with sun. At night a few dragons curled in the sky, breathing their smoke. One Sunday ('to catch the last of summer, Zoe') Pat took Zoe in the bus (flashing his free pass) to Richmond which Pat described as a place of beauty by the river where one could forget the cares of the city.

When they arrived they sat on the grass by the river while Pat read his Sunday newspaper and worked the competition (first prize a three-thousand-pound bungalow) filling in, in order of preference, the modern amenities that would make the bungalow more desirable. When Pat had finished with his newspaper he folded it, put it in his pocket, said something about the tide rising and how about an ice cream? Then after eating their ice-creams they travelled on the bus back to London and although Zoe searched her belongings for secret deposits, she never found out whether they had, after all, 'caught the last of summer'.

Another afternoon (was there warning in the sky?) the young artist came to visit Zoe. Peter Heron. For a moment she could not remember him.

'The coffee-bar,' he said. 'You gave me your address. I promised to take you out, one afternoon in summer.'

'In summer? How strange. But I don't know you.'

'But I'm an artist. I know where you live,' he added accusingly.

'You mean where I really live?'

'Yes.'

He was thirty, old enough to suffer the inner disappointment that his paintings had not yet received the recognition which he felt they deserved; young enough to refer to himself as a possible 'late developer'. But his true despair was that he had stopped painting, that people had begun to address him with remarks like

'You've got a voice like a schoolteacher. Why don't you try it?'

'Why don't you take up advertising?'

'There's money in these agencies.'

But he was a painter, he kept telling them.

He dressed like a painter, or how he thought a painter should dress, so that there would be fewer mistakes about his identity. He wore corduroy trousers (paint-spattered), a dark velvet jacket, and at that time he had a beard and side-whiskers. Fortunately neither Ma Crane nor Pat was at home when he called or they would have been alarmed. They would have thought of him as a microbe in human form.

Painting was all right – Ma Crane had said many times that she was fond of pictures – but the painters themselves, unless they were dead or their intimate tragic life was featured in the Sunday papers, were not to be tolerated. In Pat's view painters were the type of people who threatened the foundations of society, and although he sometimes realized vaguely that the foundations of society needed threatening (and in those moments his fear made him more determined to drive in the rivets of conformity), he looked upon these whom he called 'painters in general' as 'idlers' who 'ought to be forced to do a day's hard work on the buses'.

'I really didn't think you would visit me,' Zoe said, fussing with her hair and putting on her brown imitation suede jacket which she too sometimes wore as a last refuge of identity; at one with the tribe, in lion-skins, dancing around the circle of darkness. 'And I don't even know you,' she added.

'But I know you, Zoe Bryce,' he said, again accusingly, and Zoe blushed. He guesses, she thought. He guesses everything.

Then he frowned and sighed. 'If only,' he said. 'My God, if only!'

They went to Soho, riding on top of the bus, and when they arrived at the club they sat at the bar with a drink.

A fair man, going bald, with a smooth pale handsome face sat next to them. He smiled at Peter.

'I'm Lawrence,' he said. 'Will you and your girlfriend come with me to the Serpentine? I'm meeting friends there and I'm going swimming.'

He gave a slight giggle.

Zoe was suspicious. Why did he want them to go to the Serpentine? Without introductions – just like that! What would Ma Crane think?

She listened as he outlined in careful detail the route they would take. Have I met you before? she asked, talking to him in the way that was her habit now to address people – without opening her mouth and uttering words – tell me have I met you before? Of course I have met you, in dreams and myths. You are one of those people who, because they have lost their bearings, have acquired a special interest and skill in being a compass for others, swinging yourself, tremblingly, like a needle, this way and that. You appear at crossroads, at the entrance to mazes, on the outskirts of cities, at the edge of the alphabet. It is you who give warning to the lost children and the tired eldest son out to seek his fortune. You do all this because, poor Lawrence, you are confused, so confused that you would even triumphantly autograph the sky – East West Home's Best because you are yourself homeless. Due north has snapped; variations are dead.

'So you'll come with me to the Serpentine?'

'Why not?' Peter said. 'We all understand each other.'

Now you pay to enter the precincts of the Serpentine, as it is the custom to enclose places, to construct an entrance whose staccato teeth swallow people one at a time, exercising an economical judgment upon the correct boundaries between person and person. How one envies those teeth and turning iron gates because they *know*! They are trained never to reject one half of you as a stranger or to demand from you in moments when your life is divided the price of three or four. But you have to be quick, and stand alone, and not try to attach yourself to the person before you or after you.

Singly Peter, Lawrence, Zoe each paid, entered, and stood, considering, uncertain.

'Ah,' Lawrence said. 'This is Zara. Zara this is Peter and Zoe.'

Zara was slim, dressed in black, with long dark hair. Lawrence had told them that she was a prostitute, a Russian, who lived with him on easy terms without discount.

She spoke angrily to him now. 'Why have you not come before? I waited. I pick for you. I pick for you. You promise to come. I have a nice Irish boy waiting for you.'

She turned and smiled at Peter and Zoe.

'I'm sorry,' she said. 'Hello Peter, Hello Zoe. Lawrence is like a little boy to be arranged for.'

She took Lawrence by the arm. 'He is waiting at the table over there. He is just a poor lonely sailor. You will like him, Lawrence.'

Lawrence was standing clutching his rolled swimming togs to his plump body, gazing dreamily at the summer battlefield and all the bodies, wounded in one place or another, strewn there, and the bright crimson and blue toys rising and falling in the air and caught by the children, the only inhabitants left alive. Yet it seemed that others moved. Some screamed. With joy. Or leaned in languor upon their death. And all the eyes which were snot blinded were searching, as Lawrence searched now, for someone to share a moment, an act, of his lonely life. The Irish sailor was waiting. But Lawrence needed the mastery bestowed upon him by his own choosing. He seemed suddenly excited and eager.

'I'll change first and have a dip,' he said confidently, his eyes roving to the men's sheds where the muscular young warriors were emerging. He disappeared to change while Zara led Zoe and Peter to the table where the young sailor sat drinking Coca-Cola, and glancing now and then uneasily about him. He blushed when Zara introduced him to the others. 'Lawrence is changing,' Zara told him.

The young sailor blushed again. It was obvious that he was not used to being procured and was beginning to have regrets. He sat silent while the others drank their coffee and smoked and Peter told Zara about his painting while Zoe listened, envying Zara's rootless transplantation and blossoming, with tiny blue flowers, among the salt marshes, and the way her identity, preserved in and nourished by bitterness, did not fall to pieces when one tried to grasp it but remained set, dimensional, its shadow completely coerced by light.

And now the sun plunged into the afternoon swamping the air with waves of heat. Only Zara seemed to stay cool and pale. Zoe felt the sweat running down inside the sleeves of her coat and beading her forehead, and her nylon stockings were damp against her legs. She surged with hate against her clothes, and with envy of Zara in her plain black dress accommodated as a tree by its leaves. Then Zoe thought of the chain store where she bought her dress and jerseys and skirts, and she felt safe – did not the skirts hang in neatly labelled and priced rows, and the jerseys lie one upon the other, packed in polythene?

'So you do private research?' Zara was saying.

She is a prostitute, Zoe thought. I, Zoe Bryce, who have had no further experience of men than a kiss from a stranger, am sitting drinking coffee, talking, smoking, on a late summer afternoon, with a prostitute who is also a stranger. I could be writing letters – to whom? Doing crossword puzzles. Eating sixpence worth of peanuts and raisins. Knitting. Reading books which beat gongs up and down the tiled bareness of my heart. Listening, looking, and all the time working furiously, uselessly, at my nothingness of creation. But I am sitting here with a prostitute. She waits for men. Beat me, tie my hands, they say. She beats them. She ties their hands. Or, say the others, Let me lie down with you in pretence. Let us be empty shapes of people, like those negatives of photographs where the developed prints have been destroyed and all that remain are shadows enclosed in a boundary of frothing light.

Her occupation is with boundaries, in a border country where people still carry their worn maps, trying to read them and knowing the directions are useless. Her life is spent with men naked red and panting and her love is grated away and buried, like pebbles on the beach.

'Yes, I do private research,' Zoe said. 'And I'm an usherette.'

Zara was looking with concern at the sailor, casting anxious glances about him. 'Lawrence will be here soon,' she said. 'Look, there is Lawrence!'

Yes, there was Lawrence coming out of the men's changing rooms. He wore trunks, black, pulled tight about his sagging belly. There was a defiant expression on his face as if he knew he was deceiving himself and must continue the deception. He could not believe his aspect of middle age. Ten years ago, he thought, I cut a fine figure, attracted people. I am still handsome, I still attract them. He walked regally past Zara's table, giving them all a slight smile and peering at them in a short-sighted manner, as one peers to identify and extract these little insects that are brought inside by the weather and lie in the folds of curtains and upholstery.

He waved to them then. He was making for the diving-board. He walked on and stood at the end of it, looking around him. There was an air of loneliness about him. For a moment it seemed that he was afraid. Some younger men were larking about on the board, waiting their turn. Someone shouted to Lawrence to get a move on, that the diving-board didn't belong to him and what was he doing standing there if he wasn't going to dive?

Lawrence looked around him once more. He hesitated. Then with his hands clasped above his head he dived, a belly-flop, landing with a great splash in the water. He came up gasping, half-choking, and flayed the water with his arms.

The people around the diving-board stopped looking at him then, for his ration of attention as the man-on-the-end-of-the-diving-board was finished and all eyes were upon the young boy, a champion, some said, preparing for his one-and-a-half somersault.

'Lawrence will swim for a while,' Zara explained. 'Lawrence likes to swim.'

She tried to make conversation with the sailor but he was obstinately shy. He murmured something about having to go. Zara persuaded him to stay a while longer.

Zoe and Peter and Zara talked and smoked. An empty cigarette packet lay on the table. Zoe picked it up, took out the silver paper, and began twisting it with her fingers, making a shape. At first her movement was absent-minded, then she began to concentrate on her making. It was absurd, how absurd it was, but it was silver trees and people with hats like silver planets, like priests, lost in the forest. How absurd, how conventional, Zoe thought. I am in a fury of making, among strangers, but it is the loneliest shape I have ever seen, that little dent, this twist at the top of the dead silver branch, the eyes in the silver faces of the dead people, the layers of snow on their faces, their clothes bunched, hiding the loneliness of their body. I am making something at last. And it snows, out of the sun and the hollow sky, and Zara is here – a stranger, and Peter whose life did not keep its promise to core for ever the skipping-ropes of paint while he dodged back and forth dancing, see his movements under yellow ochre chinese white gamboge tint, two little boys in navy blue, these are the actions I can do; and the sad sailor, and Lawrence running running in the outer circle on the cinder-track into the darkness. I create from silver paper but no one sees. Where is Toby, Pat?

'Oh,' Zara was exclaiming, 'Look what you have made. Look, Peter, what Zoe has made.'

They admired it. 'How did you do it?' they asked.

'It's only silver paper,' Zoe said, flushing with pride. The sailor admired it too. Then 'I have to go,' he said. He hurried away through the crowd and they never saw him again. Later, Lawrence came up shivering with cold his skin patchy and blue. He was trying to look brave and handsome; he looked neither.

'The sailor's gone,' Zara cried. 'I pick for you and you never come. Now where will you find another sailor?'

'Never mind.' Lawrence smiled at her. 'I've met some people. We're having a party tonight.'

Zara looked forlorn. 'Party?'

Then Lawrence noticed the silver paper shape. 'Did you make it?' he asked Zoe. 'How did you think of it?'

Everyone admired the shape once again. Zoe was not used to being the centre of admiring attention; not for something she had made – when in her life had she ever made anything? It's only a bit of paper, she said to herself, but she throbbed with warmth. How strange that it had so affected the others, had evoked in them feelings which they could only consider and explore by sitting there, as all three were doing now, silent, staring at the silver sculpture.

'It reminds me,' Lawrence began. But he could not identify his memory.

How extraordinary, Zoe thought, that such feeling should be roused by seeing a conventional paper shape twisted at random, in idleness, among strangers whom I shall never meet again.

'Can I keep it?' Zara said. 'I'd like to keep it.'

Zoe wondered, Shall I give it to her or shall I crush it, one twist in my fingers to destroy the silver forest and its meaning? Is this the only word I shall ever speak and do I now retreat into silence? My creation. Not knitting. Not the answers in a crossword puzzle. Not a child given to me in gentleness and despair with the open sky flowing over two bodies voyaging hooked and coupled on their coffin-narrow gauge of love. The communication of my life – a kiss in mid-ocean between myself and a half-drunken seaman. The creation of my life – oh my God! – a silver paper shape fashioned from the remains of an empty cigarette packet! Surely now it is time for my death? Here by the Serpentine – a smear of water – on a hot crowded afternoon in late summer, with the sweat running down inside the arms of my imitation suede jacket, and the veins bulging on my feet; here among the striped innocence, and the children's toys circling in the air

Was anything real at all? Nothing, only the balls,
   their glorious curving,
Though one would ever pass ah! fleetingly under
   the falling ball.

Here among the lonely people searching to appease their
loneliness which blooms in its hunger like an insectiv-
orous plant and the more it feeds the more powerful its
blooms become; with the bitter prostitute Zara sitting
near me, and Peter, the artist, dreaming of the painting
which he will never complete (he also longing to stand
for one moment of his life beneath the brilliance of the
perfect circle), and the young sailor who was nameless,
earnest, rueful, sampling the vice of the city which means
the back-street hunger of his own skin, and Lawrence pathetic prim turning his hands this way and that, like shadows, disowned in the dark, trying to lure the substance
which will at last claim and shelter them; here, have not
I, Zoe Bryce, arrived at the time of my death? Has it not
risen with 'deliberate rightness'? Zoe said, 'Yes, you may
keep the silver paper shape.'

Zara put it in her handbag.

And that night after Zoe had shut her window against the
intruders and locked the door and made ready her bed,
she swallowed the eighty-one tablets, the number which
she had calculated from the dread foundation of three,
and she lay down, arranged and ordered, to die. And Ma
Crane found her dead the next morning. There was no
note – as the coroners say.

Why need one write a note if one can communicate
with a left-over wrapping of silver paper from an empty
cigarette packet?

264

XXXVII

So Miss Zoe Bryce, schoolteacher, usherette, engaged in private research, plunged from the small cliff-area where she lived at the edge of the alphabet and achieved that most dramatic and convenient change in habits which we call Death. Alarm, horror, formalities, the *South London Star* – 'kept herself to herself, but cheerful always,' no next-of-kin, problem of the lonely, says vicar, house of death, anyone's house, striped awning over the front door, letterbox, the dustbins out for the weekly collection, I knew her I spoke to her –

But only a fortnight later the tobacconist at the end of The Elms, just opposite the bus stop, attacked his wife with a garden fork, and the suicide affair was layered over with new incident and speculation; though buried events, like compost, fume and fertilize.

Leaving Pat in charge of the house Ma Crane went north to the Lake District to visit her daughter and be comforted by her and to give her comfort, for Nan was lonely living, as she described it, 'miles from anywhere' and neither Ma Crane nor her daughter dared to investigate the exact locality of 'anywhere'. When the story of Zoe's suicide had been told and Ma Crane had received gratefully the versatile forms of commiseration from early morning cups of tea to requests to 'put her feet up' during the day, she began to grow more cheerful. She entertained the children. She played the piano and sang *Oh for the Wings of a Dove* and *Jerusalem* which were her favourites.

Yet she too began to pine for 'anywhere'.

And did those feet in ancient time walk upon England's mountains green, she sang, looking disconsolately out of the window at the shadow of the atom station. She longed for the crowded city. She did not want to be ignored in a wilderness beneath a vast shunning sky which seemed to have turned its protective light elsewhere. She began to share her daughter's feeling of banishment. Death in her lap cried for its meal, and when she leaned to feed it, it changed into the telly licking hungry chops at her. And the picture on the screen stretched like rumours and lies; there was interference from a source unknown, and that frightened Ma Crane.

'Come south with me for a holiday,' she urged her daughter. 'The scandal will have died. Christmas will be here soon, and they are having angels in Regent Street.'

In the meantime Pat, whose annual holiday had 'come up' at last, stayed in The Elms looking after the house and Chummy and clearing Zoe's possessions from the upstairs room. Death usually arrives wrapped in a shock-absorber, like those parcels marked *Fragile* which are nested in straw and surrounded by layers of corrugated cardboard. The removal of the wrappers occurs only in the final stages of realisation, and Pat had not yet arrived at that stage; he was postponing it by conventional mutterings of 'It doesn't seem real, I can't believe it.'

He supervised all proceedings carefully. He washed Zoe's room with disinfectant – a ritual which helps people to imagine they are made immune from the infection of violent death. He washed, ironed and packed her clothing, including the little white, knitted dress which he found in its locked suitcase. Had she been leading an immoral life? he wondered. Immorality, secret books on sex, suicide – all were grave crimes. Her soul would never rest in peace.

'Why did she do it?' he asked. She was educated, a

schoolteacher engaged in private research but she could have been earning over ten pounds a week as a secretary, they were crying out for secretaries, three to four columns in the papers each day, all high wages, luncheon vouchers, pension schemes, staff discount, she could have been set up for life, like me.

'Like a guy above a bonfire' – but what exactly, he wondered, was the nature of her private research?

His curiosity was intense. He had to know. He looked for papers or letters; he found none. Books, clothes, postcards, cutlery, tea-towels, gave no clue. In one small suitcase, however, he found three or four toy musical instruments – he thought they were clarinets – painted blue and gold with the paint peeling from them, and a record – he had never heard her play it, she had no gramophone – Schubert's *Shepherd on the Rock*.

He studied the title. 'Classical,' he said, dismissing it. And with his curiosity still unsatisfied he went downstairs to attend to Chummy whose needs habits and loyalties were more easily understood and controlled. Pat had grown fond of Chummy. He liked to prolong his preparation of Chummy's meal, buying the half-pound of coley each day and boiling it on the gas stove in Ma's kitchen; and on the days when he could not buy fish he would get a tin of cat food which, he always suspected, did not contain the ingredients the label claimed for it. 'Rather you than me,' he would say as he emptied it into Chummy's plate.

Rather you than me, Zoe Bryce. I have to take more care, Pat thought. The way things are I can't keep driving the buses, not getting older as I am, one mistake and it's too late. I'll get a nine-to-five job with a big establishment in town. Things are not the same now. Winter will be here again before we know it, and my pullover has worn thin, there's no warmth in it.

A sidelong look at death. I will hide my face in the blue robes of a woman, Our Lady. I will sneak under the wing of the mother swan.

So Pat changed his job. He became stationery supervisor in a large city store.

Just how much blank paper do you need, sir, to match your blank life?

XXXVIII

Though life offers machines for the purpose –
monotonously turning wheels that sweat their trained
    perplexities and despairs,
guarded on the assembly-line by creatures with covered
    heads, gloved minds and sealed memories,
with canned music playing – a windfall of cherries
gashed in the black heart while they danced
hammocking the worm to sleep,
Tonight I devise my own simple time for dying,
without rules or help from neighbouring factories,
without the mid-week sustenance of pork-pie and
    penis,
only with brown paper, sticks, flour paste, I make
a little kite on a string of loneliness, not anchored
    anymore
to earth, habits, houses, trees, people, or thorned
    wishes
where nations prick their finger and cry –

Tonight I devise my time. I make a little kite
to follow the tides of death in the sky.

I, Thora Pattern, have chosen Toby Withers, Zoe Bryce,
Pat Keenan and all others whom I have known or dreamed
of or constructed from tree-fern brains found on bombed
sites and mountains of the interior, as inheritors of my last
will and testament, as if I bequeathed to them the parts of
myself which I cannot invite as guests to this lonely house
with its stoned-out windows and worm-eaten sashes and
frames and its pile of sawdust which Time places in careful droppings (confectionery, icing-forced) in the corners

of the rooms; and the ripped-up floorboards revealing the treasure, the riddled earth, the casks of worms brewing the ferment of death.

Outside, all the buildings have toppled. Men in white suits, as if for tennis, prance about the debris in search of the last victims. The woman next door, blinded, has found a pot of whitewash which trickles down the windowpane; like toothpaste – 'you'll wonder where the yellow went when you brush the sky' but the sun, the merry-go-round sun bearing the full blame and journeying of the flat immoveable earth, blares its music while the painted horses rise and fall under the tall streamered poles of light.

And where is the Keeper of the Merry-Go-Round?

He is away, they say, in the city, abroad, overseas, on holiday, or skin-diving sharp as a mosquito in the human swamp.

Now the day is smoothed out, like a specimen, its identity searched for, its household name and the academic name compared, explained, the household name praised for its twist of life, like a curl cut from the forehead of a corpse, the academic name admired for the golden cage it builds between man and his experience, enabling him to study its habits, to feed it, care for it without being torn to pieces by its claws or teeth and stalked by it along the leaf-blown avenues of darkness.

Stop unwinding the days. Are you also a draper strangled by your tape-measure?

What shall I, Thora Pattern, make from the bolted material of these days? Snip measure charge pay and walk adorned with patches of cloud and frost and words, in a string of beads, around my neck; strong polished beads which do not break at the first tug of anger or confusion; there is no scattering of them in the room and blood-to-the-head search for them beneath furniture... I have one table, three chairs. No one visits me. Why should I wear words, like beads, around my neck if no one will visit me?

White is the colour I shall remember when dying. What purity, you say – the confirmation dresses of the girls in the South Church or those standing in ceremony under the trees planted in memory of those 'who shall not grow old' – who lie unable to walk across their fields of paradise; trench-deep, worm-laced, medals like poppies spitting sleep in their eyes, their lives caked slowly under each burning personal sun. White? I say evil, the swans, the white-wash on the day the Bomb fell, the housewife arranging the contemporary droppings on her window-panes and walls, the action painter throwing his white garbage to get a meaning, a communication, on the day when those who will die slowly will die slowly, chipping off the years and generations like convicts imprisoned in their lives, forced to work the white quarry of hopeless time; and those who die immediately will flash like a firework a catherine-wheel or sparkler or human throw-down, although their lives may have been merely a damp hiss in the gutter or a wet clogging of a council drain.

White, the evil colour, my flag which I hang from my heart and wave in the snow and the silver forest and none recognize it because they keep saying, How pure the clock-face, the sheets untouched by lovers; white that pockets the spectrum that lies like skin on the backs of mirrors that flies in my head like a moth in darkness that wears the shell of night and death, that is host to words, black words, and the hooks and infinities of musical notation and the beetle-diarrhoea of newsprint and the entreaties in letters that are never answered. Letters for help.

XXXIX

WHEN Peter Heron heard of Zoe's death he destroyed his few paintings – those of the bottle phase, bottles in armies, parties, wedding-groups, bottles in green and blue mist with their corks out and the mysterious fumes rising from their personalities, like people with the top sliced off their head. And he destroyed the city painting he had made on the evening Zoe died – a deserted city in vivid pink with buildings whose texture resembled human skin, and the whole city a shape of a magnified human fingerprint whorled with streets, empty of people, filled only with traces of humanity – newspapers, packets, cars, like the debris floating on the surface of the water after the flood and the wreck, or relics of memory rising to the surface of dreams. The painting was called *Tracing the Crime*. 'The city of the human face,' he said to himself. 'A face lost in a supermarket among the polythene bags with their little round sweating-holes, like synthetic arrangements for excrement.'

He spent a confused week wandering on the Heath and sitting in the coffee-bar with others like him who were afraid to be alone and face the fact that they wouldn't ever paint again. He sat there with his coffee, renewing it every half-hour in order not to be thrown out, arguing about painters and painting and the latest exhibitions, and feeling cheap pleasure when he was told that Herbert or Jo or Will was holding a one-man show in the Grand Feu Gallery and he was able to say to everyone, exciting envy, 'Oh yes, I know Herbert, I know Jo.'

And the searchlight of fame picked him up on the outskirts of other people's lives, illuminating him for a moment, accentuating his resemblance to one of those weird growths half-discerned on the edge of the moon.

He spent the days in pubs and clubs, cadging drinks, or in the dark of a cheap suburban cinema where the seats rattled, the upholstery had a burst appendix, and the old men were slinking and snoring. He picked up women in the evenings and went to bed with them. They despised him. He despised them. I'm not an ordinary layabout, he told them. I'm not a ponce, a pimp. I'm an artist, a painter, I'm sensitive...

On the Thursday of the following week he watched the remains of his paintings being emptied into the back of the dust-cart with the food scraps, empty tins, the choked insides of vacuum cleaners. He watched the dustman who was always on guard in case something valuable was thrown away, retrieving a few paperbacks and clean newspapers and putting them carefully in a little pile. He gave the man sixpence.

'Good taste,' he said.

Then he went inside and dressed carefully and answered the advertisement from the Hire-Purchase Company.

'Wanted. Salesman. Opportunities for promotion.'

XL

TOBY RARELY BOUGHT a newspaper now. He could never find the news which he desired but could not name. He used to buy a paper every morning, scan it from beginning to end, discard it with a feeling of defeat and disillusionment. Now the only newspapers he read were those which Mike and John brought home – Friday wrappings for fish and chips, Saturday Pink Classified. During the week he sometimes bought an advertising paper and read every line of it as if it were powerful fiction. He was excited by the Used Car Sales and the general For Sale Column; the Accommodation Advertisements with their proclamations *Business men only, No children, pets, or coloured.* (Where, Toby wondered, are all the rainbow people they speak of? I have never seen rainbow people walking in the street.) But it was the matrimonial advertisements which disturbed and interested him, reminding him that he was a bachelor, an epileptic, and that Evelina had refused to marry him.

'She turned me down,' he kept saying to himself. 'She turned me down. And I suppose she's still there in Waimaru and her mother going about the house and her old man sitting sewing leather, under the window to get the light.' He would read the advertisements and consider them. *Likeable spinster*, he read. *Sweet young unmarried mother, Charming nurse, attractive widow with house...* All wanted husbands. Would they want him? How would he describe himself? He read the men's columns – *Sincere West Indian. Bronzed Australian farmer. Executive with Sports Car...*

How could he describe himself?

Epileptic, income now National Assistance because

of poisoned arm, would like to meet –

'Dad, this is my wife. This is my father – Melissande, Beatrice, Peggy –'

'What, you with your fits, married?'

Then Melissande or Beatrice or Peggy would give a cry of horror and fear and run from Toby, catching the beautiful white wedding dress on one of the nails sticking out of the wharf shed. And Toby would hurry after his new wife and find only the torn piece of wedding dress which he would fold and put in his pocket. And he would return then to where his father was waiting to welcome him home from overseas, and his father would be complaining about the bitter wind 'passing right through' his left shoulder. 'It cripples me, Toby.'

Then severe and powerful his father would refer to Toby's marriage, beginning each sentence with 'I've told you all along. You know as well as I do – I thought going overseas would have dinned some sense into you, who do you think you are to go bringing –'

Melissande, Beatrice, Peggy –

Then Toby's father would change his expression, wrinkle his face and begin to cry and then thump his fist against the wharf shed, 'Where's the spirit-level? Mum, what did you do with the spirit-level? And the awl? Where is the awl?'

The spirit-level, the awl, the soldering bolt that sizzled against the leaden sky, causing thunder; and statues to pour from the clouds and set solid on squares of waste land. The awl? The all? the tin-snips, the plane – the plain? Home of the nor'wester blowing all day warm across the wheat and between the gum trees and the pine trees.

'No, there's nothing you can do,' Pat said. 'But don't keep sweeping the streets when your arm gets better, and living in that filthy room, they'll bring you down to their level –'

spirit-level –

'You can have Zoe's room, you could smarten up, get a job in a shop, grocer's or supermarket or warehouse –'

'Why?' Toby asked.

'I blame the cinema, her working there as an usherette; the sea-voyage, unhealthy books, and perhaps aspects of her life that we never dreamed of –'

'It's going to rain.'

'You won't get caught in it. I'd lend you my umbrella but I've had it re-covered, expensive; but it means everything to me these days going to work; my umbrella.'

'You've changed your work?'

'Yes, it's going to rain.'

'It's raining now.'

'Only spitting. Yes, I supervise stationery. As I said to the little foreign girl in the Deferred Payments Section – '

'I didn't see it in the paper. She was a schoolteacher, wasn't she? I wrote home and told Dad I had met a schoolteacher from the Midlands. It's stopped raining.'

'I knew it wasn't going to last.'

Be careful, the stairs are dangerously spiked, there are spirits to poke your eyes out, tiny bubbles of spirits to bring you down to their final level beneath the pavement, beneath the roots of trees and the sewers.

Yes, it had stopped raining. The day was grey bordered with black. On the way to the bus stop Toby passed a hearse with its swing doors open to receive the dust-free super-polished slim-line coffin. The coffin was put in. The doors were closed. The wreaths on the roof of the hearse were adjusted. Two of the men (their faces rosy with the mark of health provided by the branding-iron of a lurking killer-frost) climbed into the front seat and sat high and solemn, taller because of their top hats which touched the roof. One of the men glanced anxiously at his watch. They were behind time, he thought. It was a long drive out of the city to the crematorium and traffic was building up.

At last the cortège began on its way but stopped almost immediately at the traffic lights. The undertakers and the relatives packed into the following limousines tried not to change their expressions from discreet gloom at the thought of death (their death), to exasperation at being delayed by the traffic; while the day's cause and cargo stayed silent, enclosed separately in death like a bean growing alone, lying beside the shrunken remnants of its black-eyed brothers in a vast green pod, a sound-proofed flannel cathedral.

The lights changed. The hearse rushed forward indecorously, the other cars accelerating to catch up. We might get there in time, the driver thought. He could feel the sweat inside the rim of his top hat, the silk pressing damply on his forehead. Stage-fright, he thought, and was proud. He liked driving the hearse. He liked to be present at a cremation and later to be shown, as a favour by the relatives, what he called to himself the 'diminishing returns' of the occasion, which in his experience were regarded partly as a big game trophy, partly as a convenient mantelpiece memory, and partly as a kind of harvest reaped from the desolate sparkless fields of mortality.

Toby watched the cortège until it was lost in the traffic. He got on the bus. He felt self-possessed and important. He wanted to be in charge of a ceremony, to arrange a proceeding. A woman was standing in the aisle of the bus. He offered his seat.

'Thank you,' she said, and thought, 'What a polite man.'

Toby nodded gravely. Every now and again he kept inclining his head as if in assent to a remark unheard by the other passengers.

'Gentlemen,' he said. 'We shall not at this stage make war upon the enemy. But the mirrors arrived then, sidling and circling.'

'Get rid of yourself,' they said.

Toby laughed. 'Haw Haw. No thank you. I've my Lost Tribe to think of.'

'Zoe Bryce got rid of herself,' they said. 'She made the fatal mistake of trying to communicate from so far on the edge of the alphabet. And Pat Keenan has got rid of himself by hiding in stationery, in envelopes with no address on them, on blank account forms where no one dares to write the cost; in aluminium-lined paper bags, between Metric Measurements and the First Aid (Wounds, Bleeding, Shock and Broken Bones) of last year's unused diaries. All people are getting rid of themselves, Toby; they can't stay lonely on the edge for ever –'

'Haw Haw but I'll not get rid of myself, I have my dream of the Lost Tribe.'

But in the meantime the mirrors claimed him. He got off the bus and walked in the gates of the Pleasure Gardens. He said, 'Good afternoon, the weather's not all it should be, Haw Haw,' to an elderly man who was spearing half-heartedly at the scraps of paper and packets littered on the grass.

'You spearing flounder?' Toby said. 'With the tide half-out? What price survival? Haw Haw.'

The old man waved. He could not quite hear what Toby was saying. He pointed with his spear along the path.

'That way to the Fun Fair,' he said.

'I don't need the Fun Fair,' Toby answered, 'it's outside the Fun Fair that the mirrors are waiting for me.'

He shouted so that the old man heard him and came over to him. 'No larking about here,' he said. 'We don't want cranks. If it's a mirror you're after I can't help you sir.'

He leaned on his spear.

'I must have misheard what you were saying, sir.'

Words change in the air, they get to me all minced up, topped and tailed, and sometimes it's nothing but static. You can't get those disguised modern ones on the National Health.

'You mean those you put in your spectacles,' Toby said.

The man drew a black box from his pocket. 'I'm not a bomb disposal unit,' he said. 'I can't get rid of the danger. There's cavities everywhere, cavities in the ground that you'd never dream of.'

'And mirrors?'

'Mirrors too. But I like to spear cigarette packets, and the ice cream tubs, so if you don't mind I won't fritter my time away – just look at the sky, blurred and coming down on us like the telly with the Horizontal Hold broken.'

There was no old man. The mirrors persisted. They surrounded Toby and he stared into them and walked up and down inside their circle. He began to laugh again, the kind of laughter which the family always tried to make him suppress. 'Don't laugh like that, Toby, you're making people turn to look at you, stop that awful laugh.'

His voice echoed. 'Haw Haw.'

One moment the mirrors transferred him into a dwarf with his legs too short, his face elongated, his hair like tussock overgrown. Then his body was a palace of width, a huge doorway of flesh and fat and the smile on his lips wound like a creek through his face. And then his lips were telephone lines and his eyes were capstans unwinding, winding coils of sight that anchored there; his cheeks swung from their hooks, dripping with blood; his legs were avenues, overhanging the lonely road out of town.

And suddenly he was thin, he was tissue-paper and distance. He grew afraid then. He looked for a mirror which would show himself, Toby Withers, his distinct identity; but in all the images he stared at, he was nowhere to be found. There, look, was the boy down the road, the Mongol boy, and the woman who kept the store, and there were his aunts, Aunty Marge, Aunt Cora, Aunt Norma, his family, his father – why should he look in the mirror and see his father? – and his mother. Why had he surrendered the right to be himself? Why had the mirrors given him the terrible responsibility of being other people? He had been driven from himself as a rabbit is driven from its burrow, and here he was now, unprotected, unhoused, like a rabbit alone under a sky of circling hawks, of hungry identities preying upon him.

The mirrors had stolen his very shape, and rearranged it into something which did not belong to him anymore. Why, he could even see the top-hatted undertaker staring at him. And Evelina, and Pat Keenan, and Mike and John, and the woman who painted the eyes and expressions in the faces of the tiny people and animals, and Zoe and her strange life and death.

'She learned her lesson,' Pat had said to him. What did he mean? What move did she make that condemned her to death?

'One thing you learn in stationery,' Pat said, 'is to keep things in their place; things and people.'

Toby closed and opened his eyes and gazed once more in the mirror, and there was his mother, staking her claim.

'Yes,' he said, in answer to her unspoken question, 'I'll

not spatter you with mud when I drive by in my fine coach. And if a swagger comes to the door asking for food, I'll let him in and not mind the state of the house. I'll not bother to stack the newspapers under a cushion or hide the dirty dishes or sweep the dust under the mat. I promise to give him something to eat and a cup of tea – perhaps a piece of salmon or trout or a whitebait patty. I'll see that the blankets are aired for the night. I promise, Mum.'

Toby did not laugh any more Haw Haw at the mirrors. If they've stolen me away, he thought, who am I? Have I got rid of myself? But there's still my dream, my Lost Tribe. But his mother persisted in the mirror and he spoke again to her.

'Yes, I can hear the swamp-hens calling, and the ducks, and blackbirds twittering in the moss-grown apple trees.'

'There's a germ got into the apple trees, Toby. The boughs die, and break off. They don't carry any blossom.'

'My arm's giving me trouble, Mum.'

'You take your proper nourishment, Toby, and get something done about your arm.'

'I'm taking your advice. I'm having it seen to.'

'And your Lost Tribe? The story that you're going to write and astonish everyone with what you have to say?'

But the sky then in its frame of light slipped from the Horizontal Hold. The mirrors and the world blurred. Darkness came. And the bomb disposal squad went diligently about its work, tracing and removing the ticking menace concealed in the ever unidentified human lives.

The next morning, on his mother's advice, Toby went to the Shipping Company and arranged for his return to New Zealand.

HOW STRANGE human beings are – their lamplit eyes, their raspberry peaked and infested skulls with the twisted thought impressed beneath leaving a faint print of meaning that soon wears away; the shell is hollow, the creature has departed or died.

And the weapons of people – their built-in defence policy of sting, tooth, nail, dream dive-bombing in the night; their brave explosions of love in the house of those dear to them; their secret robberies from themselves, their lives swinging at last like the door of an empty safe where Death, gloved, has forced an entry, leaving no trace. So the definitions return to their lairs, lick the wounds got in human combat, and sleep.

It is winter now. The frosts visit during the night and in the ceremony known as the laying-on of hands they touch the windowpanes stark beneath the lace curtains, resurrect the buried thought of snow; and the merciless morning wind passes like an X-ray through people and buildings, tracing the chill shadow of ribs and planks and rafters, abolishing flesh, all solidity, with its keen pitiless vision. People move like shadows in the afternoon light. Curtains are drawn early. Through the windows of rooms not yet lit one sees the flash of television, the last bid of light for rescue, in the composite form of custards, detergents, horses, smoothly cardiganed men, all crossing the screen like self-possessed shades flitting through the abominable desert. Later in the evening the sodium lamps with a crazy glare on their faces lean like wicked concrete stepmothers over the people hurrying on the pavements...

Toby is living again in New Zealand, in the southern

city, with an aunt whose bones are 'turning to chalk', Aunt Cora. Toby still dreams of the Lost Tribe. You and I know that he will never write it, that once he finds the real expression of it beyond the childhood story which the teacher read out in front of the class, he will be in as much danger as Zoe in her lonely wandering through the silver forest. And who will help Toby then?

He lives with Aunt Cora. Her late husband was a tobacconist. He used to sit in a box-shaped cigarette-lined kiosk in Herd Street from nine to five every day except Saturday and Sunday, and when he died he was laid quiet and still in a coffin shaped like his work-day retreat, but lined with padded satin instead of with cigarettes.

Toby makes himself useful at Aunt Cora's. He paints the front door, mends the leak in the roof. He tells her of his experiences in England, of the book he will be writing when he sees his 'way clear'. And when she attends her classes in True Health Aunt Cora tells her friends that her nephew Toby is a 'much-travelled' man. And when people in the family who have known Toby since he was a small boy and have always tried to avoid him and not to accept responsibility for him, express surprise that Aunt Cora who once acted in the same way, making excuses when holidays at her home were suggested, agreeing with everyone that Toby was 'not all there', has 'taken up with' Toby, Aunt Cora replies mysteriously, 'There's more to Toby than you think.'

She is not ashamed of him anymore. She mentions him in letters to her niece. Toby is like a son to her – Aunt Cora whose only interesting attribute is that her bones are 'turning to chalk'. She never had children. It was always her sister's children whom she cared for, making them clothes, buying them presents, taking them for holidays. In the company of friends when the conversation turned

'My daughter Mary, My Johnny, Now my Eric –' Aunt Cora had to provide special anecdotes about Winona and Wally – 'My sister's little girl Winona, Now my nephew Wally...' And sometimes it seemed too much like being excluded from the mystical long division sum, like being the odd number at the bottom or at the side of the column, the mental afterthought, the carrying number put there for mere convenience and erased when the answer to the sum is worked out.

Yet there were moments of pleasure in Aunt Cora's life. The time Winona won third prize in the singing competition with 'Come Follow Follow Follow the Merry Merry Pipes of Pan'; when Winona's photo appeared in the newspapers and Aunt Cora sent copies to friends, writing down the margin near the photo — *My niece Winona*. And then there was the time when Wally, going to Medical School, passed his Preliminary Exams and had his name in the University List.

'My nephew, he's a medical student, studying to be a doctor you know.'

Although Wally did not pass the remainder of his exams and gave up studying to operate a milk-bar up north, Aunt Cora still referred to him as 'My nephew Wally, a former medical student.'

And now there is Toby.

'Toby, my nephew, who's been Overseas. Toby.'

And Aunt Cora's bones.

The doctors say they can do nothing for her, that the dissolution of her bones (why do they turn to chalk? What script will they form at last?) is a gradual process that cannot be halted. She walks with a stick now, and wears heavy chocolate-coloured stockings. Hearing the mysterious tale of her crumbling bones her relatives up north have written down to express their sympathy and to say that they would invite her to stay with them if they had room. Wally has been considerate, too, sending a card on behalf of himself and his family, a large card with roses encircling a mound of padded satin and words printed inside

The sky is blue
The birds are singing.
Get Well, Get Well
the bells are ringing.

But Aunt Cora does not know that among relatives closest to her there have been fierce letters arguing the responsibility of one of them to 'take' her. For when one is ageing or ill, when one's bones, turning to chalk, are in danger of breaking into articulate language, one is often put out for someone to 'collect' like the weekly refuse.

One must submit, in the end, to being 'taken'. The time came once for Toby's grandparents. It has come for Aunt Cora. Soon it will come for Toby's father living alone in Waimaru. Toby knows, he knows, for the time has been extended for him all his life, with people saying, 'You can't keep him, you'll have to put him somewhere. Who will take him, someone will have to take him!'

Now the State is a kindly mother. She has built homes for people who are in need of being 'taken', whose relatives and friends suffer at that time a paralysis of their favourite and rewarding habit of acquisition which showers human life with possessions as diverse as rattles, bottles, flowers, jobs, televisions, bank accounts, pictures, stamps; and other people.

The State has built homes, some large and rambling with names like Sunset Corner, Eventide Vista; some divided into small flats. If they are situated on the coast they have a fine view of the sea, and if they are inland they overlook mountains or lakes. The rooms are spacious, well furnished. And walking up and down the polished corridors and sitting in the contemporary sun-lounges are all the bewildered people whom no one has offered to 'take'. But how blue the sea glitters beneath the window, and the pohutukawa blossoms flame like torches being carried in hell...

It is still winter. The day is grey with a tidewash of leaves and nagging blustering winds that for weeks now have encircled the trees in the grove, trying by violence and persuasion to conscript the last leaves for their annual march-past and display of flame-coloured death. Zoe Bryce is dead, I say to myself. Toby is with Aunt Cora. Pat? Peter? All the other people whom I have known and put in my secret writing?

I must stop somewhere and begin my own life... Is it true that self-discovery ends in death?

And is death the vacant lot out of town, full of rusty sharp-edged tins, motor tyres, human debris which only death volunteers to store? Or is it the oasis in the desert, with men constantly in search of it to build their homes and lives around it, that it may satisfy their hunger and thirst? Is it a pool which the years and their rotting vegetation have made stagnant but which in time can be freed to flow and irrigate our lives without the nightmare mosquito-sucking of our blood?

How I am haunted by death and the dead! And by the division of humanity into so many people when one birth, one mind, one death would be enough to end the tributary tears that flow in every acre of the earth in the stone obstructions of the heart that are called stars. What mathematical trick has divided the whole into the sum of so many people, only to set working in our hearts the process by which we continually strive to reduce the sum once more to its indivisible whole – until millions in one city become for us two or three people and finally one person. We pass our mother fifty times in a few seconds in the street, and our father, and the only people we have ever really known; and if we love, everyone we meet is our lover.

And what if the person who meets us for ever is ourselves? What if we meet ourselves on the edge of the alphabet and can make no sign, no speech?

So it is the end of self-discovery. I have arrived at the dead. The dead follow me in the street, turning their lives over and over like stained leaves, shuffling like the hesitant footsteps of leaves. I feel their hands on my cheek and I turn to exclaim, 'Why do you follow me? Why don't you stay in the grave where you were buried with so much expense and ceremony, you in your slim-line coffin with the new tadpole look which everyone chooses, you in your silver-gilled casket, why don't you stay there, make peace with the worms and the flames, sift over your ashes like grains of sand when the tide has gone out for ever and the sun has exploded into darkness?'

The dead follow me in the street, along the grove with its avenue of bare trees, the trodden hands of the chestnut leaves lying everywhere on the pavement, as if in flying from their lives they reached to grasp at a dream and had their hands stamped on, to teach them a lesson. No meddling. It is the will of the season.

The dead intrude in my sleep, the dead who do not belong to me, whom I have never known; the human dead, and the material corpses, the litter and refuse associated with human lives – the stray papers and empty silver packets blown through the streets of the city.

The dead wave the shadow of their lives, of their silence, across my night-pursuits of peace. A handful of flowers to give –

To whom? Export or die.

Beaten with the wand the memories weep, and cities run like sparkling tears from their eyes; houses of salt spring from the earth. The inhabitants of the city and the forest fight to kill one another in order to become one. They fight to eliminate themselves, their shadows, their speech.

Each night, I say, the dead creep between my sheets. They share my hot water bottle with its velvet cover, and my handkerchief tucked beneath the pillow; during the night they glance with cunning at my alarm clock on the chair by the bed. What a crude face man has given to Time! What a strained white face of a worried constipated being! And the hook there, see, at the top, for hanging.

In the morning it is the dead who seek first the warmth of my slippers and my clothes slung over the chair; it is they who claim my breakfast and drink my coffee. And always, day by day, they follow me in the street. I do not know them. I have never met them in their lives, yet they follow me like stray dogs that have picked up a scent which they do not understand but which they will follow until it leads them home.

Home?

The edge of the alphabet where words crumble and all forms of communication between the living are useless. One day we who live at the edge of the alphabet will find our speech.

Meanwhile our lives are solitary; we are captives of the captive dead. We are like those yellow birds which are kept apart from their kind – you see their cages hanging in windows, in the sun – because otherwise they would never learn the language of their captors.

But like the yellow birds have we not our pleasures? We look long in mirrors. We have tiny ladders to climb up and down, little wheels to set our feet and our heart racing nowhere; toys to play with.

Should we not be happy?

ACKNOWLEDGEMENTS

Grateful acknowledgement is made to the copyright
holders of the extracts used on the following pages:
pages 108 and 264, W. W. Norton Company Inc for the
lines from *Sonnets to Orpheus* by Rainer Maria Rilke,
translated by M.D.H. Norton; p. 161, Pia Glover and the
Denis Glover Estate for the lines from *The Magpies*,
by Denis Glover.